The Sheriff's Unexpected Wife

~~~

STAND-ALONE NOVEL

A Western Historical Romance Book

by

Nora J. Callaway

Disclaimer & Copyright

This is a work of fiction. Names, characters, places, and incidents either are products of the author's imagination or are used fictitiously. Any resemblance to actual events or locales or persons, living or dead, is entirely coincidental.

Copyright© 2025 by Nora J. Callaway

All Rights Reserved.

This book may not be reproduced or transmitted in any form without the written permission of the publisher.

In no way is it legal to reproduce, duplicate, or transmit any part of this document in either electronic means or in printed format. Recording of this publication is strictly prohibited, and any storage of this document is not allowed unless with written permission from the publisher

Table of Contents

The Sheriff's Unexpected Wife 1
   Disclaimer & Copyright 2
   Table of Contents 3
   Letter from Nora J. Callaway 5
Prologue 6
Chapter One 15
Chapter Two 24
Chapter Three 32
Chapter Four 42
Chapter Five 50
Chapter Six 59
Chapter Seven 68
Chapter Eight 83
Chapter Nine 90
Chapter Ten 99
Chapter Eleven 107
Chapter Twelve 115
Chapter Thirteen 123
Chapter Fourteen 131
Chapter Fifteen 140
Chapter Sixteen 149
Chapter Seventeen 155
Chapter Eighteen 164
Chapter Nineteen 172

Chapter Twenty 179
Chapter Twenty-One 188
Chapter Twenty-Two 197
Chapter Twenty-Three... 205
Chapter Twenty-Four 212
Chapter Twenty-Five 220
Chapter Twenty-Six 226
Chapter Twenty-Seven 235
Chapter Twenty-Eight 244
Chapter Twenty-Nine 252
Chapter Thirty 260
Chapter Thirty-One... 267
Chapter Thirty-Two 274
Chapter Thirty-Three 281
Epilogue 289
   Also by Nora J. Callaway.. 296

Letter from Nora J. Callaway

"How vain it is to sit down to write when you have not stood up to live." -Henry David Thoreau

I'm a lover of nature in the mornings and a writing soul at nights. My name is Nora J. Callaway and I come from Nevada, the beautiful Silver State.

I hold a BA in English Literature and an MA in Creative Writing. For years, I've wanted to get my stories out there, my own 'babies' as I like to call them, inspired by my own experience leaving out West and my research of 19th-century American history.

All my life, I have been breeding horses, cows, and sheep, and I've been tending to the land. It's time to tend now to my inner need to grow my stories, my heart-warming Western romance stories, and share them with the rest of you!

I'm here to learn and connect with others who enjoy a cup of black coffee, a humble sunset, and a ride with a horse! Bless your hearts, as my nana used to say! Come on, hop in!

Until next time,

Nora J. Callaway

Prologue

Butte, Montana 1865

"I should have died in Tennessee," Allen Strauss muttered under his breath as he reached down to massage his leg. He'd been shot during the last battle, and it was taking a while to heal.

Allen looked over the railing of the steamboat into the Missouri River. He stared sightlessly at the murky waves as the paddlewheel churned up the muddy water. The scent of damp earth and sagebrush wafted on the warm breeze. It was a sharp contrast to the acrid smoke from the gunpowder that had burned his lungs for the last four years.

He rolled his shoulders, the tension making them stiff.

His eyes glazed over, and the river, the boat, and everything around him disappeared. The image of his brother's face as he lay dying in the field haunted him. His eyes had been wide with pain, and the ground below them was soaked with blood. Joseph's angular face and dark brown eyes mirrored Allen's, and Allen felt a piece of him dying with his brother. The brothers had been the same height, and since Joseph had only been a year older than Allen, they'd done everything together. Allen thought his brother was invincible.

Allen could still hear his brother's last words echoing in his mind. "Stay the course, Brother, and may God watch over you. Don't grieve. We're fighting for something bigger than ourselves."

Then, he'd exhaled his last breath.

Allen had dug his brother's grave and put a cross at the top. He'd said a few words and then walked away. There was no time to mourn because the soldiers had to keep moving.

Once the dead were buried, Captain Strauss led his company further south to their next battle point. He fought like a man who had nothing to lose. Their father had been killed at Gettysburg and had been buried in the Soldiers' National Cemetery a month before Joseph had been killed. Their losses devastated him. His brother's voice haunted him, sneaking into his mind and punching him in the gut with pain.

Allen's white-knuckled grip tightened on the railing of the ship as the memories flooded back. He swallowed hard, barely able to breathe as the pain of losing them ripped him apart inside like a jagged knife tears into a piece of meat. A guttural sound of anguish tore from the depths of his soul.

The only thing that kept him going was that his sweet love, Angelica, was waiting for him at home. Occasionally, her letters caught up with him. They were full of stories about what was happening in Montana Territory, which sounded perfectly ordinary.

He'd sit down and picture her beautiful face. Her flashing green eyes were always full of laughter and fire. She'd help any person or animal who was in need, but she could put the toughest men in their place when necessary. She had long black hair, which she kept in a braid that trailed down her back.

Finally, when the war was over, he used his muster-out pay to book a passage back home. Allen boarded the steamer in St. Joseph, Missouri, in June, heading for Fort Benton, Montana.

A deep voice brought him out of his reverie. "Are you doin' all right, Capt'n?" one of the sailors asked.

"Fine, Monty. Thanks."

As he looked out over the countryside, Allen found it hard to believe that the land was pure and untouched by the war. Green bluffs lined the riverbank. Clusters of cottonwood trees grew along the winding waterway. Occasionally, he spotted a settler's cabin and a herd of deer or bison as they grazed on the tall prairie grass.

The sixty-day journey by steamboat seemed to take forever. After three years of fighting and moving, each day was tedious, with nothing to occupy his time. Not that he would ever want to go back to war—not in a million years—but he itched to do something to keep active and to occupy his mind.

Scenes from the war constantly haunted him. He could hear the cries of the men as they fell, and he was certain that he'd never get the smell of gunpowder off of him. He simply wanted to go home, leave all the death and destruction behind, and start a life with Angelica.

Allen stayed on deck as much as possible. When he was forced to be inside his cabin, it felt as though the walls were closing in on him and suffocating him.

Finally, after what seemed like an eternity, the steamboat arrived at Fort Benton. His heart beat faster because he was so close to home, anticipation and dread tangling together in his chest. The death of Joseph and their father would make Butte so different, and he felt the never-ending grief crushing his heart. It wouldn't be the same without them.

He smelled the familiar scent of pine, and Allen took slow, uneven breaths, trying to ease the tightness in his chest. The thought of setting foot in Butte without his father and brother by his side sent a sharp, excruciating pain through him. Their deaths created an achy emptiness inside of him that hurt as much as the day he'd buried his brother.

Still, he hoped to build a life with Angelica, and while that would never make the pain disappear, it would be something beautiful and good.

The three-day stagecoach ride from Fort Benton to Butte dragged on. The minutes wore on with agonizing slowness. The terrain was rough, and the cramped passengers were thrown from side to side like a ship in a violent storm. Allen was pretty sure that every organ inside his body was mush by the time they finally arrived.

Allen was still in uniform as he stepped off the stagecoach and grabbed his bag. Several people welcomed him home. Eventually, he was able to untangle himself from the old women's hugs and handshakes from the men. He didn't bother going home to the ranch first.

Determined to greet the woman he loved, kiss her, and marry her, he limped to the small house she shared with her mother.

Allen hesitated for a moment before he knocked on the door. His heart raced, and a huge knot had formed in the pit of his stomach. He wasn't the same man who'd left three years ago. Would Angelica recognize him? Allen felt as though he'd aged a million years, and the horrific scenes he'd witnessed were etched on his face.

Biting his bottom lip, he knocked. After a few moments, an older woman answered the door.

She smiled warmly at him. "Hello, Allen. I heard the war was over and hoped that you'd be coming back soon."

"Yes, ma'am. Can I see Angelica, please?"

Her smile faded, and her face turned white. A hint of tears sprang in her eyes. She put her hand on his arm and said, "Oh, Allen, I'm so sorry. She died a few months ago from the fever that swept through the town. We lost a lot of people. I tried sending you a letter, but I guess it never caught up with you."

Allen's heart and soul shattered into a million pieces. The world tilted around him. He couldn't breathe, and his insides twisted. He slumped against the door frame, as his legs could no longer hold him up, and he stared at the older woman in disbelief.

"I kept the ring you gave her. I know it was your mother's. Hang on a minute."

She turned, and as soon as she was out of sight, Allen walked away, putting distance between him and the unbearable agony that devoured him. The whole world had gone dark. Allen's mother had died giving birth to him. His father and brother were dead, and now he'd lost his sweet Angelica.

***

"I see you're home, boy," Uncle Amos said when Allen walked into the ranch house.

"It would seem so."

"Got your letter about James and Joseph. Darn shame." Amos's voice reflected his usual gruffness, which made it hard to tell if he felt anything at all about the loss of his brother and nephew.

"Yes." Allen's soul felt empty, and he didn't have another ounce of himself to give to the man who'd taught him how to be a rancher but never showed a bit of affection for him or Joseph.

"You can have the second room."

Allen nodded. He went into the room and lay down on the first bed that didn't move and was comfortable. The cots and bedrolls he slept on in the war were hard, and the bed on the ship had continuously rocked with the motion of the waves.

He slept through the rest of the afternoon and all night.

He groaned when he woke up the next morning, unhappy to discover that he was still alive. Allen had hoped that the sleep had taken him away from his grief, and he wouldn't have to face a world where everyone he loved had been ripped away from him. A crushing weight settled on his chest, and he stared at the ceiling, knowing he was trapped in this world.

Uncle Amos already had breakfast ready when Allen limped to the table. "I'm getting too old to run this ranch. I ain't got no other kin. If you take over the ranch, it's yours when I'm gone."

Allen looked at his uncle. The shriveled man was several years older than his father and didn't look too healthy. He thought about the offer. Allen had no other prospects and no other plans. He honestly hadn't thought much about his future except to marry Angelica.

"That sounds reasonable."

He almost regretted his decision when he discovered the deplorable state the ranch was in. Uncle Amos owned five thousand acres and had approximately two hundred fifty head of Hereford cattle. The only smart thing he'd done was to contract with one of the local farmers for hay so the animals could be fed in the winter.

Allen threw himself into the task of making the ranch successful. He never allowed himself to stop and think about the war, his father, his brother, or Angelica. Allen was up with the first light of day and worked until it was too dark to see an inch in front of him.

On the rare occasions that his uncle showed any concern for him, he'd say, "Boy, you're going to work yourself to death."

Allen simply shrugged him off.

He seldom ventured into town, letting his uncle get any supplies they needed. It was too hard dealing with people. Even though the war had been over for a while, the country was still healing. For the people in Montana Territory, who'd been so far away from it, it was a fascinating topic. Luckily, most people understood when he didn't want to talk about it.

Allen dreaded nights. As captain, he'd been in charge of the lives of around a hundred men. In his nightmares, he could see them being mowed down by the enemy. Their screams echoed in the night air, and the stench of blood and gunpowder hung heavily in the air.

He'd get two or three hours of sleep before his eyes popped open from the terror and heartache that burned deep inside of him. Occasionally, he screamed. His body was drenched with sweat, and his heart pounded so hard that he was sure it was going to rip out of his chest. He'd fumble for a weapon that wasn't there.

Finally, after several agonizing minutes, it registered that Allen wasn't on the battlefield. He was in his room, far away from the blood, the death, and the terror of what was to come next.

The first couple of times, Uncle Amos had rushed into his room to find out what was wrong. The conversation had always been the same.

"Why are you screaming, boy?" Amos asked, sounding more annoyed than concerned.

"I see them dying. I see the bullets ripping open the wounds in their sides," Allen whispered, the horror echoed in his voice.

"Boy, the war is over." Amos sounded more disgusted than sympathetic.

"I wish it was." Allen pressed his hands against his head as though it would make the visions disappear.

Now, Uncle Amos stayed in his room and didn't bother checking on Allen, much to his relief. He was humiliated by the nightmares. Real men didn't scream like children in the middle of the night.

Conversations with the old man were mostly about what supplies were needed, what chores had to be taken care of, and when the breeding cows were due. That suited Allen just fine.

Most of the time, Uncle Amos was a nuisance. He seemed to resent the fact that Allen had turned the ranch around and made it profitable. He grumbled and complained constantly, and more than once, Allen wondered whether the hassle was worth it. He had money saved, and he could buy land and start his own ranch. Then, he reminded himself of all the hard work he put in and didn't want to see it go downhill.

Allen did his best to focus only on the ranch's progress. He had fifty purebred Herefords that were breeders and ten bulls that serviced them. Cows on the range were also breeding, so the herd was growing.

After about a year, the ranch was more than Allen could handle by himself. He contacted his buddy, Ben, who'd been in his company, and invited him to come to work on the ranch. Ben, who was about to muster out, needed a job and agreed.

Shortly after Ben arrived, the old sheriff retired. Allen, following in his father's footsteps, ran for office and easily won the election. Any time a memory snaked its way into his brain, Allen pushed it away and forced himself to work harder. His sole focus was on the ranch and keeping order in town. He soon gained a reputation as a fair but hard man.

Most importantly, Allen didn't have to think or remember when he pushed himself. At night, most of the time, he was so exhausted he didn't dream—or didn't remember anything if he did dream. That was the way he wanted it. As long as he kept his hands busy and his mind focused on the tasks at hand, the past couldn't catch him.

Chapter One

New York City, 1875

Virginia looked up from her sewing machine and rubbed her eyes. The low lighting in the factory made it hard for her to see the seams, so she had to focus hard on the fabric and thread to make sure that not a single stitch was out of place. Her leg hurt from pumping the treadle. Sighing heavily, she cut the string from the dress that she'd never have enough money to buy for herself. The fine wool crepe dress was dark forest green and would have perfectly offset her bright emerald eyes.

She stretched out her hands, which trembled like a woman three times her age. The calluses on her fingertips were bleeding from where the needles had pricked her several times a day. Her back ached from being hunched over the sewing machine for hours, and her neck was so tense that she could scarcely turn her head without a jolt of pain shooting down her spine.

The endless clatter of machines had dulled her senses. The cotton she stuffed in her ears didn't block out much of the sound. Her head pounded until she was sure that it was going to explode.

Sighing heavily, she put the dress on the stack with the other dresses she'd made. At the end of the shift, the foreman, Jack, would count the pieces completed by each person so they could be paid at the end of the week.

Virginia looked up at the clock. Her twelve-hour shift was almost over. There were twenty minutes left, so she wound the empty bobbins. She checked the tension on the machine, cleaned it to ensure there was no dust, lint, or thread around it, and then oiled it to make sure that it would be ready to go first thing in the morning. After checking the needle, she changed it since it had dulled.

Finally, after what seemed like an entire year had gone by, the whistle blew, indicating that her shift was over. She quickly grabbed her shawl and waited for the foreman to note the time she left.

Meaghan grabbed her arm as she stepped onto the street, breathing in and relishing the fresh air. "We're getting together later at my and Ian's apartment. Would you like to stop by and play rummy?"

"I wish I could, but my aunt will want me to help out with the children."

"She's a slave driver," Meaghan said. "It's bad enough that she takes all of your pay."

Virginia shrugged. "She took me in after my father died. It's the least I can do."

Meaghan hugged her. "You're a saint. I know that I wouldn't be taking her attitude and treatment as well. I'd best be getting home. Ian will be getting off work soon and will want his supper."

"Have fun tonight."

Virginia's stomach rumbled, as the two pieces of bread she'd had for lunch didn't come close to filling her up, although that was her usual fare. She was pretty sure that if her aunt didn't know she had to have some kind of nourishment to keep going, she wouldn't even get the bread.

She walked ten blocks to the tall tenement building she lived in with her aunt, uncle, and three cousins. It was seven stories tall and had a dingy brick exterior stained with coal smoke.

The single entrance led to dark hallways with apartments lined on either side.

She climbed the narrow, steep staircase to the third-floor apartment. Virginia closed her eyes briefly and took a huge breath before entering. She could hear her youngest cousin, Samuel, screaming at the top of his lungs and her aunt Fiona yelling over him.

As soon as she entered the three-room apartment, her aunt yelled, "It's about time you got here. You're late—again. How many times have I told you not to lollygag and hurry home? You're needed here."

Virginia knew better than to argue with her. It would simply earn her a slap in the face.

"Set the table. Dinner will be ready shortly."

"Can I change my dress? I'll be quick about it."

Virginia cringed as Aunt Fiona turned around with a wooden spoon raised high in her hand as though she was going to strike her niece.

"You ungrateful wench. You should be grateful to have a roof over your head. Don't talk back to me. When I tell you to do something, you do it immediately. Am I understood?"

Aunt Fiona's green eyes narrowed, and her lips pressed together in her haggard, thin face. Her frizzy red hair curled around her cheekbones, making her look like a madwoman.

Virginia bowed her head. "Yes, ma'am."

Biting her lip, she knew better than to say anything back to her aunt. The woman had always treated her as an unwanted slave who had no thoughts or feelings of her own. Virginia wanted so badly to escape the tiny tenement apartment, to be able to breathe and have a life of her own, but it would be so hard with the mere pittance she received from the factory and the fact that her aunt took every penny of her pay.

There were days that she almost hated her aunt, but then forced herself to push away the feelings. She did have a roof over her head and food, which is more than what other people had. Some had to live on the streets, or even worse, in the poorhouse.

She quickly set the table and then picked up her seven-year-old cousin, who was almost as big as she was. The boy had been spoiled by his mother and had a tendency to scream when he didn't get his own way.

"What's going on, Seth?"

"I'm hungry."

"I understand, but your mother's making dinner. Screaming isn't going to make her cook any faster."

"I was mad because I'm hungry."

Virginia hid her smile. "I get that way, too, but we have to be patient. She's cooking as fast as she can."

"You're not his mother. Don't talk to him like that," Aunt Fiona snapped as she put the stew on the table.

Seth looked at Virginia sympathetically. Even though he was a brat, he did have a fondness for her.

"Yes, ma'am," Virginia said.

Uncle Arthur walked into the apartment just as Aunt Fiona was putting the fresh bread on the table. He kissed his wife on the cheek and barely nodded at Virginia to acknowledge her existence.

Ten-year-old Patrick and twelve-year-old Bridget followed behind their father. They'd been playing on the streets with their friends. They sat down at the table and prayed over the stew, potatoes, and bread.

"The stew is wonderful," Arthur said.

"Thank you. I had just enough money to get a little bit of meat from the butcher."

There was barely enough food for the six of them. Seth gulped his down hungrily and eyed Virginia's plate as she ate more slowly. He licked his lips, and his gaze was sharp with want.

Virginia briefly closed her eyes, knowing that her hunger pains would keep her up all night; still, she gave half of her meal to him. She already got the least amount of food of everyone. She was so thin that sometimes her friends pitied her and shared their lunch with her.

She helped clean up after the dishes were done and then went outside to sit on the steps, longing for some peace and quiet and fresh air. The factory was dusty and dirty, and the apartment smelled like unwashed bodies and boiled potatoes.

Finally, though, it got late, and she didn't want to be forced to sleep in the hallway since her aunt locked the door after a certain time and would refuse to open it.

Virginia quietly opened the door. She could hear her uncle snoring in the only bedroom in the apartment. The three children were sleeping on the floor in the corner of the room, but Virginia was usually allowed to sleep on the couch.

Aunt Fiona patted the couch. "Come sit next to me."

Nervous, since her aunt never spoke kindly to her, Virginia slowly approached the couch and sat as far away from the woman as she possibly could. She sat on her hands to keep them from trembling and swallowed hard. Virginia stared at her lap—anything to keep from looking at her aunt.

"As you know, times are tough. We barely have enough money to pay rent and buy food, as well as the other things that your cousins need. We've taken care of you since you were ten."

Virginia's head snapped up, and she looked at her aunt. "I started working at the factory when I came to live with you and brought home money to cover the costs of my clothes and food."

Aunt Fiona held up her hand to stop her.

"You brought in money, and it wasn't nearly enough. After Arthur got hurt and couldn't work anymore, money got really short. Now, with three kids, we're barely surviving. I've had to take in laundry to help support us." She gestured around the room. "There's not enough room for us, let alone you."

"I bring in enough to cover my expenses," Virginia argued. "I work very hard."

"Yes, I know you do, but it's not enough." Aunt Fiona held Virginia's chin in her hand and squeezed, causing Virginia to wince. "Plus, you're twenty-three years old. It's time you started your own life."

Virginia's heart sank, and her stomach twisted into knots. She envisioned herself sleeping in the alley with a threadbare blanket wrapped around her like some of the other homeless people. "What am I supposed to do? Where am I supposed to go?"

Aunt Fiona gave a sly smile that sent icy chills running up and down Virginia's back. She shivered as she waited to hear what awful plan her aunt had.

"You don't think that I'd throw my only niece out in the streets, do you? Why, my brother would turn in his grave and come back to haunt me." The feral smile returned, and Virginia shrank inside herself. "I have something better. You're going to be married. Isn't that wonderful?"

Virginia's eyes widened, and her jaw dropped as she tried to process what her aunt had just said. "What?"

"You heard me. You're going to be married." She handed Virginia an advertisement.

Virginia, who couldn't read, stared blankly at it. "What is this?"

"It's an advertisement for a mail-order bride. It's very common these days for lonely men out West to put advertisements in newspapers, looking for a woman to marry."

She tapped the paper in Virginia's hand. "This ad is from a wealthy rancher in Montana who needs a wife. His name is Allen Strauss. I wrote to him, and he's agreed to marry you. He sent money for you to travel to Montana. The man was nice enough to send enough money for you to buy food along the way, although I *should* keep some of it for setting this up for you."

"I can't go all the way to Montana to marry a man I've never met. How could you do this to me?" Her heart thundered in her chest, and she struggled to breathe. Her aunt had given her to a man she'd never met before, like she was a plaything.

Aunt Fiona yanked hard on Virginia's braid, pulling her head painfully to one side. "Now, you listen to me," she said through gritted teeth. "You should be grateful to me. First, no man here is going to want you. Look at you. Second, you'll have a safe place to live and food in your belly."

She let go of the braid, and Virginia rubbed her head, blinking back the tears. There was no way that she was going to let Aunt Fiona see her cry. The woman took a wicked delight in watching her torment.

Virginia took a deep breath and swallowed hard, resigned to her fate. She knew that if she didn't go to Montana to marry Allen, her aunt would be happy to throw her out. "When am I supposed to leave?"

"Next Monday. That gives you enough time to finish out the week at the factory and collect the rest of your salary, which you'll give to me. You won't be needing any of it since you have enough money for your train fare and food."

She swallowed hard. She wasn't surprised that her aunt took her last bit of pay. Virginia understood that they needed the money, but so did she. She briefly wondered how Aunt Fiona planned on buying food and paying rent without her income, but decided not to ask. That really wasn't her problem anymore.

"Now that's settled, I can only give you an old canvas bag to pack your belongings in. It should be fine since you only have a couple of dresses and a few other clothes, your mother's Bible, and the wooden rosary that your father had," Aunt Fiona said, her voice suddenly condescendingly sweet.

"Thank you," Virginia whispered.

She still couldn't wrap her mind around the idea that she was going to Montana to marry someone she'd never met before.

The next day, when she told Meaghan what happened, Meaghan almost dropped her sandwich in shock. "You're foolin', right? You're leaving next week to marry a perfect stranger? What if he looks like Genghis Khan and has a personality to match?"

"What choice do I have? If I don't agree to marry him, she'll turn me out on the streets."

"You can always come stay with us," Meaghan said. "We'll make room."

"You barely have room for yourselves. You live in a three-room apartment with Sean's mother and sister, plus your son. It's best that I just go."

No matter how much Meaghan argued, Virginia wouldn't change her mind. There was no way that she was going to be a burden on anyone else. She'd go to Montana and make the best of it. Anything had to be better than working long hours in the factory, bent over a sewing machine, and then going back to Aunt Fiona's to be treated like an unpaid servant.

Three days later, she stood on the platform, waiting to board the train. None of her family had come to see her off. Virginia hadn't expected them to. She felt so utterly alone and small as she stood there among the bustling people moving around her, and terrified of venturing into the unknown.

Beneath it all, though, a flicker of excitement stirred inside of her as she prepared to set out into her new life. It would be something different. Instead of the cramped city life, she would get to experience wide open spaces. Meaghan, who read, told her about Montana Territory, after she finally accepted that Virginia wasn't going to stay in New York City.

With a deep breath, Virginia stood straight and tall, holding her head up high as she stepped onto the train. Fear still gnawed at her, but a little bit of anticipation followed close behind. She would be starting a new life, like the ones in the dime novels Meaghan told her about.

Virginia closed her eyes.

Goodbye, New York City. Hello, Montana Territory.

Chapter Two

Butte, Montana 1875

Allen took the cuffs off the short, bald man and watched him stagger into the jail cell. "This is the last time I'm telling you, Earl. You cannot get drunk and start fights in the saloon."

"I was just letting off a little steam, Sheriff. You know how it is. Besides, I didn't start the fight. Nick threw the first punch."

"He punched you after you accused him of cheating again, and then you insulted his family and his manhood. This time, you're done blowing off steam. You're going to pay for all the damages you caused, and Paul said you aren't allowed back in the saloon anymore."

Earl puffed up his chest and pressed his face against the bars. "He can't do that."

"Yes, he can. The saloon is private property, and he gets to say who can and cannot come into his place. This is your third fight in three months, and he's done with you."

"What's he gonter do?" Earl slurred.

"For starters, as soon as you walk in, he's going to have one of his guys beat the living tarnation out of you and throw you out in the street. Then, if he decides to make a complaint against you, I'll toss you in jail and fine you," Allen said.

"That just ain't fair, Sheriff. A man gotter have a spot to take the edge off."

"Well, maybe after you pay for all the damages you caused, he'll think about it, but if he tells you that you can't go in, then

I guess you'd better buy your liquor from Mick's general store and take it home."

"It ain't no fun ter drink by myself."

"Guess you should have thought of that before you started the fight with Nick."

Allen shook his head as he walked back to his desk to make a note of the arrest and the fine in the ledger.

Butte had its share of crime, and Allen and his deputies were kept busy, although most of it was limited to fights. The miners and cowboys would come in, start drinking, and throw punches. Once in a while, some outlaw gangs passed through, someone stole horses, or there was a claim jump, but Allen managed to keep the crime rates low and the citizens safe.

About once a year, a couple of people decided the best way to settle the score was a shootout on Main Street. Allen managed to calm most of the people down before anyone was killed, but if the idiots were stupid enough to risk their lives to settle some kind of honor issue, then he wasn't going to arrest them. They would do it anyway once they got out of jail.

Stephen, one of the deputies, came in, hung his hat on the rack, and plopped into his chair. "We need to do something about Miss Katie. She's got to keep those girls under control. One of them broke a man's nose because he tried to get away without paying."

"I say that he deserves what he got. The men know the rules when they go upstairs with the ladies. It's well-known that most of them can hold their own in a fight against any man," Allen said. "I'm headed home. You know where to find me."

Allen saddled Blaze and rode back to Uncle Amos's ranch slowly. He enjoyed looking at the land and the brief moments of peace when he didn't think about anything. If thoughts from the past intruded, he simply focused his mind on the details of a tree or the number of bucks, does, and fawns in a deer herd. Montana was truly a beautiful state, even if the wind blew three hundred days out of the year.

He was glad that Uncle Amos wasn't in sight when he ducked into his room to change clothes. Ben, his best friend and foreman, caught him as he walked outside.

"Ferdinand and Oscar managed to break through the fence again in the north pasture."

Allen groaned. "If those bulls weren't such great studs, we'd have a year's worth of meat. It seems like they are busting through the fence every other week."

Ben laughed. "It gives you something to do. You wouldn't want to be bored, would you?

"No chance of that. I'm pretty sure I could find a way of entertaining myself that doesn't involve fixing fences."

They hitched up the wagon and put in a couple of fence posts since the bulls had a tendency to break them as they tore down the fence. Ben and Allen loaded up the post-hole digger, a sledgehammer, wire stretchers, pliers, and nails, and headed out.

Allen groaned when he saw the damage. "Why can't they just make one hole and go out through the same hole? Why do they have to tear down an eighth of a mile worth of fence?"

"They care about you, Allen. They know you like to keep busy and that fixin' fences is your favorite thing in the world to do."

Shaking his head, Allen grinned. "So, they have a conspiracy against me, huh? Is that why something seems to break on this blasted ranch every day? It's wearing me out."

"You have two other ranch hands besides me. It's wearing you out because you're doing too much. Not only are you a full-time sheriff, but then you come out here and work until dark."

"I'm just trying to keep it going. It didn't take me long to make it profitable again, but it seems like every time I turn around, that old man is doing something to hurt the ranch. It's almost like he wants to fail."

"He's just mad that you're a better businessman than he is. Amos doesn't know how to manage money and tries to undermine you when it's time to sell because he doesn't understand the law of demand or how the market works." Ben sighed. "He's jealous and resents you because you are doing what he can't."

"I guess," Allen said. "I just figured it was because he's a mean old man and always has been."

Sweat poured off his forehead as the hot summer sun beat down on them. The turkey vultures circled overhead outside of the fence line, looking for carrion or even small live prey. The air was eerily quiet except for the sounds of Allen and Ben working on the fence.

Allen looked up when he heard hooves pounding the ground, coming toward them. Uncle Amos swung off his horse. The old man's face was bright red, and a storm brewed in his rheumy blue eyes. A steady throb in his neck was a clear sign that he was angry.

What now? If it's not one thing, it's the other.

"Why did you buy such a huge supply of hay for the cattle? It's the middle of July. We don't need it now." Uncle Amos's voice was raspy.

"Joshua Turner harvested and baled the hay and wanted to plant for a second season. Demand was low, so I was able to get a lot of feed for a very low price. We'll use all that I bought and more during the winter." Allen made sure that his voice was calm and measured.

"You don't know nothing about running this ranch, do you? You don't just buy up a bunch of hay that we don't need right now. There will be hay in September. Right now, we need the money for other things," Uncle Amos spat.

Allen continued working and refused to let Uncle Amos see he was irritated. "It'll be twice as expensive then. This was a good deal and a smart move. Right this minute, we're caught up on supplies, and all our accounts are paid up. It was the right thing to do."

Uncle Amos crossed his arms over his chest and glared at him. "Sometimes, I think that you ain't got the good sense that God gave a goose."

Allen didn't bother replying. He knew when his uncle was spoiling for a fight, and he just wasn't in the mood.

"I'm getting hungry. You need to get home and make me some food. We've got hands who can take care of this. Those lazy good-for-nothings need to earn the salary I pay them."

Uncle Amos got back on his horse and tore off across the field.

"It's too hot for him to be riding that old horse like that," Ben said, shaking his head. "Not to mention the prairie dog holes. If Pepper steps in one of those, he'll break a leg for sure."

"At least Keith will make sure to brush him down really well and give him some oats."

They worked for a few minutes, and Ben paused, looked at Allen, and grinned. "You know what I think you need?"

"What's that?"

"A woman."

Allen coughed, startled by the suggestion. "What in the world makes you think that?"

"A wife would help you keep the house clean, cook meals, and take care of some of the chores." Ben cocked his head to one side. "She might also be able to keep your uncle busy so he has less time to harass you."

"I doubt that. Do you have anyone in particular in mind?" Allen playfully smacked Ben's back. "Don't you dare say Miss Katie."

"She *has* been after you for quite some time. I've heard her say that she'd give up her establishment for you."

"Not in this lifetime or the next three," Allen said, shivering exaggeratedly. "I'm not interested in getting fleas."

Ben laughed and said, "There's always Mrs. Stillwell. She's a widow and always brings you small pastries."

"No. She's old enough to be my mother." He paused, nailed a wire to the fence post, and looked at Ben. "As it happens, I've thought about finding a wife already and took steps."

"Steps? I didn't think you'd have time to visit Anaconda, Deer Lodge, or Helena to find someone."

"I haven't. I put in an ad for a mail-order bride."

"I'm sorry. You did *what*?"

Allen chuckled. "I placed an ad in *The New York Times* and *New York Herald*."

"What in the world did you say?"

"Man in need of a hardworking, reliable young woman of good moral character to help run a cattle ranch and marry. Must be strong and capable. If interested, write to Allen Strauss, Box 112, Butte, Montana."

Ben stopped dead in his tracks and stared at him disbelievingly.

"What?"

"You might as well be ordering a sack of potatoes or hiring a servant."

Allen shrugged. "The papers charged by the word, and I didn't want anyone to get any kind of romantic notions."

"Wow." Ben shook his head. "Has anyone answered yet?"

"Yes. I've been conversing with Mrs. Fiona Williams about her niece, Virginia. She said that Virginia is willing to come to Montana. She wants to get away from the city and start a new life for herself. According to Mrs. Williams, Virginia worked long hours in a musty warehouse, bent over a sewing machine, and didn't want to spend the rest of her life working hard for little pay."

"Aren't you a little curious about why you were talking to the aunt and not the woman?"

"Nope. I figured that they've got their reasons. I sent her the money for the train fare and food. She'll be here in about a week."

"Aren't you worried that she's gonna look like the north end of a southbound donkey?" Ben asked.

"Why do I care? It's not like we're going to be involved or anything. All I care about is that she can cook, clean, and take care of our basic needs around the ranch. Nothing more, nothing less. I don't even care if she has the nasty personality of an old battle-ax. It's not like I'm going to be spending much time with her. If you don't like her, then ignore her."

Ben sighed and rubbed his face with his hands. "I just don't know what to think about that. Maybe you should have just hired someone from town."

"No. There's no self-respecting woman who would spend a lot of time in the company of men. Even if she did, it would damage her reputation. On top of that, I don't want anyone to get any ideas and cause trouble for me in town," Allen explained.

They loaded all their supplies into the wagon.

"With a wife who understands that this is a marriage of convenience only, there won't be any problems. No kinfolk is going to come after me for tarnishing anyone's reputation. She won't be expecting any of that romantic nonsense."

Ben shook his head. "I'm a little worried about you. That's a very harsh way to put things. And if Virginia's aunt didn't tell her what to expect from you, then she's going to be very disappointed and hurt."

Allen shrugged. "She'll get over it. People do."

Chapter Three

Virginia was relieved when she sank onto the hard wooden bench, glad that she could get a window seat and that she was on the right train. Her happiness was short-lived, though. The train was soon crowded, and the person next to her pressed so hard against her that she could barely breathe. It was noisy, and the car was full of coal smoke and dust. It was sweltering hot, making sweat tickle her scalp. She was miserable.

The noise pounded in her head, and each sound was like a hammer striking her skull. The smell of unwashed bodies and various food people brought with them made her stomach churn.

It's going to be okay. I just have to get through this part, and I'll be fine. I have a new life waiting for me. There will be a lot of fresh air and room to breathe. This isn't going to kill me.

These words ran through Virginia's head every time she was overwhelmed.

Twenty-seven hours until we get to Chicago. That's all. I can deal with that.

Finally, at long last, the train pulled into the Chicago station, and she hurried off with her bag. The people rushed around her. A few of them pushed her as they rushed to disembark one train or board another.

Some of the women were wearing fancy dresses like she'd sewn at the garment factory. Others wore simple cotton shirts and skirts like she was wearing. It seemed like everyone was talking at the top of their lungs.

Her head was swimming, and for a moment she felt lost. She had no idea where to go. Fear gripped her heart like a vice.

Get yourself together. You can do this.

Taking a deep breath, she looked around. She had about an hour before she caught the next train. Her stomach grumbled, so she bought a roll with some of the money she had with her.

Virginia was certain that her aunt had taken the majority of the money that Allen had sent for food because she only had a couple of dollars until she got to Butte. That wasn't much for the seven to ten-day journey.

With a sense of relief, Virginia found a bench that was a little out of the way. She put her roll down and then set her bag on the ground. When she looked up, Virginia saw a little girl grab the roll and run off, stuffing as much of it in her mouth as she could.

Her stomach grumbled loudly, and sharp pains pierced her gut. She was incredibly hungry. Slowly, she returned to the stand and bought another roll. This time, she stood off to the side and ate it. She felt bad for the child who was likely as hungry as she was, but Virginia wasn't going to chance losing another roll.

She got a drink of water from the hand pump the station had for travelers and filled up her canteen. Then, she walked back to the bench and waited anxiously for her train.

Virginia unconsciously moved her foot as she had for the last several years while operating the treadle on the sewing machines. Virginia twisted her hands in knots and chewed on her bottom lip. She pressed her canvas bag next to her, terrified that someone would steal the precious few belongings she brought with her.

She thought about the factory and how her aunt and uncle always made her feel like a burden. The factory had almost been more like a home than her aunt's apartment had been.

At least everyone at the factory had been kind to her—even the supervisors.

This journey is taking me to a new life where I can be free. It's still going to be hard work, but at least I'll be able to breathe.

She tried to picture the face of the man she'd marry but couldn't quite conjure an image. It was merely a vague, shadowy form.

For an instant, fear gripped her heart.

What if he's mean? What if he's worse than my aunt and uncle? I can't go to anyone for help because he's the law.

Virginia closed her eyes and forced herself to take even breaths.

Stop. There's no sense in borrowing trouble. I'm sure he's a perfectly nice man.

She briefly wondered why, if he was a nice man, he couldn't find someone to marry in Butte, but she pushed the thought away.

He must have his reasons.

The next train, bound for Omaha, Nebraska, finally came, allowing Virginia a brief respite from torturing herself with the fear of what was to come. The train blew its horn, and a rush of people disembarked, pushing past the waiting passengers.

Although it was still third class, this train wasn't quite as crowded and noisy. A nice young couple, who were going West to start a new life together, sat across from her.

They were also from New York City, and the three of them shared stories about their experiences there and mentioned a few things they would miss. They talked about their dreams. Mary and Todd wanted to start a farm and a family.

Virginia simply told them that she was going to Montana to visit a relative. She was too embarrassed to say she was going out there as a mail-order bride to marry some man she'd never met. She also figured that it wasn't really a lie because, technically, a husband would be a relative.

The twelve hours passed quickly, and Virginia was sad to see them go. They'd made the trip a lot more pleasant and had taken her mind off the fear of what was to come.

She was greatly relieved to find that the station in Omaha wasn't nearly as busy. Virginia was starving and feeling a little light-headed, so she reluctantly handed over five cents for a ham sandwich and a nickel for a cup of weak coffee.

Virginia devoured the food just as the next train, headed for Cheyenne, Wyoming, arrived. She'd been awake for nearly two days, so as soon as she sat on the hard wooden bench, she rested her head on the window and quickly fell asleep.

Her head jerked as her eyes popped open. She had no idea how long she'd been asleep. Virginia quickly sat up straight. A tall, thin man with dirty clothes and an unkempt beard sat across from her. She felt his eyes on her, and the hair on the back of her neck stood up.

A wave of unease washed over her. She unconsciously touched the high collar of her blouse and smoothed her hand over her skirt. Virginia didn't acknowledge him, fearing that might give him leave to speak to her. She turned her attention out the window, although there wasn't much to see in the darkness.

Finally, he said in a leering voice, "You're such a fine lass to be traveling all alone."

Her stomach twisted in fear. Her throat tightened, and the air around her felt thick and heavy. She didn't reply, hoping that he would leave her alone.

"It's awfully rude not to speak to someone when they talk to you," he said.

The man had an accent that she couldn't place. His voice was oily, and it made her insides tremble. She clutched her hands together to keep them from shaking.

Virginia continued to ignore him until he reached out to touch her knee. Her reflexes took over, and she slapped his hand. She felt as though her lungs were exploding, and her heart stopped. Virginia hadn't ever encountered anything like this before and wasn't sure what to do.

The man stood up and acted as though he was going to backhand her. "Why, you filthy…" he started to say.

"Caroline, dear, are you okay?" an older woman asked. "I'd wondered where you'd got to."

Virginia looked at the woman, confused at first, and then saw her slight smile. "Sorry. I was tired, so I sat here. I must've fallen asleep." Virginia sighed, her shoulders sagging with relief. She looked at the woman as though she were a saint who'd stepped down from the heavens to save her.

"I understand. It's been a tiresome journey." The woman glared at the man who'd touched Virginia. "Is this man bothering you? Do I need to fetch your father?"

"I was just being friendly." The man shot a nasty look at Virginia and hurried away from the two of them.

Exhaling a long breath, Virginia smiled weakly at the woman who'd come to her rescue. "Thank you so much."

"It's my pleasure. My name is Caroline." She took the seat that the obnoxious man vacated. "I'm going to Cheyenne to live with my son. He went out to Wyoming Territory a year ago to buy some land and start a ranch. Robert's doing well, so he sent for me."

Virginia nodded and relaxed against the wooden bench, grateful for her friendly companion. "That's terrific. I'm meeting my fiancé in Montana Territory. He's a sheriff."

Although Caroline had protected her from the dirty man, she still didn't feel comfortable telling anyone that she was a mail-order bride—and worse, it was because her aunt forced her into it.

"Congratulations, my dear. I hope you have a happy life. My Fredrick died about ten years ago. He caught the fever that was going around. He was a terrific husband."

"I'm sorry for your loss." Virginia patted Caroline's arm.

Caroline put her hand over her heart. "He's still with me in here. We had thirty-three good years together."

They talked until they reached Cheyenne. Caroline hugged her and then said, "There's my son over there. Godspeed," and she hurried off.

It seemed like a sea of people at the station. Everyone was hurrying to one place or another. Three trains were lined up, and Virginia had no idea which one to get on.

Her heart raced, and she felt her throat closing up. She trembled as panic set in. Biting her bottom lip, she took several deep breaths to try to calm down.

"Excuse me, ma'am," Virginia said to one woman. "Can you...?"

The woman walked away from her without a backward glance.

Virginia tried asking several people, including two porters, which train she should get on. One porter growled at her and snapped that he was busy, and the other ignored her.

Fear gripped her heart as one of the trains got ready to depart. She didn't want to miss the one that would take her to Helena. The line to speak with the ticket seller was long, and she was afraid that her train would leave before she could figure out which one to board.

Tears pricked the back of her eyes as she frantically searched the crowd for someone who could help her. Finally, a tall blonde woman with flashing blue eyes, wearing buckskin pants, a buckskin shirt with fringes, and a cowboy hat, heard Virginia trying to ask a man about the train heading for Helena.

"Miss, I'm going in the same direction. Follow me."

Relieved, Virginia sucked in a huge breath of air. The strangely dressed woman led her to a train on the other side of the station. They boarded ten minutes before the train took off.

Virginia sat on the wooden bench and closed her eyes for a brief second, feeling the icy cold hand release her heart. She pressed her shoulders and head against the back and tried to remember to breathe.

The woman sat across from her and gave her a lopsided grin. "I'm June."

"Virginia. Thank you so much for helping me."

"I'm glad to help. I know sometimes the stations can be confusing and hard to figure out. It's taken me a while to make heads or tails of the systems."

"Do you travel a lot?" Virginia asked.

She really wanted to know why the woman was wearing pants and dressed as she was, but she didn't want to be rude and ask. The woman had helped her, and she was extremely nice, so Virginia didn't want to upset her.

June seemed to have read her mind. "I guess you haven't run into a whole lot of women running around in pants."

Virginia shook her head. "No. I can't say that I have."

She leaned against the window, a slight smirk tugging at her lips. "I'm a sharpshooter. I go from town to town, doing shows for the locals. I go by the name Shootin' June." She said the words as though it were the most common thing in the world.

Virginia's eyes opened wide. She'd never heard of a sharpshooter. "What kind of shows do you do?"

"I do tricks with my pistols. I show out the pictures on playing cards, shoot the apples on a person's head, shoot the flame off of a candle without hitting the candle."

"Wow. That is amazing." Virginia's voice was barely above a whisper, in awe of the woman who sat across from her.

"Thank you. My favorite tricks are to shoot coins out of the air or shoot a bullet at the edge of an ax blade so that it splits in two and hits two targets."

Virginia looked at June, admiring the confidence the other woman had.

"Oh, my goodness. I would love to see that," Virginia said.

June chuckled, noticing how Virginia stared wide-eyed at her. "You'll have to come to one of my shows sometime. Are you staying in Helena?"

"No. I'm going to Butte to meet my fiancé, Sheriff Allen Strauss."

June nodded. "I don't think I could ever settle down in one place. I've been on my own and moving from place to place since I was knee-high to a grasshopper." She studied Virginia for a minute and grinned. "Who knows, maybe I'll come your way. Right now, though, I'm stayin' in Helena. There's a traveling Wild West show there, and I'm hopin' to join them. I mostly do shows by myself and get paid through tips. If I can join one of the shows, I would have a steady income because they advertise before goin' to a town and charge admission."

Virginia envied June a little. She was free to go where she wanted and didn't have to answer to anyone. June dressed in pants and welcomed the attention because that was how she made money. She didn't have to rely on anyone else. The woman didn't seem to be afraid of anything.

They talked for a while, and when night fell, June went to sleep. Virginia laid her head against the train wall and tried to get some rest, but June's snoring kept her awake for a while. Finally, though, exhaustion overtook her, and she drifted off.

Once the morning sun streamed through the windows, Virginia and June woke. Virginia's stomach rumbled and clenched tightly from hunger. She hadn't had any food for almost twenty-four hours. The meager meals her aunt used to serve seemed like a feast, and her mouth watered when she thought of the beef stews her aunt made.

The news butcher walked through the car, selling sandwiches. Hesitantly, Virginia gave her last dime for a ham sandwich. June bought a beef sandwich.

June regaled her with stories from her different shows, and Virginia told her about working at the garment factory since she was ten. When she was younger, she threaded needles, wound bobbins, moved materials, pressed the clothes, and cut out patterns. When she got older, she became a seamstress.

"I can't imagine bein' stuck in a factory for twelve to sixteen hours a day," June said, shivering exaggeratedly. "That would be purgatory for me."

"It was, but there weren't many choices. I did what I had to do."

June nodded and smiled sympathetically. "I hear that."

When the train arrived in Helena, Virginia thought she'd made her first good friend out west.

"My fiancé is Sheriff Allen Strauss. Please come to visit me if you come to Butte," Virginia said.

"I surely will. So long."

June headed off to find her next show, and Virginia boarded the train that would take her to Butte, her new friend's adventurous spirit filling her soul.

Chapter Four

Allen looked up at Ben as the foreman walked into the barn.

"Have you heard from Uncle Amos?" Allen washed his hands in a bucket of water and dried them with a towel. "I've been expecting him to come out to the barn wanting breakfast."

Allen had been in the barn since before dawn because one of his prized heifers had shown signs of going into labor soon, and she'd had difficulties in the past. He was pleased because the calf had just been born and was healthy.

"I see Daisy did just fine this time." Ben patted the cow on her head. "No, I haven't seen or heard from him. Maybe he decided to make his own breakfast."

Allen looked at him out of the corner of his eye. "That old man hasn't made a meal for himself since I got back from the war. He'd rather starve than cook."

Ben chuckled. "He is a stubborn cuss."

Allen shook his head. "That's putting it mildly."

The calf wobbled to its feet, and Allen was satisfied. He smiled. New life was always precious, especially when it added to his herd.

Allen's stomach rumbled, reminding him that if he wanted to stay among the living, he needed to eat, so he headed back to the house. As he took out the pan to start the bacon, he realized Uncle Amos wasn't in the kitchen. He hadn't been on the porch either.

A sudden fear gripped his heart as he walked to his uncle's bedroom and knocked on the door.

"Uncle Amos. Are you awake?"

There was no answer.

Slowly opening the door, Allen peeked in. Uncle Amos was lying in bed with the blankets and quilt pulled up to his chin. It looked like he was sleeping peacefully.

His heart raced as he quickly covered the short space between the door and the bed. Allen had never known Uncle Amos to sleep late. He shook him, but there was no response.

Allen pressed two fingers to the man's neck.

No pulse. Darn.

He noticed that Uncle Amos seemed cold to the touch and was already starting to stiffen. Allen had seen enough death to know that he was gone.

Allen shut the door to the room and ran outside. "Ben, I need you to go fetch Dr. Simmons."

Ben nodded and started for the stables. "What's wrong?"

"Uncle Amos is gone. He must have died in his sleep."

Skidding to a stop, Ben turned to gape at Allen. "Dead?"

Allen ran his fingers through his hair. "Yes. He's cold and has already started to stiffen."

"On my way."

Not knowing what to do and realizing that the doctor would take at least an hour to arrive, he made breakfast for himself, Ben, and the two hands, Keith and John. Ben would have to eat a cold meal.

Keith and John were just as shocked as Ben was.

"He gave us a thorough tongue-lashing last night," John said. "He didn't like the way we were cleaning the tack. He seemed fine and like his normal self."

Allen nodded. "He scolded me because his fried potatoes weren't done to his satisfaction. Uncle Amos had slowed down some lately, but I know his arthritis was bothering him, and he did just turn seventy-one. I reckon it was on account of his age."

They ate in silence. Afterward, Keith and John went out to tend to chores while Allen waited for the doctor.

Ben and Dr. Simmons arrived twenty minutes later. The undertaker pulled up in front of the house with his hearse.

Dr. Simmons shook his hand. "Good morning, Sheriff. Ben tells me that your uncle has passed."

"Yes, sir. I checked on him this morning because he didn't come for breakfast. He was stiff and cold."

Mr. Martin, the undertaker, patted him on the shoulder. "Sorry for your loss."

Allen followed Mr. Martin and Dr. Simmons into the bedroom.

The doctor looked at Uncle Amos and sighed. "I've been expecting this. Frankly, I'm surprised he lived as long as he did."

"Pardon?" Allen asked, shocked, not sure he was hearing correctly.

"Amos came to me about a year ago with chest pains. He'd been experiencing shortness of breath and fatigue for a while. I noticed an irregularity in your uncle's heartbeat."

Allen's jaw dropped in surprise. "He never said anything to me."

"He didn't want you to know. He came to me twice more with the same symptoms. The last time was about a week ago."

Allen sat down in the chair and rubbed his face. "I didn't know." His voice was little more than a whisper.

Mr. Martin gestured to the board stretcher he'd brought in. "Doc, can you help me get him onto the stretcher so I can take him back?"

"Sure."

"I'll notify Father Cahill to let him know that he'll need to conduct the service tomorrow. I'll have the gravediggers get started, and we can have the service around ten in the morning." Mr. Martin spoke with the efficiency of someone who'd conducted hundreds of burials. "Do you have clothes you'd like him buried in?"

Allen hastily collected his uncle's Sunday clothes and carried them out to the hearse.

He dressed in his uniform and nodded to Ben. "I'm going in to put up some notices. Uncle Amos was well known around here. I reckon there'll be a good number of folks wanting to pay their respects at the funeral."

Ben returned the nod. "I'll take care of things on this end."

Allen quickly made up a few notices at the sheriff's office and put them in the general store, the saloon, the courthouse, the post office, and the town bulletin board. He figured that between the handbills posted in those places and word of mouth, everyone who wished to attend the funeral would know the time and place.

***

Ben, Keith, John, and Allen were at the church fifteen minutes early. They took their spot in the front pew. Mayor Jasper Johnson and his wife, Gloria, sat behind them.

The church was filled by ten, and Father Cahill stood at the pulpit. "My dear brothers and sisters in Christ, we gather here today to commend the soul of our beloved friend, Amos Strauss, into the hands of our merciful Father. Although our hearts are filled with sorrow, we can take comfort in the promise of our Lord, who said in John, Chapter Eleven, Verse Twenty-Five, 'I am the resurrection and the life. He that believeth in me, though he were dead, yet shall he live.'"

Allen felt a tug at his heart.

Although Uncle Amos had rarely, if ever, shown affection, he had given Allen a home and taught him how to run a ranch. He'd still loved the old man, even though Uncle Amos had made life difficult sometimes, not to mention he'd been the last living member of his family.

Father Cahill continued. "Amos was known to many of you as a man of strength. He lived honestly and worked hard. He never faltered during times of hardship. We mourn his loss, but we don't mourn without hope because we know that death is not the end. We pass on to the life that Christ has prepared for us. Today, as we lay him to rest, let us pray that his soul may find peace in the light of our Savior."

Everyone bowed their heads.

Allen sincerely hoped that Uncle Amos would find peace.

The father recited the traditional prayer for the dead. "Oh God, whose mercies cannot be numbered, accept our prayers on behalf of Thy servant Amos, whom Thou hast called to Thyself. Grant him an entrance into the land of light and joy, and the company of Thy saints. Wash away his sins in Thy boundless mercy, and bring him to the everlasting rest promised to all who believe in Thee.

"Eternal rest grant unto him, O Lord, and let perpetual light shine upon him. May his soul and the souls of all the faithful departed, through the mercy of God, rest in peace. Amen."

The congregation sang, "Nearer, my God, to Thee," "Amazing Grace," and "Abide with Me."

Allen, Ben, Keith, and John carried Uncle Amos's casket to the graveyard and set it on the wooden planks laid across the open grave.

Father Cahill intoned another prayer and sprinkled holy water on the casket.

A long procession made its way back to the ranch house. Several women had made dishes to share. Everyone ate and told stories about Uncle Amos. Allen was surprised that some of the townspeople had funny stories. He'd never known his uncle to have a sense of humor, but apparently, he told jokes to the blacksmith, storekeeper, and saloon owner.

"Are they talking about the same man?" Ben asked after the mayor relayed a particularly humorous story.

"I'm not sure," Allen said. "In all my years, I've barely seen the man crack a smile."

"I thought he'd been a cantankerous old cuss to everyone. He even fought with us in death since he never let on that he was sick."

Allen groaned. "I wish he had. But he wouldn't have wanted us fussing over him."

Finally, after an eternity, everyone left. Ben and Allen got busy cleaning up.

"Luckily, soon, we won't have to worry about cleaning the house since you'll have your woman here to help."

Allen's head jerked toward Ben, his heart hammering in his chest.

He rubbed his face and then froze. "Virginia! With the funeral, I got my days mixed up and completely forgot about her. She's supposed to arrive today."

He checked his pocket watch and groaned. She would have arrived several hours ago.

"Wow, you already blew it with your new wife, and you haven't even met her yet," Ben teased. "I'm not surprised since you have the worst luck of anyone I know."

"Quit your yammering, and come help me hitch up the wagon."

Ben and Allen ran outside and had the horses harnessed in ten minutes.

"I'll stay here and finish cleaning so your new bride doesn't walk into a complete mess."

Allen nodded, hopped up on the buckboard, and turned the horses toward the dirt road that led to town.

I can't believe I forgot about her. She must be terrified.

Allen had hardened himself over the years and rarely thought about how a person might feel in a particular situation, but a flash of sympathy coursed through him as he thought of the woman who'd traveled for the last ten days, sitting at the train station, alone and scared.

He had no idea what to expect. Mrs. Williams had described Virginia as having fiery red hair and being passably pretty. Of course, the woman might have been biased or simply trying to convince him to accept her niece.

As the horses expertly made their way toward town, needing little guidance from him, Allen wondered, not for the first time, whether he'd made a mistake. Ben had pointed out that he could have hired a matronly woman from town to cook and clean for them. It would have been less of a hassle, and he'd at least know the person in his house.

Allen knew nothing about Virginia except what Mrs. Williams told him. She had written that Virginia was smart, hard-working, and had a sweet disposition. Even though he'd told Ben it didn't matter what Virginia was like since they would be spending minimal time together, he hoped she hadn't been exaggerating.

His heart lurched as they passed by the graveyard. Uncle Amos had been buried in the corner, and Allen could see the raised mound of dirt and the small white cross that stood at the head of the grave until the simple headstone, carved with a cross, Uncle Amos's name, and date of birth and death could be set in its rightful place.

He guided the wagon to the station. A train had just arrived, so people were pouring out while others waited to board. His eyes scanned the platform, looking for anyone who matched Mrs. Williams's description. After several minutes of searching, his eyes landed on a small, red-haired form hunched on a bench.

I'm not sure I'm ready for this, but I guess it's too late for that.

Chapter Five

Virginia wished that Shootin' June was traveling all the way to Butte with her. She'd taken comfort in knowing she wasn't alone on the trip. Luckily, this part of the trip would only take her three hours.

She twisted her hands in her lap and bit her bottom lip as she wondered about her new life. It was so close. Soon, she would meet her fiancé and spend her days looking after him. Maybe, if they were compatible, they could start a family.

Virginia had always wanted a family with a lot of kids. She'd make sure they grew up knowing they were loved, just like she was before her father died of the fever. Moving in with her aunt and uncle had been a shock to her system, as she was treated with cold indifference on the best of days. They'd started making her work long hours in the factory a few days after she arrived on their doorstep.

No, my kids will have chores, but they will have a chance to laugh and have fun, too. I'd make sure they get an education so they can learn to read, write, and do arithmetic.

For a minute, she imagined holding her newborn baby in her arms, kissing its sweet face. She pictured running around in the yard, laughing, and playing tag with a couple of young'uns.

Virginia shook her head.

You don't know if he's going to like you or if you're going to like him. He might not want a family. For all I know, he could be a hundred years old and just want a nursemaid. A wife would be cheaper than hiring one.

Anxiety rolled up inside of her and exploded like the fancy fireworks she'd seen lit on the harbor on the Fourth of July.

Her chest hurt, and she couldn't draw a breath as she painted the worst-case scenario in her mind.

Stop it! she yelled at herself in her thoughts. *Don't create problems where there aren't any yet. He might be the nicest man on Earth. You aren't going to solve anything by working yourself into a state over nothing.*

She forced herself to push the thoughts away and stared out the window as the train rolled down the tracks. As the train left Helena, the grassy land and foothills opened up in front of her. Sagebrush dotted the landscape. The different colored flowers painted the ground, making the vast expanse look like an endless sea of color. It was breathtaking.

They passed the rushing, murky waters of the Missouri River and several streams. The landscape changed, and she saw the rugged mountains in the distance.

Virginia was delighted when she spotted the herds of elk, deer, pronghorn antelope, and bison grazing in the prairie. Rabbits hopped around, and she was certain she had seen a large snake sunbathing on a huge rock close to the tracks.

They passed by a couple of small mining towns. The train didn't stop at any of them, but it slowed as they passed, so she could see the few buildings bordering the dirt road and people doing their business.

New York City was huge and stayed busy all day and night. It was never quiet. She wondered what Butte would be like.

Aunt Fiona said he had a ranch, which meant we wouldn't live in town. Will I ever get used to the quiet without people shouting and talking all hours of the night and the horses clopping down the streets?

She shook her head.

I can and I will, she told herself firmly.

The train slowed. She saw an area where huge shafts had been dug into the hillside with small wooden headframes. Piles of greenish-blue ore glinted in the sunlight.

A large factory of some sort was closer to the town. Several stone buildings with tall chimneys were grouped together. Heavy smoke billowed out of the tall smokestacks.

Finally, they pulled into the station and stopped. Virginia hastily grabbed the old canvas bag and walked out onto the platform. She inhaled deeply, loving the fresh air that replaced the smog that had choked her in the train car.

Virginia refilled her canteen and took a long drink before she walked to the front of the station, searching the crowd for a man who looked as though he was there to greet her.

How am I going to know it's him? He's the sheriff, so I guess he'll be wearing a uniform. How will he recognize me? Did Aunt Fiona describe me?

In the back of the crowd, she saw a tall, dark, handsome man who was scanning the crowd. He grinned and walked toward the platform. Virginia's heart skipped a beat.

She took a step back, embarrassed, as a young, pretty woman with dark hair rushed toward him. He pulled the woman into his arms and lifted her into the air.

"Justin. I've missed you so much."

He grinned. "Sophia. It's good to have you home. How's your mom?"

They walked away, hand in hand.

Virginia looked hopefully at the group, but no one paid the slightest bit of attention to her. Soon, the platform was cleared, and she was left alone.

"He might be running late," she muttered under her breath. "He might have had to deal with an outlaw or something. I'm sure he'll be here soon."

Virginia waited for an hour. Her stomach was cramped from hunger, and the bench was very hard. She was exhausted and wanted nothing more than to sit on something with a cushion and sleep.

She went into the station and asked the ticket master if he knew where to find the sheriff.

"Ma'am, I really don't know. You could try him at the office, although he doesn't stay there too often. Normally, he walks around town, making sure that everyone is behaving. He could be on his ranch, too."

"Thank you," she said.

Virginia sat on the hard wooden bench again, groaning in the back of her throat. Her body ached all over from sitting on hard surfaces for the last ten days. It was a different kind of ache than she got from sewing twelve hours a day.

She looked at her fingertips. "At least my fingers aren't bleeding for a change."

Biting her lip, her foot once again worked the imaginary treadle as she tried to figure out what she should do. Virginia considered going to the sheriff's office and asking for him. The thought of explaining her business with the sheriff to a stranger, if her fiancé wasn't in, was humiliating.

Plus, he was supposed to pick her up at the train station. What if he came by and she wasn't there?

The hours ticked by, and the sun was descending in the west, painting the town in brilliant red, orange, and golden yellow light. The chilly night air shrouded her, and she was enveloped in darkness.

Virginia's guts were tied in a knot, and a huge boulder settled in the pit of her stomach. Her purse was empty. She didn't have the money to stay at a woman's hotel, even if they had one, and she certainly didn't have enough to get back to New York City.

She groaned in the back of her throat, and she fought back the tears. "I should have listened to Meaghan. I could have stayed with her until I found an affordable boarding house that took women."

Her legs ached, so she paced back and forth across the platform, biting her bottom lip. She kept a sharp eye on her canvas bag. Even though there wasn't much of value in it, she couldn't afford to lose what she had.

"Am I going to have to sleep here?" She looked at the small station and doubted that the ticket master would let her sleep in the corner of the building. Vagrants weren't welcome in any of the buildings in New York City, and she was certain that would be true here, too.

A thought occurred to her.

Did Aunt Fiona lie to me? What if she never arranged a marriage at all? Would she have really sent me out West with a one-way ticket to leave me stranded here?

Although it would have been more likely for her to simply kick her out on the streets and not waste the precious money on the train tickets, Virginia couldn't quite swallow the fear.

Sending me out here, though, would make sure that I wouldn't try to come back. She can be cruel, and she might do something like that.

Swallowing her pride, she was about to walk to the sheriff's station when she spotted a wagon coming toward the station.

A tall man wearing a cowboy hat pulled the brake on the wagon and stepped onto the platform.

"Are you Virginia Kelly?" he asked in a deep voice.

She stood tall, her shoulders back and her head held high. "I am. And you are?"

"Sheriff Allen Strauss. I believe you've come in response to my ad."

She opened her mouth to give him a piece of her mind for leaving her stranded for so long, but the words died in her throat. Virginia studied him for a minute. The man standing in front of her wasn't the grizzled old man she'd been afraid of meeting. Allen was tall, broad-shouldered, and carried himself with an air of confidence. He was muscular but lean. His brown hair peeked out from under his cowboy hat, and a curl swept over his forehead. He had an angular jaw and was clean-shaven. His tanned face spoke of spending hours in the sun.

Virginia was fascinated by his large brown eyes. They were beautiful but unreadable.

A strange warmth curled through her. Her heart skipped a beat, and she inhaled deeply. Hurriedly, she pushed aside the unfamiliar and unwelcome feeling.

She swallowed hard. "I have."

"Is that your bag?" he asked, pointing to her shabby canvas satchel next to the uncomfortable bench.

"It is."

Briefly, she wondered whether she should go anywhere with someone who'd leave his future wife stranded at the train station all day. If he was busy, the least he could do was send someone for her.

Where else am I going to go?

"Do you have a trunk or anything?"

"No. That's all I have."

Allen raised his eyebrows but didn't say anything.

She pressed her lips together. Virginia didn't feel as though she owed him an explanation.

He put her bag in the back of the wagon and held out his hand to her. A bolt of lightning exploded inside her as she put her hand in his. She quickly sat on the buckboard and pulled her hand out of his as though he had burned her.

Great. Another wooden bench.

Virginia wanted to rub her behind and back, but knew that would be very unladylike.

Once they were settled in the seat, he glanced at her, a look of regret in his eyes. He pressed his lips together for a second and said, "I'm very sorry I was late. My uncle died yesterday, and his funeral was this morning. Everyone met at the house, and I completely forgot what day it was."

Her heart softened as she realized that he'd had a trying day.

"I'm sorry for your loss. Of course, I understand why you were late picking me up."

The sun had set, and although there was a full moon and a sky full of diamond-like stars, the night was an inky darkness. In New York City, the streets were never dark as lamplighters lit the lamps each night. In some areas, electric lights lit up the streets.

Virginia swallowed a groan as the wagon traveled over the bumpy, uneven road, the seat hitting her legs, behind, and back uncomfortably. She looked around at the shadowy silhouettes of the trees, hills, and distant mountains. Coyotes were howling in the distance, and the scent of sagebrush and pine filled the air. The creak of the wagon and the plodding of the hooves hitting the dirt combined with an owl hooting from the trees and insects singing.

"So, your aunt did all the letter writing."

"Yes." Virginia had to stop herself from adding "sir" to her reply. After all, this was her future husband.

"Did you tell her what to say?"

Virginia debated about whether to tell him the truth, but decided that they should start off their marriage with honesty, especially since she had no idea what her aunt actually wrote in the letters.

"Actually, I didn't even know that she'd answered an ad until she told me that she'd arranged for me to be married, and I was to leave in a few days."

Allen looked at her sharply. "You didn't answer the ad?"

"No. I've lived with Aunt Fiona and Uncle Arthur since my father died when I was ten. She thought it was time for me to leave and decided that being a mail-order bride was the best option." Virginia spoke matter-of-factly. She was telling a story, not looking for sympathy.

"Are you sure you want to go through with this?"

Virginia thought about his question.

What choice do I have anyway?

"Yes. Living on a ranch, cooking, cleaning, and whatever other chores I need to take care of is going to be very easy compared to being hunched over a sewing machine for twelve to sixteen hours six days a week."

"It's hard work, but it does sound better than working in a factory."

An awkward silence settled on them like a wet blanket. After they drove for what seemed like hours, although Virginia knew it wasn't that long, she saw the silhouette of a barn, stables, and a house in the distance.

"We'll be home soon."

Virginia gulped nervously and nodded.

And then what?

Chapter Six

Allen had been surprised when he saw Virginia waiting for him at the station. He'd been struck by her good looks that were obvious in spite of her pale face, the dark circles under her eyes, and her slightly messy hair. It looked as though the trip had been very difficult. He could only imagine. It couldn't have been easy for a single woman to travel all that way alone.

Mrs. Williams said her niece was passably attractive, but Virginia was beautiful. Her fiery red hair and bright green eyes, which had flashed with annoyance when he finally approached her, captivated him instantly. She was a mere wisp of a woman—barely coming to his shoulders—and rail thin, but he had an idea she had a good measure of strength inside her soul.

Although she was obviously exhausted from her long journey, she had a dignity about her that impressed him more than any fancy dress or high-toned speech could have.

He felt like a complete heel. Even though he'd had a good reason to have lost track of days, he knew that being a lone woman in a strange town, stuck at the train station for hours, had to have been frightening.

What kind of man would leave his intended bride waiting for hours alone at a train station in an unfamiliar town?

Allen was shocked when Virginia told him she had nothing to do with arranging their marriage. He was under the impression that Virginia was excited about the arrangement and a willing participant.

She's a grown woman, so she didn't have to get on the train, come to Montana Territory, and marry me. I'm certain that she could have found another solution to her problem.

However, he was unsettled that she wasn't the one contacting him and didn't make the agreement. Virginia did have an idea what he was asking of her. She mentioned that cleaning the house, cooking, and helping out with some of the chores would be a welcome change from being in the garment factory for twelve hours.

Of course, she likely assumed those would be her duties. That was typically what housewives did.

He gritted his teeth and felt the vein in his neck throb every time he thought about the fact that Mrs. Williams didn't tell Virginia anything about the letters or allow Virginia to have a say. For all Virginia knew, he'd been asking for a wife who'd be willing to milk cows all day and take the milk to town to peddle it.

He was relieved when they got home. It had been a very long day, and he was about to drop from fatigue. However, he still had several things to take care of before he could crawl under the blankets.

Allen jumped from the wagon and helped Virginia get down. A fire blasted through his veins when their hands touched. Embers that he thought had died out years ago flickered at the warmth of her hand in his.

He forced the feeling away.

I'm just tired. It's been a long day.

She stared at the house in disbelief. Her eyes were wide, and she had sucked her bottom lip into her mouth. She was downright adorable.

Keith walked out of the barn and looked at Virginia curiously. "I'll unhitch Star and Belle for you and take care of them."

"Thank you." Allen hesitated for a minute. "Keith, this is Virginia. She came from New York City to be my wife."

The words sounded strange coming from his mouth, and Keith was taken completely by surprise. He looked at Virginia, then back at Allen, and then back to Virginia. Allen didn't want to tell anyone, except Ben, about his mail-order bride plan until she actually arrived.

"Pleasure to meet you, Keith." Her voice was soft and sweet.

"Nice to meet you as well," he stammered out. "I best tend to the ladies."

Allen bit back a chuckle. It was amusing to see him so taken aback. Keith had never shown surprise about anything. A volcano could form in the middle of a field, and Keith would just take it in stride.

Keith glanced at Virginia as though he wasn't sure she was real. Allen figured that he'd get the same reaction from everyone in town. In everyone's mind, Allen was a confirmed bachelor for life, just like his uncle.

He grabbed Virginia's bag. "Please come inside."

As they walked through the front door, he hung his hat on the rack and led her through one door.

"This is the kitchen." He cringed as he saw that Ben hadn't finished washing the dishes from the reception, and they were piled high in the sink. "As you can see, I built a sink and a large wood-burning stove. It has a nice-sized oven." He chuckled. "You'll find out that my foreman, Ben, loves pies. Do you know how to make pies?"

She grinned. "I can make the best cherry, pumpkin, apple, berry, mincemeat, and custard pies that you've ever tasted.

That's just for dessert. I also make great meat pies when I have the ingredients."

"That's terrific. Everyone will love you for that. You'll have plenty of supplies. If you need anything, you can either tell me, and I'll get it for you, or you can go to town to fetch what you need when you feel comfortable enough to do that."

Her eyes lit up. He guessed that food had been scarce at her aunt's house.

"We have a large larder and pantry. It's full because I went to town the other day, but like I said, if you need anything, let me know."

"Thank you."

He guided her through another door, where a large dining room table took up most of the space. A cabinet held the dishes, including some China that had been gifted to his mother when she'd married his father.

"We have a sitting room and a more formal parlor. The parlor is used more as a library. We don't get a lot of guests, but when we do, everyone visits in the sitting room. It's more comfortable."

She nodded and looked around without saying anything.

He winced as he tried to see the place from her perspective. At least a year's worth of dust covered everything except for the chairs and couch. The mantel was gray and adorned with a couple of spider webs.

Ben and Allen had tried to straighten up before the funeral, knowing that everyone would meet at their place to celebrate Amos's life. Apparently, they hadn't managed to clean up the years of neglect. He briefly wondered what the townspeople had thought as they milled around and told stories about Uncle Amos.

He looked down at the floor and grimaced. Muddy footprints and other marks seemed to glow in his mind. Allen couldn't remember the last time anyone had swept and mopped.

She's going to have her work cut out for her. It'll take her a week just to make a ding in this mess.

Allen led her upstairs and opened the large room. It had been his uncle's bedroom, but Allen thought it only right that Virginia should have it. He and Ben had hastily cleaned out Amos's belongings, giving the decent clothes to charity and burning the rest. Allen had kept the important keepsakes that his uncle had cherished. They'd aired out the mattress and put clean blankets on the bed.

He put her bag next to the wardrobe. "I imagine you'd like to freshen up. There's clean water in the pitcher and soap next to the basin. Come back downstairs when you're ready."

"Thank you."

Allen sat down at the table and waited for her. He was so tired that he almost fell asleep, his head drooping down. She stepped so lightly that he barely heard her when she came into the room.

Virginia had washed her face and hair. It was still wet and braided down her back. She wore a clean dress.

"Thank you. I feel a lot better."

"Are you hungry? We have plenty of good food left over from the reception today."

She nodded shyly. "If it's no trouble."

Her face turned bright red when her stomach grumbled. Allen hid his smile, knowing she was embarrassed.

"It's no trouble at all." Allen stood and got her a plate, utensils, and a cup from the cabinet. He put a large piece of fried chicken, some mashed potatoes, and a slice of molasses cake on the plate, then poured her some lemonade.

Virginia's eyes were as round as saucers, and he had the idea that she hadn't had so much food in a long time. Although she tried to eat daintily, it was quite plain to see that she was very hungry.

"Did you eat during your trip?"

She looked at him like a deer caught in the lantern light and froze. Her mouth moved a little, but no sound came out. Finally, she said, "I had some food. My aunt said there was very little after she paid for the train fare."

Allen growled in the back of his throat. He'd sent plenty of money for second-class tickets and three meals each day.

"Did your trip go all right?"

"It was long." She kept her voice even, but Allen thought there was something in the way she said it.

"I reckon so. The ten-day trip from New York City to Butte wasn't a Sunday stroll. You traveled more than two thousand miles."

She grinned. "I feel every one of those miles in my bones."

"Did you at least have decent seats?"

"They were fine."

Fine. They weren't fine at all.

"Did you travel in the second-class cars?"

Virginia didn't answer right away. She was suddenly fascinated with the molasses cake on her plate, studying it as though she hadn't seen one before.

"Not exactly," she murmured.

Allen inhaled deeply.

She traveled third class. The poor woman endured ten days of hard wooden benches, coal smoke, and cars crowded with people.

"Did your aunt buy the tickets?"

Virginia nodded and took another bite of the chicken.

The woman had taken his money and bought Virginia the cheapest tickets she could, giving her just a small amount of money for food.

The thought riled him, and he considered writing to Mrs. Williams and telling her exactly what he thought of her theft.

Virginia looked at him, and as though she could read his thoughts, she said, "I managed. I'm okay."

He grinned at her. "I get the feeling that you would manage in almost any difficult situation."

"I'm sorry, but I can't finish this. I'm not used to...." Her voice trailed off, and he had the idea that she was going to say that she wasn't used to having so much food.

"I'm sure that Major and Thunder, my dogs, will enjoy what's left."

She nodded, and he saw her eyes starting to flutter shut. "I'm sorry, but it's been a long trip with practically no sleep."

"I figured you would be tired. Don't worry about the dishes. I'll take care of them. Let's get you upstairs."

Allen walked her upstairs and hesitated. He knew he needed to tell her something, but wasn't sure how to do it.

Just spit it out and get it over with.

"My bedroom is across the hall. Don't worry if you hear anything in the middle of the night."

She tilted her head to one side. "What do you mean?"

"Don't worry if you hear any yelling or anything coming from my room in the middle of the night, and don't come in under any circumstances. I'm a very loud sleeper."

"Do you have nightmares?" she asked, the sympathy evident in her voice.

Allen stiffened at her question, and he gritted his teeth. He rubbed the back of his neck before looking at her. "I'm just a loud sleeper," he said gruffly. "If it's good with you, we'll go into town tomorrow and make our relationship official."

She nodded. "Okay. Good night."

Virginia went into the room and closed the door behind her. He imagined she'd be asleep in about five minutes. Allen wouldn't have been surprised if she slept all the way through the night and the next day. She'd worn the weariness like a heavy cloak that weighed her down.

He was glad that she hadn't pushed the issue about his nightmares. He never spoke to anyone about them. Even Ben, who slept in the house, didn't say a word to him about them. Everyone knew just to leave him alone. He knew that something was wrong with him because even after ten years, he couldn't get the sounds of the bullets whizzing, the men screaming, or the smell of gunpowder and fresh blood out of his mind, especially at night when he couldn't push the thoughts and images away.

Allen went downstairs and looked at the mess. He tossed the scraps out to the dogs and added the dishes to the rest sitting in the sink.

"I'll get them tomorrow," he muttered and lumbered back upstairs. It had been an incredibly long day, and he was sure he'd fall asleep while he was standing at the sink.

He glanced at the closed door as he passed it.

Tomorrow, we're going to be married.

Although the plan had been in the works for a couple of months, it still didn't seem real.

Chapter Seven

Virginia pulled on her flannel nightgown and sank down onto the soft mattress, tugging the blankets up to her shoulders. She hadn't slept on an actual bed since she was ten. Her aunt's couch had been hard and lumpy, and it seemed almost impossible to get comfortable. This bed felt like heaven.

Her eyes were heavy, and she was so tired, but her mind raced.

Allen seemed very nice. He'd been courteous even though she was sure he'd been tired from his long day. She remembered the funeral when her father died, and it had been a long, drawn-out affair. Even though they'd been very poor, her father had a lot of friends, so they had the ceremony at the church and another at the graveyard. Afterward, everyone met at her old apartment to talk about him and tell her how sorry they were that he'd died.

She pictured Allen in her mind.

He was an extremely handsome man.

"I'm going to be married tomorrow," she whispered under her breath.

She could hardly believe it. It didn't seem any more real than it had when her aunt first told her that she was going to travel to Montana Territory to marry a man she'd never met.

Her heart fluttered, and a tingling sensation coursed through her body.

"What's married life going to be like? Is he going to want to…well, do what married people do right away?"

She got the idea that the answer to that would be "no." Not only was he a nice man who'd take her thoughts and feelings into consideration, but he also didn't want anyone in his room while he slept.

"Why does he have nightmares?" she wondered. "Maybe he was in the war."

The War of the Southern Rebellion had only ended ten years ago, and Allen was old enough to have served. Many men had taken up arms and fought for states' rights, to keep the Union together, and to free the slaves. She'd listened to the people talk around her and knew that the war had taken its toll on the soldiers who returned in many ways. Not only had many of the men been hurt physically, but a lot of them suffered mentally.

She pictured him in her mind and smiled. He was an extremely handsome man—much better than she'd envisioned during her trip. Her heart flip-flopped as she remembered his smile and handsome face. He was also very nice.

And I'm going to marry him tomorrow.

Finally, her eyes fluttered closed, and she drifted off to sleep.

***

The bright sun shining through the window as it rose woke Virginia. Her eyes flew open, and she looked around her, startled for a brief second. She didn't know where she was.

As she fully woke up, she recognized her new bedroom. It was the same size as the living room she'd shared with her three cousins in New York. She had a place to hang her clothes and put her meager belongings.

Virginia pictured Allen again and trembled. She really didn't know much about him, and she was going to marry him today.

I'm going to be legally bound to him.

The thought intrigued her more than it scared her. She truly believed, deep in her soul, that he was a good man, and she hoped that they could become friends and then something more. Virginia could see her dream of a house full of kids coming true.

Virginia reluctantly rolled out of bed, every bone in her body aching from the long train ride. She groaned as she splashed water on her face and tried to wake up all the way.

Her muscles screamed as she pulled off her nightgown and struggled into her work dress. She figured she'd need to make breakfast before changing into her Sunday dress for the ceremony.

The dishes were still piled in the sink when she got downstairs. There was no one around, so she opened the stove door. Relieved to see that the wood and kindling were already prepped inside, she lit a match to get it going.

Virginia looked around and saw a water bucket that was a quarter of the way full. She wasn't sure how fresh the water was, so she grabbed the bucket and stepped outside to look for the well. She was happy to see that they had a hand pump, and she didn't have to haul the water up in a bucket by hand.

She managed to get the bucket inside and poured some of the water into a pan to boil it. Once that was done, she poured it into the sink and added some of the old water so she could tolerate the hot water. She scraped some of the soap into the water, found a washcloth, and got busy.

Virginia hummed to herself as she worked. The movement loosened her muscles, and she was grateful that she wasn't sitting in front of the sewing machine. She was pretty sure that she'd rather wash dishes all day than work in the warehouse.

"Good morning," a voice behind her said.

Virginia squealed and dropped the dish she'd been scrubbing into the water. She whirled around to face the man who'd spoken to her. Her heart raced a million miles an hour, and she glanced at the cast iron skillet on the stove, ready to grab it if she needed to.

He smiled and raised his hands. "I'm sorry. I didn't mean to scare you. You must be Virginia."

"Yes," she said hesitantly, taking in the tall, blond man with twinkling blue eyes.

"My name is Ben. I'm the foreman here and Allen's friend. I guess he forgot to mention that I live in the house, as well. I have the bedroom on the end."

"He did forget to mention that little detail." Virginia wiped her hand on her apron and tucked a lock of red hair behind her ear. "It's nice to meet you."

"And you, as well." He gestured to the dishes she'd neatly stacked in the wooden dish rack on one side of the sink and on the towel on the other side of the sink. "I meant to get these done before you came downstairs today. What a welcome to you."

"I don't mind. I do need to figure out where the bacon and eggs are so I can start breakfast. I also need to know where these dishes go."

Ben pointed to the bacon and eggs. "I'll dry and put the dishes away for you. I imagine you'll want to rearrange the kitchen so it suits your needs."

"Thank you. How many people am I cooking for?"

"Five, including yourself. The two ranch hands take their meals with us."

She nodded and searched the larder for the supplies she needed. Virginia quickly mixed up the biscuit dough and put it in the oven.

Virginia glanced at the tall, blond man working next to her. He seemed very charming and helpful. She was more at ease as Ben asked her about her trip and told her about some of the encounters when he'd taken the steamboat from St. Louis to Helena several years ago. The tension melted from her shoulders, and the wariness dissolved into laughter.

She fried the bacon in one pan and carefully cracked the eggs in another. The stove heated the room quickly. Ben opened the windows to let the cool mountain air flow in. Delicious smells swirled around, making Virginia's stomach grumble hungrily.

Three men had an uncanny way of knowing when breakfast was ready. Two of them lumbered into the dining room and took their seats.

"Good morning, Virginia. Did you sleep well?" Allen asked.

Although his voice was calm and polite, Virginia detected an uneasiness in it.

"I did, thank you."

"I didn't mean for you to make breakfast on your first day here. I had some cows calving in the barn and wanted to make sure everything was okay with them." He waved at the sink. "I also didn't mean for you to do all those dishes."

She smiled at him. "I don't mind one bit. I get to stand up straight, and my fingers aren't bleeding from the needles."

Virginia glanced at the two men in the dining room. Their eyes were glued to her as though they were trying to figure out what was happening. She recognized Keith from the night before, and she figured that he'd have told the other man who she was.

"Breakfast is ready. Please have a seat."

Ben and Allen sat at the table while she placed the biscuits on a trivet. Then, she brought out a plate of bacon and eggs for each man. She set a large enamel coffee pot on another trivet. The cups and utensils had already been laid out.

Allen said grace and looked at the man she hadn't met yet.

"John, this is Virginia. We're to be married today. Virginia, this is John, the other ranch hand. I guess you've met Ben, who is the foreman."

Virginia nodded to John. "Nice to meet you."

"I'm sorry, did you say that you were to be married to her today?" John asked.

Allen glanced at him and frowned. "I don't think I stuttered."

John and Keith exchanged shocked looks but didn't ask any more questions. They quickly ate, complimented her cooking, took their dishes to the kitchen, and disappeared out the door.

Virginia smirked.

Apparently, her appearance was a surprise to them.

"There are going to be a lot of people who are shocked that you are here and you're my wife. I only told Ben about you. I wanted to make sure you'd come first."

"Here I am," she said, holding out her arms.

"As soon as you're ready, we'll head into town and have Father Cahill marry us."

He said the words as though he was ordering a piece of farm machinery or conducting some other type of business transaction.

Virginia's heart sank.

She'd hoped for more.

I knew this wasn't a fairy tale wedding like the ones Aunt Fiona always read to the kids. We don't even know each other. I can't expect him to be romantic or have any kind of feelings about it.

She quickly washed the dishes. Virginia was surprised when she opened the cabinet below the sink and saw that a pipe attached to the sink went through the wall.

"It's self-draining," Allen said when he noticed her studying it. "It's one of the upgrades I recently did. My uncle, who owned this house, had a kitchen that was out of the pioneer days."

"I love it," she said, giving him a brief smile. He returned it, and she pushed back the fluttering in her stomach as she added, "I'm going to go upstairs and change my dress."

Virginia quickly changed into her church dress. She looked down at the plain navy fabric. It had been one of her aunt's cast-offs, and Virginia had made several modifications to make it fit. Before Aunt Fiona had given her the dress, she'd removed all the lace and other adornments. There was a small patch on the side, although Virginia was sure that she'd sewn it neatly enough that it couldn't be seen.

She had no jewelry or anything fancy she could wear. Sighing heavily, Virginia unbraided her hair, brushed it out, and rebraided it. Then, she wound it around her hair like a coronet.

Her heart was heavy. She'd always hoped for a beautiful dress to get married in, like she'd sewn at the garment factory. She imagined the silk dresses with the lace around the collars, hems, and wrists. She pictured the delicate beading and the flowing skirt. The bodice would fit her perfectly, and she'd have a lacy veil to match.

Sighing again, she looked at herself in the mirror. Her face was still pale, and the dark circles under her eyes reminded her of a raccoon. The waist of her dress was loose since she'd lost a lot of weight during her trip.

She shrugged. "It's the best I have. I have nothing to be embarrassed about."

Virginia walked downstairs. Ben and Allen were sitting at the table, talking about the number of cows that were still pregnant.

She used the opportunity to stare at Allen. He took her breath away because he was so handsome. A white button-down shirt and black slacks replaced the short-sleeved shirt and denim pants he'd worn before. His curly hair framed his handsome face, and the clothes did nothing to hide his muscular body.

Allen looked her up and down, not giving any sign of whether he approved of what he saw. "Are you ready?"

She nodded, unable to say anything.

"Ben's going to accompany us to the church as a witness. I'm sure we'll be able to find someone else in town to act as the other witness we'll need."

Virginia walked outside to the wagon. Allen helped her up. Despite her nervousness, which made her feel as though she might explode, she couldn't ignore the warmth that flowed through her from his touch.

He looked sharply at her and pulled his hand away. She wondered if he'd felt something, too.

Don't be so fanciful. It's just because you're getting married to him. No man, besides your father, has ever held your hand, even for a second before.

She sat up straight as the wagon jounced down the road, making her body ache again.

Once we're done, I'm not going anywhere for a month.

The ride was awkwardly quiet, with Ben occasionally pointing out a deer or eagle as they rode to town. She wished she knew what Allen was thinking.

When they arrived, since they were only going to be there for a couple of minutes, they didn't unhitch the horses.

Allen stiffly walked into the church beside her, looking straight ahead. He didn't glance her way once. Virginia wondered if he regretted his decision.

It's too late now, for both of us.

The graying father held out both his hands to her. "I'm Father Cahill. You must be Virginia."

"Yes, Father."

"Are you entering into this marriage willingly?"

"Yes, Father."

"Very well. Margaret, would you please join us?"

The woman sitting at the organ walked over and smiled at Virginia. "I'm Margaret. I play the organ for the church and help run a lot of our events."

Virginia smiled back but couldn't find her voice to reply.

The father asked each of them to recite their vows, which they did. He pronounced them man and wife and asked Allen if he had rings to present.

Virginia was shocked when Ben handed him two golden bands. Allen put the smaller one on her left ring finger and said, "With this ring, I thee wed."

Ben pressed a larger gold band into her hand. She stared at it blankly for a second before sliding it into Allen's left ring finger. "With this ring, I thee wed."

"I now pronounce you man and wife. You may kiss your bride."

Allen grimaced as though he'd been told to kiss a toad and quickly brushed a kiss across her cheek.

"I need everyone to sign the ledger here for our records."

Virginia and Allen signed the ledger as the married couple, and Ben and Margaret signed it as witnesses. The father signed it afterward. The ceremony was over.

Disappointment settled in her soul. The wedding was nothing like she'd dreamed about. Instead of a cold exchange of words that were designed as nothing more than to create a contract, Virginia had fantasized about the love and passion that would be a part of the ceremony. She'd always wanted her wedding to be more meaningful than this. There were no family or friends gathered around—just two strangers who would be able to attest to the fact that the ceremony happened and she and Allen were legally married.

There were no soft smiles or loving looks exchanged between the two of them. As a matter of fact, he'd barely glanced at her. She looked at Allen, but his face was unreadable, and his eyes were distant.

She bowed her head. The reality of the ceremony weighed heavily on her chest, and a quiet ache and emptiness replaced her dreams of love and a beautiful wedding.

Allen finally spoke when they got to the wagon. "I noticed you just had one canvas bag, and I assume that's your Sunday dress?"

Her face blazed bright red as shame and humiliation flooded her cheeks. "Yes."

He nodded. "Let's walk over to the general store. I want you to buy enough fabric and supplies to make at least two work dresses and a Sunday dress. You'll need shoes and boots, as well."

"Thank you," she said softly.

"Do you have a cloak for very cold months?" Then, before she could answer, he added, "One that's in good condition and not patched together?"

He spoke with a matter-of-fact tone. It wasn't condescending, nor was it caring or sympathetic. Once again, she got the idea that he was conducting a business transaction.

"No."

It felt odd to have a strange man buying her things. Her logical mind reminded her that he was her husband, and that was what husbands did. However, her heart told her that he was a stranger, and it wasn't proper for him to buy her anything.

She glanced down at her dress and realized that he was probably embarrassed by the way she was dressed. He was a ranch owner and the sheriff. He couldn't have his wife looking as though she'd just escaped from the poor house.

Virginia cringed when the general store owner rang everything up. The total added up to twenty-five dollars, which was more than she made at the factory most months.

Allen pulled the money out of his pocket and handed it to the clerk, who looked at Virginia curiously.

"Mick, this is my wife, Virginia. Once she gets settled, she'll likely be coming in to pick up supplies. She can put whatever she needs on my credit."

"Sure thing, Sheriff," Jake said. He nodded at Virginia. "Mrs. Strauss."

The name sounded strange to her.

Get used to it. That's who you are now.

The ride back to the ranch was as quiet as the trip into town. Ben occasionally made a comment about the weather or that he might go hunting for some elk to supplement their food supply. Allen didn't say much of anything. He simply grunted a few times in response to whatever Ben said.

She was relieved when they got back to the house. Allen helped her off the buckboard and carried her supplies into the house. He disappeared into his room, changed his clothes, and went outside without a word.

Ben glanced at her sympathetically. "He'll come around. I think he's in shock, even though this was his idea."

"Thank you."

Feeling lost, Virginia went upstairs, put her work dress back on, and rummaged through the pantry to see what she would make for lunch. She cut some fresh beef into small cubes and tossed them into the pot, adding beans and a jar of tomato sauce. Virginia threw in some diced fresh chili peppers, salt, pepper, cumin, and oregano.

While that cooked, she rolled up her sleeves and started cleaning.

What a wedding day.

***

A week later, Virginia still felt like she was married to a stranger. He was gone all the time. During the day, he was in town, performing his duties as the sheriff. In the afternoons and evenings, he was busy on the ranch, working with the farmhands.

At night, he sat on the porch, whittling something or reading a book. His demeanor let Virginia know that he didn't want to be bothered. She wouldn't know what to talk about even if he'd been inviting.

She found peace in the large, quiet house. Virginia took pleasure in cleaning and organizing everything. It felt as though she lived in a mansion, especially compared to the tiny, cramped apartment she'd shared with five other people.

The work was hard. Virginia made sure that all of the bedding was washed weekly, along with both her and Allen's clothes. She cleaned at least four or five years of dust off the furniture and cleaned away several cobwebs. The men loved the three meals she made each day, including the desserts. Virginia had also learned how to feed the chickens and collect eggs every morning.

One afternoon, Ben strolled into the house as she worked on her Sunday dress. Sewing everything by hand took a lot longer, but she enjoyed it because it was for her, even though she did prick her fingers often with the needle.

"I don't suppose you have any snacks handy for the poor starving ranch foreman, do you?"

She laughed because he purposely sounded pitiful. Virginia really liked Ben. He was a great guy and easy to talk to. She quickly discovered that he had the appetite of a teenage boy and a bottomless pit in his stomach.

"I made some small tarts for dessert, but since you look weak and are about to faint, I can give you one now."

"You're a saint," he said teasingly.

Virginia handed him the treat. "Is Allen back on the ranch yet? I need to know when I can start supper."

"I wouldn't wait for him. He went to a neighboring town, along with several men, to help them with a wildfire. They spread quickly and are dangerous with our high winds. They destroy towns and ranches in a matter of hours and, sometimes, minutes."

She felt a rush of admiration. Virginia crossed her arms over her chest and sighed. "I don't know how he does it. He's always working and must be exhausted."

"He's the master of taking care of other people but ignoring himself."

Virginia tilted her head. "Why is a man like him single? I would think that every maiden in Butte and the surrounding towns must have had eyes on him."

"There's been a few, but he's never paid them no mind."

"Why?"

Ben hesitated as though he were trying to figure out how much to share with her. Eventually, he began, "A long time ago, he was in love with a woman and planned to marry her. However, while he was away at the war, she died. It broke his heart."

A stab of pain pierced Virginia's heart. She couldn't imagine losing someone like that.

"His father and brother died in the war, too. When he came back, the only family he had was his Uncle Amos. They weren't close because Amos wasn't one to show affection."

Virginia's heart broke for him as sympathy washed over her. "I'm sorry. That must be terrible."

Ben sighed. "Allen keeps himself busy all the time so he doesn't have to think. I suspect it's also because he doesn't want to get too close to you. Everyone that Allen ever loved ended up dead."

It's no wonder he's so closed off, Virginia mused. Her stomach curled, and she couldn't help but feel the weight that settled on her shoulders. *Is there any hope for a friendship or a real marriage? Will he ever see me as more than just another employee?*

Chapter Eight

Allen was completely exhausted when he left Coyote Creek and headed home. The wildfire had almost gotten out of control, and for a while, they were afraid they'd have to evacuate the town and nearby ranches. As it was, the fire burned up almost ten square miles before they managed to put it out.

Men and some women from several neighboring towns joined the fight. They used axes to cut trees in the fire's path, shovels to dig firebreaks, and wet blankets to attempt to smother the flames. Allen cut down trees, and he and Blaze dragged several large trees toward the river, trying to keep them out of the fire's path and giving it more fuel. Most of the people created a bucket brigade to throw water on the fire.

At one point, the wind whipped up and turned the flames in a different direction. Several people were badly burned, and one man likely wouldn't survive his injuries.

Finally, they managed to get the fire under control, tamping down the last of the burning embers.

Some fresh men, who'd had a chance to rest, came in from Anaconda, Boulder, Whitehall, and Deer Lodge to go over every inch of the burned area to make sure that nothing was left smoldering that could flare up again.

It was ten miles from Coyote Creek to Butte, and Sheriff Frank Hicks, a good friend of his, suggested that Allen stay the night with him. However, Allen had to get back. He knew Ben was very good at his job, and the deputies could handle his duties for one day, but he still wanted to be home since the rest of the cows were due at any time. They were his prized registered Herefords, and he'd paid a lot of money for them. He couldn't afford to lose a single one of them.

The moonlight reflected off his wedding ring. Allen glanced down at it. He'd still not gotten accustomed to wearing it, nor could he wrap his mind around the fact that he was married.

A flash of guilt tightened in his chest.

He hadn't spent any time at all with her. As a matter of fact, he wasn't sure that they'd had a conversation since they were married. Allen worked a lot of hours, and when he got home, he made no effort to talk to her.

He dropped his head and admitted that he'd actually been avoiding her. There was no way in the world he was going to allow himself to care for her. Allen couldn't go through the pain of losing another person he loved.

"I made no promises other than to provide a safe place for her to live and food. I bought her some fabric so she could make some dresses for herself," he muttered under his breath.

He felt like a blackguard. Allen figured that she had hopes of a real family. He never had the talk with her that he planned to have when he put the ad in the paper. Allen had intended to tell her that theirs was a marriage of convenience, and she shouldn't expect anything more than that. She'd cook and clean, and she'd get room and board.

You make her sound like an indentured servant, except that they can eventually earn their freedom.

Her big, bright green eyes flashed in his mind, and he squirmed uncomfortably in the saddle. He knew she must be lonely. She traveled thousands of miles away to marry him and didn't know anyone besides Ben, Keith, and John. She hadn't gone to town yet, either.

He wondered if she felt trapped on the ranch and sighed heavily.

She was beautiful, inside and out. He'd watched her with all the animals, and she was gentle even with the ones that would eventually be someone's dinner. The dogs adored her and followed her around everywhere.

"You could be nicer to her and have a conversation with her sometime," he scolded himself, although he wasn't sure what they would talk about. He didn't know anything about her, what she liked, or what she was interested in.

You get to know all that and her by sitting down and talking to her, he told himself. *No. You can't let her in!* screamed another part of his brain.

The conflict inside of him had gone on so long that he found himself outside the house. He hadn't paid attention to anything during the ride. Blaze had simply plodded along the familiar roads, likely more tired than Allen was.

Although it was past midnight, Keith came out of the bunkhouse. "I was waiting for you. I knew you'd come home even though it's late. I'll take care of Blaze for you."

"Thanks," Allen said, patting Keith on the back as he handed over the reins. "Give him some extra oats tonight. He worked just as hard as the rest of us."

"Will do, Boss."

Exhaustion washed over him as he walked into the kitchen. He looked over at the dining room table and saw that although Virginia was already in bed, she'd left some food on the table for him. Something tightened in his chest, and a feeling of warmth flowed through him at the kind gesture. He knew it was more than just an obligation because he could have dug food out of the pantry or larder. She was showing that she did care about him.

Rubbing his forehead, he thought, *No. Not right now.*

He lifted the lid off the pot and inhaled the rich aroma of beef stew with carrots and potatoes. Next to the pot were a couple of pieces of cornbread and an apple tart covered with cheesecloth.

Allen quickly devoured the meal, well aware that his father would have admonished him for his bad manners. The womenfolk had brought out sandwiches for lunch, but that had been a lifetime ago, and his stomach had tied itself into several knots from the hunger pains.

He put the dirty dishes in the sink, feeling a little guilty but too exhausted to wash them. Allen dragged himself up the stairs, and Ben met him in the hall.

"Is everything good?"

"It's out. There's some men combing the area now, making sure that nothing's left that can start up again. They have no idea how it even got started."

Ben looked at him appraisingly, clearly worried about him. Ben knew that the nightmares and flashbacks attacked more often when Allen was exhausted. "Are you okay?"

Allen's face flushed red from embarrassment as he knew exactly what Ben was asking. "Just tired. It was a long day."

Nodding, Ben said, "Good night."

"Night."

Allen quietly shut the door behind him and splashed water on his face, washing off the soot and ash. He sat down on the side of his bed and barely got his boots off before he collapsed, quickly drifting off to sleep.

His mind instantly went somewhere far away in the distant past.

Allen was riding as fast as he could through the field, Joseph by his side. They were dodging bullets as they tried to rescue General Atwood, who had been injured. There was no way either of them could let him get captured.

The ground shook from the cannons exploding, one after the other. His ears buzzed from the screaming men as they fell from the cannonballs or bullets that zinged through the air.

Allen tried to breathe, but the smell of gunpowder, blood, and fear was suffocating. The metallic taste of the combination of smells coated his tongue, making him nauseous. Still, he couldn't stop. They had to get to the general before the enemy realized he was hurt.

He urged his horse to go faster.

As though in slow motion, Allen saw the bullet whiz by him. He could hear the sharp whistle as it sliced through the air. Joseph's body jerked, and he cried out as the force of the hit peeled him from his horse.

Instantly, Allen stopped, dismounting at the same time. The other men behind him would continue toward the general.

"Joseph," Allen said, tears clogging his vision. "Stay with me, brother."

He saw the gaping hole in Joseph's chest and the blood spreading across his uniform.

Allen's soul splintered as Joseph began to speak, and Allen screamed out from the anguish of losing his brother.

He thrashed as he felt someone touching him.

No. I can't let go of him. I have to hold on to him.

"Allen. Allen, wake up."

A woman's voice pierced his unconsciousness. Allen's eyes flew open, and he stared at the woman standing over him. It took him a few seconds to realize that this was Virginia. His new wife.

His heart thundered in his chest, and his lungs screamed for air. Allen realized that he'd been holding his breath.

"You were screaming," she said quietly. "Everything's okay. You're safe."

Rage, humiliation, and a million other emotions exploded inside of him. Not caring how rude he sounded, he snapped, "Get out."

Virginia didn't even flinch. She just frowned. "It's okay. Nightmares are nothing to be ashamed of. It's just our mind's way of processing our experiences. I heard someone talk about it one time. My cousin used to have them all the time."

Allen gritted his teeth, the heat flooding now to his cheeks. "I'm not a child," he spat, unable to control his growing frustration—one born from embarrassment. "I told you not to come into my room, no matter what you heard. Get out."

By the time he finished speaking, tears sprang to her eyes, and she practically ran out the door, her face crumpling as she sped away.

He sat up and put his face in his hands. Allen could feel his heartbeat in his throat, choking him. His entire body was shaking.

Focusing on his breathing, he tried to calm his heart. It was beating so hard that it hurt.

Finally, the room stopped spinning, and he felt as though he could stand without collapsing to the ground. Splashing cold water on his face helped him snap out of the hazy reality he'd been trapped in.

He felt bad about yelling at Virginia. She'd only been trying to help him and to comfort him. She had no idea that his dreams were much worse than monsters who might be lurking under the bed. The reality of war was a horrific mix of blood, men crying out, and bullets screaming as they whizzed by. When he stopped for five minutes, he'd see the bodies lying in the field, and his heart hurt for all those dead—those who'd left loved ones behind and had long lives ahead of them.

"She has to learn to listen to me," he muttered. "I asked her not to come in here. She doesn't need to see me like this. I won't allow her to see me like this."

He went downstairs for a glass of water and slowly made his way back to bed.

As he closed his eyes, he prayed, "Please, God, I'm begging you. Let me have peace. Just for one night. Please, let me have peace."

Chapter Nine

Virginia lay in bed, staring up at the ceiling. She sniffed and wiped the tears from her face. She's just been trying to help. Allen's screams had been haunting and pierced her soul.

She'd just wanted to help.

"Maybe he thought I was trying to treat him like a child," she mused. "He's a grown man." She sighed and pulled the blankets up to her chin. "I'll just leave him alone from now on. If he wants to scream, then he can scream."

It took her a while to get back to sleep. Even then, she tossed and turned all night. When the first streams of sunlight came through the window, she was still sleepy and could have used a couple more hours of rest.

Sighing heavily, she rolled out of bed and made her way downstairs to start breakfast. Ben came down shortly after. He cheerily talked about the weather and that it was going to be a fine day outside, not too hot and not too cold.

She desperately wanted to ask him about Allen's nightmares, but she wasn't sure how to bring it up. It wasn't like she could just say, "Good morning. Why was he screaming last night, and why was he so upset when I tried to help him?"

Besides, Allen could come down at any minute, and she didn't want to be in the middle of talking about him.

Virginia sighed.

This is not what I envisioned married life to be like. At least he's not mean—not usually.

Life had taken a complete turnaround. Every day, she cleaned up after breakfast, fed the chickens and collected the eggs, pulled weeds out of the garden, and straightened the house. Ben, Keith, and John came in for lunch, and then Virginia had the rest of the afternoon to herself.

She thought about her life in New York. There, she was stuck at her sewing station for hours and hours, until her shoulders, back, and neck screamed in pain from being hunched over for too long. She didn't have that problem here. She was able to move around freely and get a lot of fresh air and exercise.

However, she was lonely. She talked to Ben and Allen, usually, for a few minutes during each meal, but was alone the rest of the time. There was only so much conversation she could have with herself or the dogs. She missed Meaghan and her other friends.

"Oh, well. Here I am. Make the most of it," she muttered to herself under her breath. "There are some benefits here. I have a lot more room, plenty to eat, and no one makes me feel like a burden."

Allen came in the front door as she finished cooking and put the food on the table.

"Got an early start, huh?" Ben asked.

"Yeah. I wanted to take care of the morning chores."

An awkward silence fell over the table. The tension was thick and hung in the air like a hot, humid, sweltering afternoon that sucked the breath out of a person's lungs. Keith and John came in for breakfast and quickly ate, muttering thanks and escaping.

She was surprised when Allen didn't rush upstairs to change into his uniform and head to town.

Ben raised his eyebrows as Allen leisurely finished his cup of coffee. "No sheriff's duties this morning?"

"No, Stephen and Douglas have it covered this morning. I'm going to stay home and take care of some paperwork and catch up on a few things."

Virginia's heart sank. For once, she'd been looking forward to him being gone because she wanted to sort out what happened the night before and maybe talk to Ben about it. He'd been honest with her about Allen's past.

The two men walked outside, leaving Virginia alone with her thoughts.

She had surmised that Allen's nightmare had something to do with the war.

That's probably all Ben knows, too. I highly doubt the two of them sit around rehashing what happened and talking about their memories because they certainly wouldn't be pleasant.

Virginia stared into space. The memories of his anguished cries echoed in her mind. She sat down and put her face in her hands, trying to make sense of everything. Virginia had seen the fear and sorrow in his eyes. What had he seen? What had he lived through? Why was it still haunting him so much, even after all these years?

She realized that war was brutal, and she couldn't begin to imagine what it would have been like to fight against friends and fellow Americans and to kill other countrymen. Virginia wondered whether all men who'd gone through the war had nightmares or if Allen had witnessed something particularly bad.

Had he seen his father and brother...?

"This isn't getting anything done," she cut herself off, pushing that grim thought away.

Virginia finished the kitchen, and Allen wandered back into the kitchen for another cup of coffee.

"Thanks," he muttered.

Without another glance, he sauntered back to his office.

She groaned. "I can't do this today."

Not letting herself dwell on his behavior, she changed into one of the new work dresses she'd made for herself. Virginia had a habit of wearing her old, worn-out dresses while doing chores around the house, but she didn't want to look shabby in town. She was the sheriff's wife, after all.

Ben hooked up the wagon for her, and she drove the five miles to town. The horses knew the way, so Virginia didn't have to focus on driving. She looked around at the rolling hills with the green and golden grasses. Patches of beautiful wildflowers dotted the landscape. Lupines, Indian paintbrushes, and wild daisies swayed in the warm, gentle breeze.

Virginia wouldn't ever get tired of looking at the animals. There had been so few animals in the city. Here, they were everywhere. Herds of deer watched, as though bored, and she, Belle, and Star traveled down the dusty path that masqueraded as a road. Prairie dogs popped out of their holes, and rabbits darted from bush to bush. A large bison herd grazed in the distance, and hawks and eagles flew overhead.

As she approached Butte, she detected a whiff of smoke. Sheds and small shanties hastily built on the outskirts of town looked like they might blow over with the next strong breeze.

She stopped at a trough, letting the horses drink their fill before guiding them to the general store. Virginia jumped out, petted them, and told them that she'd be right back.

Virginia picked up some cloves, cinnamon, vanilla extract, and sugar so she could bake some pies. She hesitated for a moment over a small jar of hand cream, and then looked at her cracked knuckles and added that to her purchases. She also bought some coffee and chamomile tea.

"Hello, Mrs. Strauss," Mick said. "How are you doing today?"

"Well. I hope you are."

"Yes, ma'am. I also have the horseshoe nails, gunpowder, and ammunition that Ben ordered. Would you like to pick those up today?"

She nodded. "Yes, please."

"Shall I add this to the sheriff's account?"

"Please."

Virginia was horrified. She hadn't thought about how she was going to pay for anything, although she remembered that Allen had told her that she could charge anything she wanted to his account. She'd just been desperate to leave for a while.

He wrapped everything up and handed it to her. "Give the sheriff, Ben, and the boys my best."

"I sure will," she said.

Virginia stopped by the post office. The postmaster greeted her warmly when she introduced herself.

"I heard the sheriff got married. Congratulations," the clerk said effusively. "I'm Mary Ann. Welcome to Butte."

"Thank you so much." Virginia instantly had a good feeling about the taller, stout woman with graying hair and twinkling blue eyes.

"Here's the mail for the ranch and all the boys. Tell them I say hello."

"I sure will. Thank you, ma'am."

Virginia rubbed the horses' noses and climbed back into the wagon. Her anxiety increased as they rode back to the ranch until she was certain she was going to explode. By the time she pulled the brake outside of the barn, her heart was beating a million miles an hour, and her lungs felt as though a hand had squeezed them shut.

"He'll likely be out working in the pastures, fixing fences, or something," Virginia whispered reassuringly to herself.

Keith peeked his head out of the barn and smiled as he walked toward her. "Did you have a nice ride?"

"I did." Virginia paused. "Could you help me with them? I can drive the wagon, but I'm not sure how to hook them up or unhitch them."

"Sure thing, ma'am. I'll take care of everything for you. You just keep those delicious victuals coming."

Virginia laughed at that, some of the gloom lifting, even if just for a moment. "Absolutely. Thank you."

She grabbed the large package she'd gotten from the general store and the mail and headed for the house. She stopped dead in her tracks when she saw Allen sitting on the porch, shaving. He looked up, half of his face clean-shaven and the other half covered in lather. Virginia giggled.

He smiled in return. "Light's better out here. I don't have to squint to see myself in the mirror."

"I think you missed a spot," she teased, taking his smile as a good sign.

"I was going for a new scruffy look, with just a small patch here and there."

Virginia tutted playfully. "I'm not sure the bad guys would take the sheriff seriously if he looked like he'd been drunk when he was shaving."

"I'll start a whole new style," Allen argued. "Soon, everyone will be doing it. How was your trip to town?"

"It was good. Everyone there is so nice and friendly."

Virginia was surprised at how approachable he was and realized he was likely trying to make amends for the night before without apologizing.

Her heart warmed at the thought.

Allen pulled her from her thoughts, asking, "Did we get any mail?"

"Yes." Virginia pulled an envelope out of her bag and held it out to him.

"I'd just make a mess of it. Can you read it to me?"

All at once, her heart stopped, and her throat closed up. She had a basic understanding of the alphabet but didn't know how to read.

He resumed shaving, and Virginia slowly opened the envelope. The letters were a blur. She blinked a couple of times and tried to sound out a couple of words, but couldn't.

The heat of humiliation exploded in her face, and she turned bright red. "I'm sorry, I can't," she whispered and fled into the house.

A few minutes later, Allen followed her inside, carrying her bundle. "What's wrong?"

Virginia's mouth moved, but the words didn't come out.

She nibbled on her bottom lip.

Her shoulders slumped, and she hung her head.

"I never learned to read," she admitted, her voice breaking with the revelation. "I started working in the factory when I was ten and never went to school. I just know the alphabet and the sounds they make."

Allen was quiet for a second and said, "Not to worry. I'll teach you how to read."

Virginia looked at him disbelievingly. "You will?"

"Yes. Reading is a pleasure and a skill that everyone should possess. You're very intelligent, and I'm certain that you'll pick it up very quickly."

Surprised, Virginia stared at him. He was being extremely kind to her.

"I'd like that, very much," she said. "Thank you."

He smiled warmly. "After supper, then."

She heated some stew for lunch and took care of her chores that afternoon.

Her mind was spinning a million miles an hour. Except for the incident last night, Allen had always been kind to her, although she hadn't seen him much since he was always working. Now, he was offering to teach her to read. That was no small undertaking. She'd seen how hard her cousins had worked to learn to read well.

Hope sprang into her soul that they could, at the very least, have a good friendship.

He was very upset and stressed out last night, she thought, trying to justify his previous actions. *He was probably embarrassed because he'd had the nightmares. I guess he thinks grown men aren't supposed to.*

Smiling and singing happily to herself, she changed out of her new work dress, put on her raggedy old one, and got to work. She didn't know if she was more excited about learning to read or spending time with Allen instead of being alone.

Virginia sighed as she swept the floors.

Admit it. He's an extremely handsome man, and he makes your heart flutter when you're near him.

She couldn't deny that something inside of her soul tugged every time he smiled at her and gazed at her with beautiful brown eyes.

Still, there was no use dwelling on something that would never happen.

Chapter Ten

Every time Allen recalled Virginia's bright-eyed enthusiasm when he offered to teach her to read, he grinned.

Beneath that warmth, though, his heart broke for her when he thought about what her past life must have been like. He'd also worked since he was a young boy. Every ranch kid, boy and girl, did, practically from the time that they could walk. It could be dangerous. But they still had the freedom to learn, play, and enjoy life.

Being forced to work in a factory, at least twelve hours a day, from the time she was ten for very little pay, none of which Virginia could keep, was awfully similar to slavery. It was the very thing he, his father, his brother, Ben, and millions of other men fought to eliminate.

At least he had a good home life. His father had been a good, loving man, and his brother had been his best friend. Virginia lost her father when she was ten, and it sounded as though her aunt and uncle were distant, to say the least.

He was surprised that he was looking forward to giving her reading lessons. Allen enjoyed spending time with her, the few minutes here and there that they'd had since they were married. He actually felt a little anxious while he waited for her in the sitting room.

The flames cackled in the fireplace, casting a golden glow over the room. Although it was summer, the evenings could still feel chilly, especially when the wind blew, and that was a given. Allen was sure it howled at least three hundred days out of the year.

Virginia padded into the room as though she were shy and didn't want to be seen, her cheeks pink. Allen smiled reassuringly at her. They were still practically strangers, and even though the air had cleared between them this afternoon and evening, she was going to learn something new. Allen knew that had to be intimidating. Not only would she be unsure of her ability to learn, but she wasn't sure what kind of teacher he would be.

"I've picked out a couple of books I thought we could start with. I learned to read with these when I was a kid." He grinned. "I'm afraid the stories might not be exciting for adults, but it's a good way to start. You can read more grown-up books once you get the hang of it."

Virginia managed a smile. "Sounds great. Thank you for helping me."

"My pleasure." He pointed to a couple of mugs. "I made us some hot chocolate while you were upstairs."

Now, her grin widened, lighting up her bright green eyes. "Thank you. I've never had hot chocolate before."

"Really?" he asked, unable to hide his shock.

She continued to smile, and a cute dimple in her cheek appeared. "Really. There wasn't any money left over for many treats, and if there was anything, it was for the kids."

Her aunt and uncle were using her money to treat their kids, barely giving Virginia enough to survive.

The thought of that made him furious with her aunt all over again.

It was a good thing that New York City was too far to go to give someone a piece of his mind.

"Try it and see what you think." Allen anxiously watched her face.

Virginia took a sip. After a few seconds of anticipatory silence, a delighted smile spread across her lips. "Oh, my goodness. This is delicious. Wow."

She took another sip and closed her eyes as though she was reveling in the taste.

Allen was pleased. She was like a small child who'd just been given a piece of candy for the first time.

"Thank you," she added.

"You're quite welcome." He gestured to the books. "Shall we get started?"

She nodded and gingerly sat on the couch next to him, as if she feared he might bite her.

He picked up *The McGuffey Reader* and opened it to one of the first pages that was designed to help early readers learn simple words. He held the book on his knee and pointed to a word in the first sentence.

"This is *cat*. You know the letters. Can you sound this out?"

Virginia nodded and studied the letters. "C…a…t." Her voice was barely above a whisper.

"That's right. Now say the whole word all together."

"Cat," she said a bit louder.

"Good," he said. "See, you're already getting the hang of this."

Virginia exhaled as though she'd been holding her breath.

Allen guided her through the same process for new words. Soon, she was able to read simple sentences, and each success seemed to increase her confidence.

He wasn't sure who was more pleased—Virginia or him. He loved seeing her learn to sound out the words and read her first few sentences.

Allen stayed patient throughout the entire lesson. He praised her each time she was able to decipher new words and corrected her gently when she made a mistake. Hard and soft C sounds were confusing, as were hard and soft G sounds. Those were hard for everyone.

Virginia's brows furrowed in concentration as she continued to sound out words. Eventually, he corrected her on the word "said."

Her lips pursed, and the pout there was adorable. "Why doesn't that sound the way it looks?"

Chuckling, Allen shook his head. "There are many people who say the same thing because English has a bunch of words that don't sound the way they should. You'll learn those as you go."

Virginia frowned. "That's like telling someone there are rules but then saying the rules don't matter."

"You'll get no argument from me on that one."

Allen gazed at her and noticed how beautiful she looked in the firelight. The flickering flames gave her an angelic look. Her red hair was bright in the light, and soft curls framed her delicate face.

He shook his head and forced himself to return his attention to the book. She read a couple of very simple sentences in a row: "Tom has a cat. The cat is fat. The cat has a hat."

She looked at him and grinned widely, pleasure dancing in her eyes.

"Excellent. You're getting the hang of this quickly."

Her excitement and enthusiasm, even over the simplest of things, warmed Allen from head to toe—much more than the hot chocolate ever could.

She drank the last of her hot chocolate and licked her lips. Virginia glanced up at him, catching his eye. For a moment, their gazes locked. Allen's heart thundered in his chest, and a smoldering ember deep inside of his soul sparked a feeling he hadn't had in years—not since....

He tore his eyes away.

Allen didn't want Virginia to see how much the moment affected him, especially until he could figure it out.

As she continued working, she'd look at him whenever she made a breakthrough. Their eyes continued to meet, and each time, Allen could feel something flutter in his stomach.

He couldn't deny that there was some tiny spark that ignited when their eyes locked. He was sure that she felt it, too, because of the slight smile that curved her lips and the way her voice softened a bit.

He wasn't sure what to do with his feelings. There was no way that he was going to let Virginia in. She was a friend and his wife of convenience. There would never be anything more. Even if he was willing, he couldn't be the kind of man she deserved.

Virginia followed the words in the book with her finger and read, "Jane plays with a doll." Then, she put her hand up to her mouth and yawned. She smiled at him and blushed. "I'm sorry."

He looked at his pocket watch and was surprised that they'd spent several hours together. "I didn't realize how tired you must be. You've been working hard for a long time. I guess you're ready for bed."

She nodded. Now that he noticed, he saw that her shoulders were slumped slightly, and her eyes drooped.

"I didn't even notice how much time had passed until now," she muttered. "I never would have guessed that learning could be so much fun."

"I'll leave the books on the table for you, so you can practice when you have some time."

"Thank you," she said.

She looked as though she wanted to say something else—or maybe even hug him, though that could be his own wishful thinking—but instead, she smiled, collected their mugs, and walked into the kitchen. She stepped outside for a few minutes, and then he heard her soft footsteps as she went to her room.

Allen lay back on the couch and ran his fingers through his hair. He couldn't remember the last time he'd had such an enjoyable evening. Never, in a million years, would he have thought that he would find such joy in helping someone learn the basic concepts of reading.

He closed his eyes and pictured her sweet smile and excitement when she conquered something new. Her bright emerald eyes glowed in the firelight, and his chest ached with an unfamiliar feeling.

I can't get attached to her. That's something I just can't afford to do.

He was so tired. His eyes were heavy, and his body screamed for rest.

Allen decided to stay downstairs, too afraid to go upstairs and sleep. He couldn't risk another nightmare where he screamed himself awake. He couldn't bear the humiliation of calling out in the night like a small child.

More than anything, Allen was terrified of hurting Virginia.

The night before, once he'd calmed down, he remembered the shock and pain on her face as she fled his room.

Sighing heavily, Allen rubbed his face. He hoped that by staying downstairs, he could control his nightmares and not run the risk of crying out in terror in the middle of the night, waking her. He never wanted to see the look of fear, sympathy, and hurt on her face again, *especially* caused by him.

Even as he settled in, he knew this wasn't going to work. Even if he did manage to stay awake all night long, he'd be useless and even dangerous tomorrow. Plus, eventually, he'd have to get some sleep. During the war, he'd seen men drop from sheer exhaustion, and nothing, not even the sounds of cannon fire and the war, would wake them.

He shook his head and decided to sit on the porch. The cool night air might wake him, at least a little. The new moon competed with the brilliant sparkling diamonds in the sky. There were only a few clouds that floated lazily by. The wind picked up, throwing a bit of dust everywhere. Major, one of the blue heelers who guarded the place at night, sat next to him, leaning against Allen's legs.

"How are you doing, boy?"

Major put his paw on Allen's knee, beseeching him for some pets.

Absently scratching the dog between his ears, he watched a coyote scamper off into the darkness.

The war had done this to him. It was responsible for his nightmares and his guilt. The memories of his brother dying in his arms, the sounds, and the smells haunted him every night. They would creep into his mind and take over sometimes during the day when he wasn't focused on something else.

He rubbed his face, trying to push the images and sounds away. Allen knew that he couldn't keep living like this, but he didn't know how to fix it. He was a broken man and didn't think he could ever live a normal life.

Virginia's sweet face popped into his mind. For a second, he let himself think about what having a life with her would look like. What would it mean to actually be married and have a family?

Allen vigorously shook his head.

Stop. This is a road you can't afford to go down. There's no way you can give Virginia the kind of man she deserves.

He couldn't lie next to her on the bed and wake up screaming every night. And, heaven forbid, what would happen if he accidentally hurt her while he was flailing about like an infant having a tantrum?

He sighed heavily.

Besides, I'm obviously meant to be alone. Everyone I've ever loved, besides Ben, has died.

Allen was afraid even to admit that he saw Ben as his brother because deep down inside, he knew that he'd just lose him, too.

Chapter Eleven

Virginia's favorite part of the day was after dinner when she and Allen sat together on the couch and practiced reading. She was doing very well, partly because she read as much as she could when she had the time. A little thrill coursed through whenever he praised her progress.

Tonight, she was excited because she managed to read everything in the first lessons of the primer and had started on the second. The words were a little harder, and it took her a couple of minutes to figure them out, but eventually, she was able to read them.

Virginia looked at Allen as he brought in two cups of hot chocolate, which had become their little ritual. Her heart fluttered as their fingers touched. He was so incredibly handsome, not to mention kind and gentle.

He still kept a firm barrier between them, though. Virginia would like to think that they'd become friends, but wished that there could be something more.

Sometimes, she'd lie in bed and wonder what it would feel like if he wrapped his arms around her and hugged her, holding her tight against him. Then, she'd remind herself that he'd made it clear that their marriage was in name only and that she shouldn't even tease herself or dream because nothing could ever come of it.

Now, as her mind drifted back to the present, she smiled widely at him. "I read everything in the first lesson today."

She was so excited that she was almost bouncing up and down on the couch like a schoolgirl.

Allen's smile grew, as did the warmth pooling in her stomach. "I can't wait to hear you read them to me."

Virginia noticed that his smile was genuine, but he looked exhausted. Lines and dark rings etched around his bloodshot eyes told her that Allen hadn't been sleeping much lately. His shoulders slumped, and his head tilted forward, as though he were carrying the weight of the world on his shoulders.

Sometimes, she heard him going to his room late at night, long after everyone else was in bed. She figured that he was only getting four or five hours of sleep a night, if that. There was no way in the world she could ask him about it, though. She'd learned her lesson when she woke him after his last nightmare.

"Are you ready?" he asked, interrupting her thoughts.

She nodded. "The sun rises over the hills and shines on the...." She focused hard on the word, remembering that he said "ie" words usually sounded like a long *E*. "...fields below."

Allen smiled and leaned back against the couch, watching her follow the words with her finger as she focused on each word.

"The farmer works from...dawn to dusk, tending to the land he...l...loves."

"Great job," he commended.

A thrill washed over her from his praise, which she craved. She read on, with more confidence, about how the corn grew with the help of the sun, and then the farmer harvested the crop in the fall.

When she finished, he seemed just a bit less tired when he gazed at her, his eyes shining. "Excellent job. I'm very proud of you. You learned all of that so quickly."

"Thank you," she said softly.

Virginia practically beamed with pride. She'd quickly learned how to sound out and read basic words. Although she wasn't ready to read *Middlemarch* by George Eliot, which she'd seen at the general store, she knew she was doing very well.

They spent a couple of hours together, as they usually did. Virginia was always reluctant to end their time, but she'd be so tired that she could barely hold her eyes open.

Virginia always felt awkward when it was time to go to bed. She wanted to hug him and thank him for helping her so much, but she was afraid to touch him. There was no way that she was willing to break their delicate bond.

She quickly gathered their cups, took them to the kitchen, and went to the outhouse before heading to bed. Even though she could barely stay awake while reading, her eyes popped open as soon as she lay down.

The faintest whiff of Allen's scent—the woodsy outdoors and sage—haunted her. The kindness and something else that shone in his beautiful brown eyes made her heart beat faster.

She wanted to run her fingers through his curly brown hair.

Stop it, Virginia, she admonished herself. *You cannot start to love this man.*

It didn't matter how many times she reminded herself that; it didn't matter. Just being in his presence made her stomach flutter. Once she told herself that maybe she shouldn't spend so much time with him, but she knew that was a foolish thought. She would take every second she could get.

***

Saturday morning, he asked her whether she'd finished making her new Sunday dress.

She smiled and nodded. "Daddy always called it the 'Sunday go-to-meeting clothes.' I finished hemming it last night."

"I thought we could go to services tomorrow. Father Cahill's been asking why I haven't brought you to church to meet everyone yet. I didn't want to tell him that I was waiting for you to finish your new dress." He shrugged. "I just told him I've been busy, but I'm pretty sure if I keep making excuses, he'll send the deacons out this way to hog-tie us and drag us in."

Virginia was touched that he'd wanted to spare her the embarrassment of not having something suitable to wear. "I'd love to go. It's been a while. Aunt Fiona usually wanted me to clean the apartment while they went because it's awfully hard to clean when the three kids are running around."

Virginia noticed the look of disgust that flashed over Allen's face. She didn't tell him about her past for sympathy. She was simply being honest.

He managed to school his expression, saying, "I'm sure everyone in town would love to meet you."

After breakfast the next morning, Ben hitched up the wagon. Allen helped her up, and then he took the reins while Ben sat next to her on the buckboard. Keith and John would ride to church so they could do their own things afterward, since Sunday was their day off.

They arrived just in time for the services to start, so there wasn't a lot of time for introductions. Virginia flushed as she took her seat next to Allen. Every eye in the church was focused on her. Although most people knew the sheriff had been married, Virginia had only met a few people from the town.

Ben had told her that Allen was considered a hard but fair man. The people in town respected him, but none of them personally knew him since he kept everyone at a distance. They were likely wondering what kind of woman would marry such a cold man.

Father Cahill preached about the seeds of faith, comparing them to the seeds that farmers planted in the spring, grew tall and strong over the summer, and were ready to harvest in the fall. He stated that people had to grow, learn, and live for God throughout their lives so that when their fall arrived, they were ready to face the Lord, knowing that they had lived for Him.

Although she hadn't gone to church much after her father died, as a child, she had come to know and love God, as her father taught her. They prayed together every morning and night and attended Wednesday and Sunday mass. It thrilled her to hear the father's eloquent words spoken in a way that everyone could understand.

He was one of those men who knew that in order to keep everyone's attention, the sermons needed to be short and sweet. There was no hours-long service.

Virginia suddenly felt shy as they sang their last hymn and said their final prayer. Several women began walking her way before she had a chance to slide out of the pew.

A tall woman with sharp blue eyes rushed toward Virginia. Dark brown curls framed her face. She wore a high-necked dark green light wool dress with long sleeves. White lace trimmed the cuffs and neckline. Petticoats or a crinoline gave the skirts a slight bell shape. Her silk bonnet, adorned with fancy ribbons and lily-white gloves, completed her outfit.

Virginia knew she had done a terrific job on her own dress, but still felt overshadowed by the woman who extended her hand and smiled widely at her.

"I'm Gloria Johnson, Mayor Johnson's wife. I've been meaning to come calling on you and meet you proper, but time just gets away from me." She squeezed Virginia's hand. "Welcome to Butte."

"Thank you," Virginia said softly.

"How do you like it here so far? I heard tell that you're from New York City, and I can't help but think that the two places are like black and white."

Virginia smiled. "I like Butte a lot. The people I've met here are very friendly. There's a lot of beautiful land, plants, and animals out here that I've never seen before. I really like that things move at a much slower pace."

"I can imagine so. I keep very busy being the mayor's wife here. I can't imagine how hectic it would be in New York City." Gloria beamed at Virginia. "We're having a festival in town next weekend. There are several things that we're still putting the final touches on, like games and food booths. Would you like to come into town tomorrow afternoon and help us work on getting everything arranged?"

Virginia looked around for Allen's guidance, but he was standing in a circle with a bunch of other men.

"I'd have to check with Allen first, but that sounds nice."

"*Pshaw.*" Gloria waved her hand. "I know the sheriff would be happy to have you help. He's all about the community."

Virginia nodded and opened her mouth to say something, but before she could speak, Gloria grasped her arm, apparently taking her gesture as acceptance. "Lovely! Emma, Elizabeth, Ruth, and Naomi are helping, too. I see they're speaking with Sara, who plays the organ, but you can meet them tomorrow night."

Despite how frayed her nerves had become from Gloria's seemingly endless enthusiasm, she couldn't help but let a genuine smile slip onto her lips. "I'm looking forward to meeting everyone," Virginia said, and she was surprised that she meant it.

Still, she breathed a sigh of relief when Allen walked up behind her.

"Mrs. Johnson," he started, his voice a low rumble, "it's good to see you again, but we must be going."

"Yes, of course. Virginia, we'll meet here at about two so we can do some planning and still be home in time to make supper for our families."

Gloria rushed off like a gust of wind. Virginia watched her leave, feeling a little bit in awe of the energy she exuded.

"Meeting?" Allen asked as they went outside.

"She wants me to help with the festival that'll be put on next weekend."

"Oh, shoot, I forgot all about that," Allen moaned. "I'll have to be there, at least a part of the time, making sure no one gets too riled up."

"It sounds like Mrs. Johnson will have plenty of work for me to do," Virginia said.

"Likely, but don't let her take up all your time. You should make sure you have time to enjoy yourself."

"I'll rescue her," Ben offered, joining the conversation with a playful grin.

"Thanks, my friend," Virginia said with a chuckle. "I think I might need it."

He and Ben hurriedly hitched the horses to the wagon, while Allen helped her up, and they climbed onto the buckboard.

They rode in silence for several minutes.

Virginia glanced at Allen and noticed he was frowning.

"Is everything all right?" she asked. "You look like something's bothering you."

Allen took off his cowboy hat, scratched his head, and put it back on. He sighed and said, "Well, there's been some gang activity going on in the next town over, and the violence has been increasing. The sheriffs have reported it from Helena to Coyote Creek. They're robbing banks, businesses, and the occasional home, stealing horses, and if someone gets in the way, they don't hesitate to kill them."

Virginia gasped, her stomach dropping. "Oh, my. No one can catch them?"

"A few gang members have been caught and either sent to prison or hanged, but that doesn't seem to stop them. No one's caught the leader yet, and he's a particularly nasty fellow." Allen sighed, but he must've noticed the anxiety playing on her face, because he rushed to add, "Don't worry about them, though. I highly doubt they'll come our way, and if they do, Ben, Keith, and John are handy with a gun."

Virginia nodded, though a knot of fear sent a sharp pain through her gut.

Fires and gangs. Butte is starting to sound a lot more dangerous than New York City. What have I gotten myself into?

Chapter Twelve

Allen stood outside Sheriff Hick's office, waiting for him. He wiped the sweat from his forehead as he watched the wind stir up small dust devils. These were the smaller ones that didn't rise more than waist-high on him or possess much force. However, he had seen some that were large enough and strong enough to knock a grown man off his feet.

He slapped at the horsefly that bit the back of his neck. "The blasted bug," he said as he spotted the small smear of blood the fly's cutting mouthparts had left. The flies left big welts that were usually itchy and annoying.

Allen checked his pocket watch again. Sheriff Hicks was more than half an hour late. That wasn't like him.

"Something must be going on," Allen muttered as he shifted his weight from one foot to the other. "Maybe I should just leave a note for him, and he can come to Butte when he has the time."

Peering down the road again before going inside, he finally saw the sheriff riding up the road.

Sheriff Hicks dismounted and brushed the dust off of his pants. "Sorry, I'm late, Allen. We had a problem with some horse thieves, and it took a little more time than I thought to sort everything out. Sheriff Arthur Jefferson from Buford is handling them."

Allen merely nodded. "I figured it was something like that. You're not one to be late. You're the guy who always shows up ten minutes early."

"That was the way my father raised me," the sheriff said. "Come on inside."

The two men stepped into the office. The air was much cooler than outside in the blazing sun.

The sheriff pulled out a chair and sat down heavily, grunting. He rubbed his jaw and took out a cigar. "Want one?"

"No, thanks," Allen said. "It seems like everything is getting a lot worse out there."

"It darn sure is. I can't remember a time when we've had so many violent crimes happening all the time. Sure, there are the usual fights breaking out at the saloon, drunks tripping over themselves in the streets, and the occasional mine jump or horse theft, but nothing like this. Buford's bank has been hit twice in the last four months." The sheriff puffed on his cigar. "Today was the third time a ranch had been hit in the last two months. So far, at least twenty-six horses are missing, and three hundred forty head of cattle have been stolen."

A stone lodged in his stomach at the news.

"That's pretty bad," Allen said, his mind racing.

He was going to have to hire more deputies because it was only a matter of time before they made their way to Butte. He was surprised they hadn't come through yet, since Butte was so much bigger.

"I'm afraid it's getting worse," Sheriff Hicks muttered with a dejected shake of his head. "They've hit a couple of the wealthier homes and a few businesses here, in Buford, and other nearby towns. People are afraid to leave their homes." He removed his hat and ran his fingers through his hair, causing it to stand up on end.

His face still had traces of the dusty ride he'd just returned from, and heavy bags under his eyes showed he hadn't been getting a lot of sleep lately.

As if he read Allen's mind, he said, "Sally has been a little frustrated with me because I've been spending a lot of nights here. We all take turns. We want to be ready when trouble hits."

Allen smiled and shook his head. "Sally is a good woman. She understands, I'm sure."

"She is, and she does, but she still wants her husband home." Sheriff Hicks pinched the end off of his cigar and splashed water on his face. "We need some rain to dampen down the dust. It can be hard to breathe when you're chasing after someone." He dried his face and sat down again. "She wants me to give them up. Says they're nasty."

Allen just grinned and didn't say anything. He didn't care to smoke but knew his friend enjoyed it. "Do you have any idea who's leading this particular gang?"

"Well, it could be a couple of men who are supposed to be in this area. Cody Millen is one."

"He was that fella who led the gang robbing stagecoaches, banks, and trains. They hit the Wells Fargo stages several times until each coach had at least ten armed riders running with them."

"That's him. The other possibility is Sheldon O'Toole."

Allen's gut clenched. O'Toole was a particularly vicious man who didn't care who he hurt. He would cut down a woman or child just as fast as he would a man.

"He's not even human," Allen muttered.

Sheriff Hicks nodded in agreement. "No, he's the devil right here on Earth."

"Let's hope that it's Cody, although neither of them is ideal. Do we have a plan?"

"The deputies you sent, mine, and a few others from neighboring towns have created a posse. They're hunting down every single possible hiding spot they could be in. The trouble is that the gangs always seem to be one step ahead of the posse." Sheriff Hicks sighed heavily.

"Is someone feeding them information?"

"That's a possibility. There are always those who can be bribed or threatened. This is like the fever that passed this way all those years ago and spread across the territory. The gang is going to be completely uncontrollable and will cause complete chaos everywhere if something isn't done soon."

Allen started to respond, but before he could say anything, the door flew open with a bang. A woman stumbled into the offices, her bonnet falling off, her face pale, and her eyes wide. "Sheriff Hicks, you have to help me."

Both men instantly stood.

"Mrs. Woods. What's wrong?"

The woman stumbled over to the desk and held on as though she was going to fall down. "My son is missing. I was inside sewing, and he was playing in the yard. When I checked on him, he was gone. Someone must've taken him!" she sobbed.

An icy cold hand squeezed Allen's heart, the shiver traveling up his spine as the hairs on his arms stood on end. "When did you last see him?"

"Not more than half an hour ago!" she exclaimed, her lip wobbling. "Like I said, he was playing in the yard. I checked on him half an hour later, but he wasn't there. I searched everywhere. I looked in the barn, under the porch, at his friend's house, and even at the general store. Mr. Sam gives him a cent candy sometimes. He's nowhere!" Her voice had risen to a high-pitched scream. She was shaking, and her eyes were wide with terror.

Sheriff Hicks was already heading for the door. Allen grabbed his hat and was hot on his heels. Blaze remained saddled since Allen hadn't intended to stay more than a few minutes to discuss the gang situation.

Mrs. Woods pointed down the road. "We live just beyond the bend. Please hurry and find Jimmy."

They rode hard, the horses' hooves pounding loudly into the ground, kicking up a tornado of dust. When they reached the small house, Allen scanned the yard. Except for some toys scattered around, there was no sign of the child.

Sheriff Hicks pointed at the road in front of the house. "There's been several riders here. I'd say at least three or four."

Allen's gut knotted. "They must've taken him."

"They've gone that way. If we hurry, we might catch them."

Both men urged their horses into a full run in spite of the scorching heat bearing down on them. Blaze had already worked up a sweat, and they just started.

Allen finally spotted them in the distance. A small group of riders was barely discernible through the dust and shimmering heat. "Up there. That has to be them."

The two men charged toward the group. The outlaws heard them coming and spurred their horses into a run. Allen choked on the dust stirred up by the pounding hooves.

Allen leaned over his horse, urging him to go faster. The wind whipped into his face, and he reached for his revolver. Before he could aim, one of the gang members turned around and fired off several shots.

One of the bullets whizzed by Allen's head, and suddenly, he was no longer chasing outlaws on a Montana Territory prairie. He was transported back to the bloody grounds of the war. The acrid smell of gunpowder and blood suffocated him, causing his throat to close. He could hear the sounds of men crying out as they were wounded, and the screaming horses as they fell.

Panic squeezed his heart and lungs. He loosened his grip on the reins, and Blaze slowed. He tried to breathe, but it was as though he was underwater and couldn't claw his way out. He could hear the shots fired, although they were muffled.

His vision darkened around the edges, and Blaze stopped completely. Allen gasped for air, trying to control himself.

"Allen!" Sheriff Hicks yelled.

He continued to race toward the outlaws, his horse weaving through the bullets. Allen could only stare, completely frozen in fear, as though he were trapped in a horrific dream.

Sheriff Hicks drew his rifle from the scabbard and fired at the nearest outlaw. The man screamed and toppled from his horse. The rider next to him threw Jimmy off his horse and sped after the other gang members.

Allen watched numbly as Sheriff Hicks jumped off his horse, practically while it was still moving, and scooped up the sobbing little boy.

A few minutes later, the sheriff rode back toward Allen, holding the child, who was starting to calm down.

Hunched over the saddle horn, Allen finally managed to catch his breath, although his heart was thundering. He forced himself to look around, chasing off the lingering images of the battlefield. He couldn't let the sheriff see him this way.

Sheriff Hicks stopped beside him. "What happened? Are you all right?"

Allen forced himself to grin and nod. "Yeah. I got a massive cramp in my side. I actually checked for blood, it was so sharp. I had to slow down."

The sheriff studied him for a minute and then clicked his horse, urging him to walk back to town. Although he didn't say anything, Allen wondered whether Sheriff Hicks knew the truth about what just happened.

Jimmy spoke in a rapid torrent of words. "I was playing with my blocks, and the bad men rode by. One of them leaned down, grabbed my arm, and lifted me onto the horse. They said the town would pay a ransom." Jimmy paused to take a breath. "What's a ransom?"

Sheriff Hicks glanced down at him. "They wanted the town to give them money and buy you back."

"People can't be bought or sold. That's what my daddy says," Jimmy said solemnly, clearly starting to calm down a little.

"You're right, little man."

Mrs. Woods was pacing in the front yard, wringing her hands, when they rode up to her. Sheriff Hicks carefully handed Jimmy to his mother.

"My baby!" she exclaimed, tears spilling down her reddened cheeks. "You got my baby back. Thank you. How can I ever thank you?" The raw emotion in her voice cut Allen to his core.

"We're just doing our duty, ma'am," Sheriff Hicks said.

"I guess we've seen firsthand what they're capable of. We're going to have to figure out some way to take them down," Allen said through gritted teeth.

"Yeah. I'll talk to the other sheriffs and get back to you. We'll figure something out."

"I'm heading home," Allen said. "I'll water Blaze down here at the trough. See you soon."

Sheriff Hicks nodded, and Allen turned his horse toward home, pausing long enough for Blaze to drink his fill.

His mind was numb, and he didn't notice any of the beautiful countryside he usually loved to admire. He felt the wave of humiliation engulf him completely.

What kind of sheriff am I? He shook his head, adding, *What kind of man am I? I got terrified at the first sound of danger. If Frank hadn't been with me, that child would have ended up dead, and it would have been my fault.*

The shroud of guilt and shame clung to him as he and Blaze slowly made their way back to Butte, and Allen had the sense it wouldn't be leaving anytime soon.

Chapter Thirteen

Virginia walked out to the stables, uncertain whether she wanted someone there to help her saddle a horse for the meeting or preferred no one was there so she could avoid going.

She was very unsure of herself, and the thought of getting acquainted with a bunch of women all at once terrified her, no matter how much she craved companionship. Virginia was sure they were all just as nice as Mrs. Johnson was, but she would have preferred meeting them one at a time.

Ben was in one of the stalls with a mare that was pure black except for a white lightning bolt on her forehead and white fetlocks. He looked up when he heard her coming and put his finger to his mouth.

"Storm about to foal," Ben said very quietly, petting the horse. "Do you need something?"

"Well, not really, if you're busy," Virginia said, taking a step back.

Ben petted Storm again and stepped out of the stall. "What do you need?" he asked kindly.

"Mrs. Johnson wanted me to go to that meeting today in town," she murmured, referring to the conversation Ben had overheard after church. "The summer festival is next weekend, and they want to talk about finalizing the plans. I don't need to go."

Ben grinned, though his look was knowing. "You should go and make friends. They're a nosy bunch, and boy, do they like to gossip, but they're a good group of ladies. As soon as they find out someone's sick or having a baby, they're all there trying to help."

Virginia bit her bottom lip and twisted her hands together. "I know how to ride, and I can mostly saddle a horse, but I've never been good with a girth. Plus, I don't know which horse I could take. It's a little too far to walk."

"It is definitely too far to walk," Ben agreed. "I'll saddle Belle for you. Belle's a sweet old girl and a great ride. She'll get you there quick enough. It'll just take a couple of minutes. Go ahead and grab your bag and whatever else you need to take with you."

"Thank you," she said, sighing as she willed her heart to slow its frantic rhythm.

Virginia grabbed her bonnet, shawl, and a small bag she carried necessities in and walked back outside, still not sure if she really wanted to go. Ben thought she should, though, and he probably wouldn't let her back out of it.

"She's ready to go," Ben said, smiling. "We have a mounting post if you'd like to use that."

Nodding, Virginia led Belle over to the spot Ben indicated. She could get on a horse without it, but didn't like the idea of hiking up her skirt in front of Ben.

After hooking her bag on the saddle horn, she used the mounting post and quickly arranged her skirts around her.

"I'm sorry we don't have any sidesaddles," Ben said. "I'm not sure a whole lot of the women out here use them anyway. It's easier and safer to ride astride."

"I don't mind. If they're going to hold the way I ride against me, then I don't want to be their friend, anyway," Virginia said in an exaggerated, defiant voice as she lifted her nose into the air.

"That's the spirit," he said with a chuckle. "Have fun, and don't let them rope you into doing anything you don't feel comfortable doing."

"I promise," she said.

"Do you remember how to get to the church?"

"When I get into town, take a left. Go down past the general store and go right. It's the big white building on the right."

Ben nodded, a grin still on his lips. "You've got it. Try to have a little fun."

She nodded and gently prodded Belle. True to Ben's promise, Belle was a dream to ride. Her smooth, even gait nearly lulled Virginia to sleep. The horse knew the way into town, allowing Virginia to do nothing but loosely hold the reins.

Virginia's thoughts turned, as they so often did, to Allen. He had been so kind to her. He was very patient when she made a mistake during their lessons. They sometimes talked about other topics as well, such as the wildlife in the Montana Territory.

She'd always loved animals, but according to Allen, rattlesnakes were a particular threat. Although they normally stayed in the forests, grizzly bears could be aggressive, especially mamas with cubs. Mountain lions could also cause problems. He warned her that although bison, elk, and moose were beautiful to look at, they could be aggressive, particularly if they had young. He did mention that the last three animals were very tasty.

Allen said that when they had time, he and Ben would go on a hunting trip.

No dangerous creatures lurked about the prairie as she and Belle made their way through town. There were just the usual prairie dogs, deer, and rabbits.

All too soon, the church appeared. Virginia dismounted and led Belle to a shaded area with a water trough. She patted the horse's neck and kissed her nose. "I'll be back as soon as I can."

Taking a deep breath, Virginia forced herself to walk up the stairs to the church. The room was crowded and buzzing, with everyone seemingly talking at once. Everyone obviously already knew each other, their laughter and conversations filling the air.

She already regretted her decision to come, and she wondered if she could slip back out the door before anyone noticed.

Virginia stood at the entrance, rooted in place. She adjusted the sleeves of her dress and smoothed her skirt, trying to remember to breathe.

She stepped back, but suddenly, Mrs. Johnson noticed her and hurried over.

"Virginia, I'm so glad you could make it." Mrs. Johnson touched her arm gently and led her toward the front of the room. "Come sit with us."

Virginia nodded stiffly and smiled. She still wasn't sure about Mrs. Johnson, who was a little more effusive than Virginia was used to.

The chatter quieted, and everyone looked at her curiously. Virginia forced herself not to squirm in the pew.

THE SHERIFF'S UNEXPECTED WIFE

"Everyone, this is Mrs. Strauss, Sheriff Strauss's wife. Please show her a warm welcome to our humble town," Mrs. Johnson said.

She smiled and waved at everyone staring at her. Virginia's stomach tightened, and she was terrified that she was going to humiliate herself and throw up everywhere.

"I'm sure you'll get to know everyone soon. You'd never remember everyone's name if I rattled them off," Mrs. Johnson said. She clapped her hands to get everyone's attention. "Everyone's here, so let's get this meeting started."

Virginia listened as the women discussed the upcoming festival. Occasionally, they interrupted one another or spoke over each other, tossing ideas around as if they'd done this a hundred times. Virginia folded her hands in her lap, attempting to keep up with everyone's thoughts, even when they overlapped.

She slipped her finger under the collar of her dress. It seemed to have tightened a little and threatened to choke her. Virginia felt small, almost invisible, and was definitely out of place. She'd never been to any kind of meeting like this and didn't have anything she could say. As a matter of fact, she pressed her lips tightly together so she didn't have to say anything at all, fearing that something silly or awkward would slip out.

Everyone knew everyone else. They shared a common history together and knew each other's families and life stories. Virginia glanced at the door, wondering what her chances of escaping were if she just quietly slid down the pew and crept down the aisle.

Suddenly, a woman she didn't recognize turned to her and thrust a pen and piece of paper at her. "Mrs. Strauss, would you mind taking notes? It'll be good to have a written record of what we decide, plus a list of all the games, booths, and contests, as well as who will be in charge of those.

Virginia's heart stopped, and her breath caught in her throat. Her eyes opened wide, and her stomach tightened so much she was sure she was going to be sick. She tried to think of something to say, but her mind was spinning. She'd barely learned to read and could only write her name.

She swallowed hard, trying to think of a way out of it, without drawing attention to herself. How could she tell a room full of well-spoken, educated women that she'd never learned to do what they had in primary school?

"Oh, well…" Virginia said, twisting her skirt in her fingers. "I don't know if—"

Mrs. Johnson took the pen and paper. "Now, Sarah, let's not overwhelm her with all the work her first time here. She should take part in the conversation, but she doesn't need to record it." She looked around the room, and her eyes landed on a young blonde woman sitting in the middle. "Ruth, you have lovely handwriting. Would you mind recording our decisions?"

"I'll be happy to," Ruth said.

Relief flooded through Virginia so quickly that she almost felt dizzy.

"Thank you," she said quietly, hoping that no one noticed that she'd panicked.

A few of the women smiled and nodded at her, and the conversations resumed. Virginia looked around, wondering if any of them suspected that she had no idea how to write.

She focused on controlling her breathing without making it obvious to everyone in the room. Her secret shame had almost been exposed. Everyone would look down on her and probably pity the sheriff for having such an uneducated wife. If anyone ever found out, she'd never be treated as an equal.

Finally, she was able to return her attention to the lively conversation that had been going on.

"We still need someone to organize the children's games," someone said.

"I can do that," Virginia said. The words had slipped out of her mouth before she even thought about them.

The women's heads turned toward her. They seemed surprised but pleased to have a volunteer.

"Are you sure?" one of them asked.

Virginia nodded and sat up straighter, her voice gaining strength. "I used to make up games for my cousins and the neighborhood children back home. I'd be happy to help."

There was a brief pause as everyone looked around at each other as though silently asking if she could actually take on the responsibility.

Mrs. Johnson clapped her hands. "That's wonderful, Virginia," she said excitedly. "I'm sure the children will love your ideas."

A few of the women suggested popular games, and Virginia listened intently. She was good at remembering what she'd heard when she wanted to.

For the first time, Virginia felt as though she was a part of something, and she had something valuable to offer. Some of the other women even asked her opinion about whether she thought certain games would work.

Her stomach gradually settled, and the nausea she felt earlier passed. Virginia was surprised that she was actually laughing and talking to the other women. She was still a little nervous and chose her words carefully so she didn't sound like a fool, but for now, at least, she didn't feel like her secret was going to be exposed. Instead, she focused on what she could do and what she could offer her new community. Planning games for children was something she did well.

When the meeting finally wrapped up, she felt hopeful. Not only had she survived the meeting, but she had contributed to it, and she was sure that the women were starting to accept her. If everything went well at the festival, she'd be closer to belonging.

Virginia hugged Belle and rubbed her nose before mounting. "Let's go home, girl."

Her mind was full of different games she could plan and the supplies she'd need to make them successful, and the trip passed quickly. As she neared the ranch, the sight of the house, stables, and barn made her smile. She loved her new home, and it was a welcome scene.

Her heart stopped, though, and dread filled her as she reached the stables and dismounted.

Allen's voice sounded very serious and urgent, laced with frustration. "We're going to have to do something. They've been terrorizing Coyote Creek and even kidnapped a young boy today. I think it's going to get a lot worse before it gets better."

All at once, the previous peace she'd found was shattered, giving way to a coiling fear.

A lot worse...? she wondered. *Just how bad will things get?*

Chapter Fourteen

Allen rolled his shoulders and stretched his back. The stress made it feel as if every single muscle in his body was so tense that it was going to explode.

"Why on God's green Earth would they kidnap a child?" Ben asked incredulously.

"I think it was the spur of the moment." Allen scrubbed his face with his hand. "They were likely a bunch of reckless idiots in town, and their leader had no idea what they did. The boy said he heard something to the effect that they were going to hold him until the town paid a ransom."

"It was lucky that you and Sheriff Hicks were ready to go after them. You got the boy back, and one of them is dead."

"Yeah, lucky," Allen said, grimacing as he thought about how he'd frozen up when it was most important.

A loud gasp made both of them turn their heads to Virginia, who was standing in the stable doors, holding Belle's reins. Her face was pale, and her eyes were wide.

"An outlaw gang a few miles from here? They kidnapped a child?"

He hadn't heard her ride up. Allen could tell that she was upset, and he couldn't blame her. Virginia wasn't the type of woman to start crying, panicking, or throwing a fit, but his heart sank as he saw her trembling.

Ben stood up, quietly left Storm's stall, and walked over to Virginia. He smiled grimly at her as he took Belle's reins. "I'll unsaddle her, brush her down, and give her some oats," he said softly.

"Thank you," Virginia replied absently.

Allen walked toward her, shaking his head with regret. "I didn't know you were there."

"It's that bad?" she whispered.

He nodded, unable to lie to her. "I'm not going to sugarcoat. It's bad right now. At least one gang is in the area, terrorizing the towns and robbing banks, businesses, stagecoaches, and even the wagon trains traveling through."

Her bottom lip started to quiver, and she bit it to hold it steady. "They took a child." It was a statement, not a question.

"Yes. Luckily, we caught up to them and rescued him. He's safe and sound with his family tonight."

A wave of humiliation flushed through him as he mentally corrected himself: Frank *caught up to them and rescued the child. I choked on my own nightmares.*

"You got one of the gang members?"

Allen nodded.

"But the rest got away?"

Again, he nodded. He swallowed his growl of frustration, not wanting to upset her further. "We're working on a plan. All of the sheriffs in the area, including me, have asked our deputies to form a posse. They're out hunting the gang now. Sooner or later, the bad men will slip up, and sooner or later, they will be found."

"Have they been in town yet?"

Allen could hear the fear in her voice—in the way it caught on her words. His jaw tightened, and he cursed himself for not hearing Belle's hooves ride up to the stables.

"Not yet, but I'm not going to lie to you," he said, essentially repeating his earlier promise. "They likely will come to Butte. It's a mining town with a couple of banks and other places they might be interested in. I promise that you'll be safe here on the ranch. Ben, Keith, John, or I will always be around. If you want, I'll even teach you how to shoot a rifle or a shotgun."

She looked at him for a long minute and nodded her head. "Maybe tomorrow. Right now, I've got to see about dinner."

Virginia left the stables, and Allen leaned against one of the stall gates. He closed his eyes and sighed heavily. Virginia had gone through enough in her life and certainly didn't need to worry about whether some bad men were going to come out here to hurt her.

He'd told her that someone was always near, and that was the truth. He hadn't lied to her and said that they wouldn't come to the ranch. They were in the business of cattle rustling and horse theft. If they found out that this ranch was his, it would make the perfect target.

Ben walked in, led Belle to her stall, and slapped Allen on the shoulder. "That was rough."

Allen picked up the bucket of oats, poured some into her manger, and checked the water trough. He absently rubbed the horse's face.

"She's scared, and I can't blame her."

"Anyone in their right mind would be. I'll be honest and tell you that I can't say I'm pleased at the thought of killer gangs roaming the territory," Ben said. "Virginia handles it well. She didn't break down into a sobbing mass of hysteria."

Allen smiled grimly. "I don't think she's the type to go quite that far. She's got way too much grit for that."

"That's for sure," Ben said. "You got lucky and managed to get yourself a good wife. It's like you were shooting craps and rolled the perfect number."

Allen simply shook his head and went back to his chores.

***

Virginia seemed to be her usual self during dinner that night. She excitedly told the men about the meeting and how she'd volunteered to organize the children's games.

"I think we can have a different game every hour. That's six games, taking time out for lunch. The women said they could round up small prizes for the winners of each game." Allen smiled. Virginia, meanwhile, became increasingly excited as she explained her ideas, forgetting to eat. "I was thinking they could do gunny sack races, bean bag toss, ring toss, egg races, leapfrog races, and musical chairs. The games would be easy to set up. The younger kids could compete first, and then the older kids."

"I might want to play, too," Keith teased.

"You never did grow out of your childhood," John ribbed him good-naturedly.

"I'll be glad to help you set up if you need me," Ben offered. "I'm sure Allen would, too, but unfortunately, he'll be needed for sheriffing duties. Even during fun times, some people can get a little rowdy."

"I appreciate it," Virginia said, her smile warm.

After she finished cleaning the kitchen, Virginia asked if he could show her how to write and told him what had happened during the meeting. He noticed the heat that flooded her cheeks as she recounted the moment, and he could relate to her embarrassment. Though he knew she had no reason to feel such a thing, he experienced the exact same thing with his nightmares.

"It'll take a little practice," he said. "But I'll be glad to teach you. Unfortunately, tonight's my night at the office, so I have to go back into town. We'll work on it soon."

She nodded, not seeming upset about the delay, and he got ready to take his shift. He never asked any of his deputies to do a duty he wasn't willing to take on.

The next day, Allen came home with some mail. One of the letters was addressed to her.

He raised his eyebrows. "You got a letter from someone named...*Shootin' June*? No last name? Or is June her last name?"

Virginia laughed and told him about the woman she'd met on the train. As she finished sharing the tale, her eyes lit up with excitement. "I've never gotten a letter before."

"Well, congratulations," Allen teased, dramatically handing over the envelope. "Here's your first one."

She carefully opened the letter and unfolded the paper. Virginia tried to sound out the letters, but they were still a bit too difficult for her.

Allen's heart twisted when he saw her disappointment.

"Don't worry about it," he said. "Sit down. I'll help you. Let me change my clothes, and I'll be down in a few minutes."

Normally, he would be itching to get out and get some work done, but he looked forward to helping Virginia decipher her letter.

When he came back downstairs, she was still trying to find the words she could read. Her fingers slowly moved over the lines, and she sounded out the letters as best she could.

"You're doing very well. Just think, a few days ago, you couldn't read anything, but now you're reading like a champ. It'll take practice, but soon you'll be buying every book Mick can get in his store."

She grinned. "I don't know about that. Maybe most of the books, though."

He laughed and sat down next to her.

Bit by bit, Virginia read June's letter.

Dear Virginia,

I hope this letter finds you well and your new married life suits you.

I've been very busy, traveling from town to town, putting on shows, and proving to all the men out here that there's a woman who can shoot better than they can. And guess what? I've managed to get a spot in a traveling show that will be in Butte in a couple of weeks. It'll be big crowds, big names, and a chance to prove myself.

I'm having fun, but I miss having a woman to talk to. I hope we'll meet up in Butte. Maybe I'll come visit you on the ranch.

Take care of yourself, and if anyone ever gives you trouble, just tell 'em that you've got Shootin' June as a friend. That'll scare 'em away.

I hope to hear from you soon.

Your friend always,

Shootin' June

"Would that be okay if she came to visit?" Virginia asked excitedly.

"Yes. This is your home, too," Allen said.

"That would be great. I'm sure you'd like her. She's a lot of fun."

"She sounds like it," Allen agreed. "Would you like to write back to her?"

Virginia nodded, but then her face clouded, a frown pulling at her lips. "I don't know how."

Allen already saw this coming, so he was quick to make his offer. "I'll help you."

He went into his office and came back with paper, a bottle of ink, and a steel-nib pen.

"Okay, tell me what you want to say," he said. "I'll write it here first, and then you can write your letter."

Dear June,

It was real good to get your letter. I was very glad to hear from you. I knew that you'd find a group to be with. I'm very happy for you.

I stay busy here, working on the ranch, sewing, and cooking. I even got involved with the festival in town. I'll be running the children's games. Can you believe that?

It would be great to see you again. I enjoyed talking to you and would love to hear some of your stories.

I'll make sure to go to Butte when your show comes to town. I can't wait to see your fancy shooting.

Your friend,

Virginia

He read her letter back to her. "Does that sound good?"

She nodded.

Allen wrapped his hand around hers, showing her how to hold the pen. "You dip it into the inkwell like this. You want just enough ink to cover the tip."

He guided her hand as he demonstrated. "Wipe the underside on the rim, like this."

With his hand still wrapped around hers, he said, "When you write, don't press too hard, or the tip of the pen will go through the paper. Let the pen glide smoothly."

He guided her hand for a few letters and then let her practice on her own.

The tip of her tongue peeked out from between her lips as she focused, her brows furrowed with concentration. She was so adorable, and Allen's heart skipped a beat as he watched her work.

Occasionally, he reached around her to hold her hand again. His body tingled from the touch, and something stirred inside of him. He loved being close to her. The sweet smell of lavender and vanilla was intoxicating. The heat from her body made him ache with a longing he couldn't quite name—or wasn't ready to name.

He had to resist the sudden urge to pull her into his arms and hold her close. Allen never would have guessed that this small, red-haired spitfire of a woman would come to mean so much to him. He truly enjoyed spending time with her, helping her learn to read, and now, he was going to teach her to write.

She's your wife of convenience, and she's a friend. That's all it can be, he reminded himself.

Even though he knew he was right, he couldn't stop the feelings he got just by being close to her.

Chapter Fifteen

The morning sun bathed the town square in a warm golden glow as Virginia adjusted the sign she had painted the night before on a scrap board that Allen had given her. He had written the words for her on paper, and she had copied them onto the board carefully, using white paint.

"You did a terrific job on that," he said. "I'm proud of you."

Virginia smiled at him. "Thank you. I had a terrific teacher—the best."

Their eyes locked, and for a moment, the world around them disappeared, leaving just the two of them in their own little bubble. She licked her lips, desperately trying to find some moisture, and her heart thundered so hard in her chest that she was sure Allen could hear it.

A warmth spread throughout her body, and she took a step toward him, almost touching him....

"Hello, Sheriff and Virginia. Do you have everything you need?" Mrs. Johnson's voice broke the moment, causing Virginia to flinch..

Regaining her composure, she stepped back and nodded. "I do. Thank you."

"Okay. Holler if you need me," she said, waving her hand as she walked away.

Disappointment hit Virginia hard, causing her shoulders to droop. She had hoped that Allen might reach for her and hold her, but now, he busied himself, pounding a stake into the ground for the rope that would mark off her game area.

There wasn't much time to sulk, though.

She glanced at her surroundings and smiled. Everyone rushed around, preparing their booths for the day. Some set up food booths while others hosted games for adults. An area was set aside for a petting zoo and horse rides.

Delicious smells filled the air. The aromas of freshly baked bread and roasting meat wafted around, making her stomach rumble although she'd eaten breakfast a couple of hours ago.

She stacked the boxes that held the gunny sacks, eggs, spoons, and the few other supplies she needed for the games on one corner. The prize boxes, with an assortment of carved animals, balls, whistles, and metal noisemakers, as well as small paper fans and corn husk dolls, were in another corner.

Virginia looked up to see Allen watching her with a huge smile.

"You could make yourself useful instead of just watching," she teased.

"You're doing such a good job that I didn't want to interfere," he countered playfully. "You're taking this very seriously."

She grinned at him and put her hands on her hips. "Well, of course I am, Sheriff. The kids are counting on me to have a good time today, and I don't mean to let them down."

Unable to help herself, Virginia tossed one of the bean bags at him. "Do you think you could hit one of those buckets over there? If you get ten points, you get a prize. The furthest bucket is ten points." She pointed to the ground. "You have to stand here."

He smirked at her, stood on the line, and easily tossed the bean bag into the ten-point bucket.

Allen casually dropped a hand on her shoulder and asked, "What prize do I get, Mrs. Strauss?"

Her heart nearly stopped, and a million butterflies exploded in her stomach. She wished she were brave enough to give him a kiss, but there was no way she could do that, especially in front of everyone.

"Would you like a whistle or a noisemaker?" she managed to squeak out.

"What would make you the craziest if I played with it at home?"

Virginia laughed, and her cheeks warmed. "Right. You get to have a carved dog."

She bent down to pick up the dog and put it in his hand. A tingle coursed through her from the touch, and she felt as though the wind had been knocked out of her.

"I'll treasure it always," he said, winking at her and putting the toy in his pocket.

"I bet that was a one-time shot," she said. "Do you think you could do it again?"

"A one-time shot?" he scoffed, pretending to be insulted. "I tell you what. Why don't we have a contest? If I win, you have to bake an apple pie for me. If you win, I'll get you a present from the general store."

"Fair enough, as long as the present doesn't involve me baking you something like an apple pie."

He laughed. "Have I ever given you a cause to be so suspicious of my character?"

She tapped her chin and pretended to think about it. "Can I get back to you?"

They each tossed five bean bags. He hit the ten-point bucket every time. She managed to get all of her bean bags into the ten-point bucket except one.

"Not bad," he acknowledged. "But you still owe me a pie."

"I'm a pro at these games since I kept my cousins and the neighborhood kids entertained when I wasn't working." She picked up the bean bags and put them near the other supplies. "I'll concede your victory, Sheriff. You shall have pie tomorrow."

Allen grinned.

Virginia watched him for a moment, thinking about how much he'd changed in just the short time she'd been there. She wasn't conceited enough to believe that he'd changed because of her. He just learned that she wasn't going to make any demands of him, and they could be friends.

She hadn't been sure that the man she first met when she came to Butte even knew how to smile. Now, he was laughing with her and playing a silly child's game.

"All right, now that we've got that settled, what's next?" Allen said, breaking the silence.

Virginia shook herself out of her thoughts. "Well, I have to sort the ribbons for first, second, and third place. Mick donated peppermint sticks for the first-place winner for each age group in the different games. Everyone else can choose from one of the toys."

Allen raised his eyebrows. "Peppermint sticks?"

"What's wrong with that?"

"I just figured you as a molasses candy type of girl."

Virginia wrinkled her nose. "No way."

They arranged the ribbons and candy on the prize table, making sure to put something heavy on the ribbons so they wouldn't fly away. She and Allen bumped into each other, and their hands touched a few times, making Virginia's knees weak.

If he ever did hug me, I'd probably fall apart and melt into a pool of water.

She shook her head to try to suppress the incessant thoughts. Virginia knew that she'd developed some very strong feelings for Allen, but also knew that nothing could come of them.

Searching for a distraction, Virginia said, "Mrs. Johnson said that she has a couple of the older kids who will help me distribute the prizes. That way, none of the candy will accidentally disappear."

"You mean like this?" Allen said, pulling one of the sticks out of the glass jar and popping it into his mouth.

A laugh spilled from her lips. "I'm going to call the law on you," she said. "I've heard that the sheriff is very tough around here and doesn't cotton to any law-breakers."

"I'm not afraid of him. I can take him."

"That might be a fight worth watching."

Allen grinned and was about to reply when Mrs. Johnson stopped by. "We're ready to begin. This is Alice and her brother, Caleb. They'll be helping you this morning."

"Sounds great. Thank you, Mrs. Johnson." She turned to the teenagers and said, "Nice to meet you."

Allen touched her shoulder. "I guess that's my cue to begin my duties. Have fun today."

She watched him stroll away, the warmth from where he had touched her shoulder lingering far longer than she'd care to admit.

The kids loved her games. Everyone was polite, waited their turns to play, and happily accepted their prizes. The town square was filled with laughter and conversation. Between games, several people stopped by to introduce themselves to her.

She spotted Allen a few times walking through the area, ensuring that people were on their best behavior. Her heart raced faster each time she saw her handsome husband.

He always caught her eye when he was near and grinned at her.

If I didn't know better, I'd think that he was starting to have a softness for me, too.

The festival was in full swing when chaos erupted.

Breaking through the cheer, someone screamed, "The general store is on fire!"

Virginia's heart thundered in her chest, and fear exploded inside of her.

It was almost like she'd been awakened from a pleasant dream with a bucket of ice-cold water.

All it took was one fire, and the entire town could be destroyed. Even in New York City, they'd heard about the Great Chicago Fire. Apparently, there were at least two hundred fifty to three hundred people who'd been killed, and more than three miles of businesses and houses burned to the ground.

Everyone froze, silence coming before the storm. After they processed the words, many people started yelling. Then, as though some unforeseen force had given the signal, several of the men, women, and older children ran toward the general store to help.

It seemed the city had installed underground water mains after news of the Great Chicago Fire reached city officials. They even had fire hydrants and large canvas sheets that could be attached to the hydrants. Someone had to keep pumping water from the underground cistern.

Other people grabbed fire buckets from the sheriff's office and started a bucket brigade, dipping water from the town well.

Virginia did her best to keep the children calm. She gathered them close to her and repeatedly told them that everything was going to be okay. All the while, she kept a close eye on the fire, ready to herd the children to the creek if the fire spread. All it would take was a slight gust of wind.

Suddenly, loud gunfire erupted, and several men on horses stampeded into the town square. They shot their guns into the air and made strange screaming sounds that sent an icy cold hand racing down Virginia's spine.

She trembled, and her lungs felt as though they had closed up. She couldn't draw a breath—couldn't force any air into her clogged windpipes.

"The gangs are here!" someone screamed. "Outlaws!"

The children! Virginia's mind raced. *I have to protect them. If they'd kidnap a boy, it wouldn't bother them one bit to hurt one of them.*

Some of them cried, while others stared at the chaos in utter shock. Each fearful expression broke her heart, but their panic only served to further strengthen her resolve.

"I need you guys to run to the church," Virginia said loudly but calmly, clapping her hands to get their attention.

"Everyone needs to hold someone's hands and run as fast as you can. Don't stop for anything. If some of you bigger kids could carry the little ones, that would be helpful."

Even though the children were obviously terrified, they followed Virginia's instructions. The teenagers scooped up the smaller kids and ran as fast as they could toward the church. A couple of women heard her and ran alongside the group, shielding the children from the outlaws. Virginia trailed behind them, ensuring that they weren't attacked from behind.

When the last member of the group entered the church, she hurried back to the market square. She had lost sight of Allen when the fire began. Virginia was acutely aware that he and the deputies would be targets for the outlaws. Killing the sheriff would only enhance their terror.

I can't lose him now, she found herself thinking, her blood rushing in her ears. *Things are just starting to be good between us. I can't lose him. Please, God.*

She searched frantically through the crowd, trying to catch a glimpse of him. All the while, her entire body felt as though it was vibrating, as if she were about to jump out of her skin.

One of the outlaws charged straight at her, as if he intended to ride *over* her. She jumped behind a tree, and as she did, she heard him laughing as he rode by. He leaped off his horse long enough to scoop up small nuggets of gold and silver that one of the vendors had been selling. Another outlaw was pocketing jewelry from a different booth. Others were stealing food and anything else they could grab.

She noticed that Mrs. Franklin's handmade quilts had been thrown to the ground and trampled. Years of work were destroyed by these dastardly men.

Virginia felt sickened by the destruction. She knew she should be terrified of the men, but her rage was overpowering her fear. She was angry that they were hurting people, either by scaring them, trampling them, or destroying their goods.

Her main focus, though, was Allen as she continued to fight her way toward the general store, thinking that he would be there.

Virginia prayed with every fiber of her soul. "Please, Lord God, let him be safe. The outlaws would want to kill him. Please, don't take him from me."

Chapter Sixteen

Allen smiled as he wandered around the festival. He was amazed that he'd had such a great time with Virginia this morning, helping her set up for the carnival games.

Every time they touched, a flame ignited inside him, an aching need that he'd thought had died a long time ago. Allen enjoyed spending time with her, whether helping her learn to read, teaching her how to write a letter to her friend, or having a goofy bean bag contest.

He passed by her area often. Allen was pretty sure that she was looking for him. He never wanted there to be a connection between them, and he wasn't sure how it happened.

The festival was going great. Laughter was in the air, and excited conversations buzzed around him. The younger children finished their sack races and happily chose their prizes.

Couples held hands as they walked around, looking at the various items for sale. A tent had been set up for men who wanted to play cards, literally for peanuts.

The sun was shining, and the air smelled delicious, making his tummy rumble. Allen was looking forward to having lunch with Virginia.

Then, he heard hooves pounding down the street—unnaturally loud. He wasted no time running toward the sound, his heart racing and his breath caught in his throat. The hairs on the back of his neck stood on end as he watched three men throw bottles of kerosene, with lit rags sticking out of them, through the glass windows of Mick's general store. Other men split off and headed straight for the town square.

They're going to destroy the town! Allen's mind screamed.

The people closest to the store shouted, and Mick and several customers exploded through the door as the building burst into flames.

Screams of "Fire!" echoed throughout the street and town square. Emergency crews trained to use the new water main system and hydrants quickly mobilized, while others rushed over from the town square to form a water brigade. Even if they couldn't save Mick's store, no one wanted the fire to spread.

Spread... Allen considered, pausing in his ministrations. *The fire is a diversion!*

For half a second, Allen debated whether to help with the fire or to chase down the gang members.

There are plenty of people handling the fire. We have to stop the outlaws.

Allen rushed toward Blaze and quickly saddled him. He ran into the sheriff's office, grabbed his rifles, and mounted Blaze, guiding him toward the town square.

He noticed that Stephen and Douglas had followed suit and were on his heels as they tried to chase the outlaws from the area. Allen motioned for them to split up so they could surround the men and drive them out of town.

Allen noticed Virginia and a couple of other women herding the children toward the church.

Smart women.

Virginia looked around as if she were searching for him. He wanted to reassure her, but there wasn't time for that. He had to get the outlaws out of town before someone got hurt. Maybe he could even capture or, if necessary, kill a couple to thin their numbers.

The town square was in utter chaos. People were running around, screaming as the outlaw's horses trampled everything. The men knocked over booths, stealing anything they could grab, and fired their guns into the air, instilling even more fear and chaos. Their loud "Yeehaws" and taunts of "Ain't nobody safe today" terrified people even more.

One of the outlaws saw Allen running toward him and fired. The bullet whizzed past his head and lodged in the tree behind him. Allen urged Blaze forward and fired his own shot, striking the outlaw in the arm. The man cried out as blood spurted from the wound.

"Round up!" yelled one of the men.

Immediately, the gang members left the town square and headed back toward Main Street, where a group of people were working diligently to put out the fire.

People screamed, and the horses' hooves pounded on the road. One of the horses reared up, and its sharp hooves caught a man in the temple. He crumbled to the ground as the outlaw trampled over him.

Allen guided his horse around the fallen man as others rushed to tend to him.

The fire was thick, and a sickening knot formed in his stomach when he heard several explosions going off inside the general store. The flames must have reached the ammunition. If it reached the kegs of gunpowder, the entire store would explode. The walls would be blown out, and it would be almost impossible to contain the fire. Toxic gas and intense heat would be released, and even more people would be hurt.

Ben ran into the store and straight into the flames, holding the fire hose and directing water at the source, hoping to extinguish the blaze before it reached the back room. Other men rushed in with buckets, throwing water on the fire and likely the back wall to prevent the blaze from spreading there.

Everything played out in slow motion. His senses were heightened, and it was as though he could see everything at once. Allen watched the men in front of him racing down the street while still seeing the people working hard to put out the fire. Screams of terror pierced through his brain, and the acrid smell of burning wood, material, leather, and other goods singed his nose.

He sent up a silent prayer that they put the fire out before it reached that part of the store and continued chasing the outlaws.

There were seven ahead of him, including the one who was rapidly losing blood. Stephen and Douglas were coming toward him. He motioned for them to spread out.

The two deputies veered off in different directions, trying to head off the gang members. One of the gang members shot at Stephen, who immediately slowed down as blood burst from his leg.

"I'm all right. Get those scoundrels!" Stephen screamed, though he grunted a bit. "Don't let them get away!"

He veered back toward town, and Allen and Douglas continued riding as fast as they could.

Allen pictured the landscape ahead, trying to figure out which way they could be going. If they went west, there were several caves in the foothills and mountains where they could hide.

If they went east, there were a couple of abandoned homesteads they could hunker down in and have an advantage if anyone came their way.

We have to cut these men off. If we can get just one, maybe we can get some information out of them.

Allen felt the power of Blaze's muscles as the horse raced toward the band of men. The men separated and went in three different directions. Allen sped forward, trying to capture the outlaw who was falling behind the others.

The man glanced back at Allen, and his eyes widened with fear when he saw that Allen was gaining on him.

Allen tightened his hands on his reins until his knuckles were white. He shifted in his saddle, bending low over Blaze's neck.

He could still smell the smoke from the fire as a large gust of wind swept by them. Allen prayed that they could put the fire out before it spread, or the outlaw gang would succeed in completely destroying the town.

The outlaw veered next to the smelter just outside of town, likely trying to hide among the outbuildings. Allen saw his plan and turned Blaze, intercepting the man as he emerged from the side of the large plant.

"Stop!" Allen yelled, pulling his pistol from his holster and aiming it at the man's chest. "You're done."

The man snarled and aimed his pistol at Allen. Before he could pull the trigger, Allen leaped off Blaze toward the man and knocked him to the ground.

Allen felt the impact in his bones, but he couldn't stop to assess any injuries. The outlaw was fighting, beating Allen with his fists and trying to kick Allen off of him. The man's pistol was lying a couple of feet away, and he was trying desperately to reach it.

Swinging wildly, the outlaw's fist struck Allen's jaw. Allen hardly felt it. His heart raced, and he sensed an intense heat and energy exploding within him as he fought to subdue the man beneath him.

The outlaw twisted his body and slammed Allen in the ribs with his elbow. The man cursed and tried to land another punch in Allen's face, but Allen moved just in time.

Allen brought his knee up hard, catching the outlaw right between the legs. The man cried out in pain, and Allen followed up with a swift punch to the chin.

As the outlaw swung his arm toward Allen's face again, Allen snapped one of the handcuffs around his wrist.

In one swift movement, he stood up, turned the man over, and locked the other wrist in the handcuff, tightening it.

"You son of a…" the man started, but Allen stood and yanked him to his feet by the collar of his shirt.

"You're under arrest," Allen growled, his voice low and hard.

He whistled, and Blaze trotted up to him. Allen threw the reins over Blaze's head, knowing the horse would follow him.

Allen shoved the man forward. "Start walking," he ordered. "I've got a nice cell waiting for you."

He felt a sense of satisfaction as he led the outlaw back to town. There were still several others out there who would terrorize the area, but he'd gotten one of them. And he wouldn't stop until he brought them all down.

Chapter Seventeen

Virginia thought she saw a glimpse of Allen as he rode after the outlaws leaving town. Two men followed him, and she assumed they were deputies. She knew that even if Allen had assistance, they were still outnumbered at least two to one.

Her heart twisted with agony as she pictured him being shot down.

Breathe. He survived the war. He's a sheriff. He knows what he's doing. He'll be fine.

She took several deep breaths to try to calm herself, but her worry persisted.

No man is invincible.

"Stop," she muttered to herself. "I have to help. Me worrying isn't going to help anyone."

A crowd of people stood near the general store. Black, heavy smoke poured out of the building, but she was sure the fire was under control. She'd heard the explosions when the fire reached the ammunition, but soon after, she thought she caught people saying Ben and a few other men had managed to get the flames put out before they reached the gunpowder kegs in the back room.

She looked around, trying to figure out where to start. Although several people had cuts and bruises, no one looked seriously hurt.

Thank God for that.

Deciding to start where she was standing, she bent down to pick up the quilts that had been trampled on by the horses and pushed down into the dirt. Mrs. Franklin, who walked with a cane, hobbled up to her.

"Honey, I don't know if they can be saved," she muttered, shaking her head. "Look at them."

"I think they can," Virginia argued. "I'll help you. We'll use a broom to beat as much of the dirt and stuff off as we can. We can soak them in soapy water for a while and then scrub them. Ben and I came in the wagon today, so we can bundle them up and take them home."

Mrs. Franklin pursed her lips, but Virginia didn't miss the light that sparked in her eyes. "Are you sure? I don't have money to pay you for all that."

"Ma'am, I don't want your money. I want to help you. I heard Mrs. Johnson say something about a fall festival. We'll have them ready for that."

Mrs. Franklin looked around as though she was afraid that the outlaws were going to bust in on the scene again. "Do you think we'll have a fall festival after today?"

"Yes, for two reasons." She held up a finger. "One: Allen and his men will have managed to round up all the outlaws by then. He said all of the sheriffs and their deputies are hunting them." She held up a second finger. "Two: People here aren't the type to let something like this get them down. It'll be hard for a while, but they'll rally. One thing I've learned is that you have to have a strong spirit to live in Montana Territory, whether you're a rancher, miner, or business owner."

The older lady nodded, really seeming to mull over Virginia's words. "That's true."

With her go-ahead, Virginia picked up all the quilts, folded them, and put them near her game supplies.

The rest of the day was spent helping the people pick up the items they were trying to sell and cleaning up the mess caused by the outlaws. Although it seemed like hours, the men had only been there for ten minutes at most. Virginia suspected it might have been even less time. During that period, though, they had caused a lot of destruction.

She continuously scanned the area but never saw Allen riding back. When she blinked, she couldn't get rid of the sight of him lying injured or dead on the road.

Ben joined her as the sun started to set. "We need to get back to the house. Although the road is pretty safe, we don't want the horses stepping in any new holes the prairie dogs might have created. We also don't want to be caught in the open in complete darkness if the outlaws are out roaming around."

Virginia turned toward him, biting her lip. "What about Allen? What if he's hurt?"

"I'm sure he's fine," Ben said, his tone softening. "I promised him I'd watch over you and get you back to the house safe. What do we need to take with us?"

Virginia looked at him carefully for the first time since chaos had erupted. His eyebrows and arm hair had been singed off, and his hands and face were burned.

"Oh, my heavens. You're hurt," she gasped.

Ben just shook his head with a chuckle. "Nothing that a little aloe vera won't cure, and we have a nice big plant at the house. It's also nothing that I won't suffer if Allen thinks I didn't take care of you properly."

She studied him for a few more minutes and, with a heavy heart, nodded. "I need to take Mrs. Franklin's quilts home. I told her that I'd wash them for her. I'll mend what I can if it's needed."

"Mrs. Franklin is a sweetheart," Ben said, picking up the pile of quilts. "Her husband died ten years ago in a mining accident, and she does what she can to get by. Everyone in town helps her out."

"I also need to take home the crates of rewards and games," she added.

Alice and Caleb ran over. "We'll help you carry your stuff. It's on our way home," Caleb said, stacking a couple of crates on top of each other and picking them up.

"Thank you," Virginia said, offering the teens a tired smile.

It didn't take long for them to load the wagon and for Ben to hitch up Belle and Star.

She wrapped her shawl tightly around herself and kept glancing over her shoulder, hoping for any sign of Allen. No matter how many times she tried to reassure herself that he was fine, she couldn't help the way her leg bounced and her chest ached.

"I promise he's fine," Ben murmured, giving her another glance. "Remember that he has a lot of things he has to do. He'll have to write up the reports for the fire and what happened at the festival, and document as much of the losses as he can. He'll also have to send word to Sheriff Hicks and the other sheriffs in the area."

Virginia looked at him and nodded. She knew he was right, but that didn't stop her from worrying.

They finally made it home, quickly unloaded the wagon, and Ben unhitched the horses. She helped him brush the horses and feed them oats. Keith and John had gotten home a little earlier and had already started some stew. Virginia forced herself to eat, even though she wasn't hungry.

She fussed over Ben's burns. A couple of them were already blistered on his face. He protested but sat still until she was done.

As soon as the kitchen was clean, she went outside and paced back and forth, straining her eyes as far as she could in the darkness. Ben followed her, setting the lantern carefully on the table next to him.

He started whittling on a block of wood. After a minute, he said, "You really care about him, don't you?"

Virginia turned around and stared at him, her heartbeat picking up at first. She almost didn't want to admit the truth—that would make her feelings real—but she knew she couldn't hide from his watchful gaze.

"Yes, I do," she admitted, her words no louder than a whisper.

Ben smiled, nodded, and continued working on his carving. Thankfully, he changed the subject. "Mick is going to have a tough time for a while, but not as bad as he might have. He had the foresight to get fire insurance from the Mutual Life Insurance Company of New York."

She stopped short and looked at Ben. "There's such a thing as fire insurance?"

He nodded. "Apparently, there are a couple of companies that offer it. They'll pay to rebuild the store and replace his inventory. It's a good thing that Mick kept meticulous records."

"Interesting," Virginia muttered. "I'm glad for Mick. He's a nice man." She turned her gaze to the sky. "It's kind of interesting that there's a full moon tonight. Everyone knows that full moons make people crazy."

Ben chuckled. "Nonsense. That's just a superstition. These outlaws have been doing their business for a while now, regardless of the moon phase."

Virginia pressed her lips together and continued to stare at the sky. She knew that it was just an old wives' tale, but she couldn't suppress a shudder as she heard the wolves begin to howl in the distance.

She took a deep breath and stared down the road, willing Allen to appear. The road stretched out endlessly, empty, with no sign of her husband.

Just as she was about to turn away, she saw movement. Her breath caught in her throat as she watched the shadow grow closer and closer to the house.

Virginia ran over to the barn as Allen slid off of Blaze.

"Allen!" she cried.

He barely had time to react before she threw herself into his arms. She hardly even processed that she was going to do so until she was already flying in his direction.

The moment she felt the warmth of his body, relief rushed over her.

He's home. He's safe. Thank you, God.

His arms wrapped around her, holding her close.

She felt a tear trickle down her cheek. "I was so afraid...." Her voice broke, and she swallowed hard, sniffling. "I thought...."

Allen exhaled slowly, his hand sliding up her back, comforting her. "I'm all right," he muttered, his fingers tracing circles into her skin.

Virginia pulled back to look into his eyes, still holding onto him, as though she was terrified that he'd disappear if she let him go.

The moonlight highlighted the cut on his cheekbones and the dirt smudged on his forehead. He looked exhausted. There was something else in his expression, though, and Virginia's heart pounded in her chest.

They leaned toward each other at the same time, and his lips met hers. Fire exploded deep inside of her, rushing through her, consuming her, as the kiss deepened. She melted against him, and her entire body came to life—sparks shooting through her limbs and prickling along her skin.

The world disappeared. Only she and Allen stood there in the night, holding on to one another. Their hearts connected through a kiss that communicated all the unspoken words and desires they'd held back.

When the kiss finally ended, Allen's forehead rested on hers. He blinked and raised his eyebrows as though he was processing what had just happened.

Virginia smiled at him and giggled. "Well, I didn't see that coming."

"Me, either, but it was nice."

She gave him another once-over, unable to help herself. "Are you sure that you're okay?"

He nodded. "I'm fine." He gently touched her face and kissed her forehead. Then, he stepped away to unsaddle Blaze, who snorted impatiently. "I caught one of the outlaws."

Ben had waited until the moment between them was over before he joined them and asked, "You did, huh? Did he give you any information?"

"Nope, not yet, but I'm sure he will once he's been in there a while. He seems to think that his boys will break him out before he gets a chance to talk. I deputized a couple more men who'll watch over him tonight." He carried the saddle into the stables, with Virginia and Ben following him in and Ben leading Blaze. "Stephen was shot in the leg, but he was just grazed, so he'll be fine. Douglas tailed a couple of them for a while but lost them in the woods."

"Do you think he'll talk?" Ben asked. "Some of them have a pretty strong allegiance to their leaders, and they're more afraid of them than they are of the law."

"I think he will. I'm pretty sure that with the mood in this area, the circuit judge would have no trouble sentencing him to hang. If he talks, he might just be sent to prison."

"I think I'd rather hang. I've heard about the conditions of some of those prisons," Ben said, shivering. "Eight hours or more of hard labor, very little food, freezing cold in the winter and burning hot in the summer."

Allen shrugged. "Where there's life, there's hope, I guess. He might think that if he chances prison, he can escape." He gently brushed Blaze, who was happily snacking on the oats that Virginia had poured for him. "Even if he doesn't tell us where the others are holed up, we'll find them. They won't get away with coming into my town and hurting my people. This incident today in Butte will make all of the other sheriffs double down on their efforts, too."

Virginia reached up and gently touched the cut on his face. "Just promise me that you'll be careful."

He caught her hand, held it against his chest, and smiled at her. "I promise."

Virginia believed him. Still, she knew she'd worry until every single man involved in the gang was captured.

Chapter Eighteen

After reassuring Virginia once more that he was fine, he walked to the creek. He needed to wash off the day's grime. The water was cold despite the hot summer day and shocked his system.

It felt good, though, as he washed the dust and remaining scent of the fire off of him. He felt a mixture of emotions bubbling up inside of him.

Allen was furious that the outlaws dared to ride into his town and terrify the people. They had stolen goods worth thousands of dollars as they rampaged through town. Mick's place was completely destroyed, and it would take him a long time to rebuild. Several people had been hurt, including Ben, while they put out the fire. Allen had already thanked the Good Lord above many times that no one had been seriously injured or killed.

He was triumphant that he didn't freeze up when chasing the outlaws, even when they started shooting back. On top of that, he managed to capture one of them. The man wasn't talking tonight, but hopefully, he would tomorrow.

Then, there was Virginia. He realized that his feelings for her gradually grew soon after he began teaching her how to read. There was so much about her that made him smile. Her perseverance was one reason. Once she bit into something, she held on to it until the bitter end. She was tough, sweet, and intelligent, although he knew her inability to read and write made her feel less smart sometimes.

The kiss had startled him.

He put his fingers to his lips and replayed the moment in his mind.

Virginia had rushed to him, wrapping her arms around him, and looked at him with so much feeling blazing in her emerald green eyes. The aching need to kiss her was overwhelming.

It stirred the smoldering embers deep inside him and made him realize the depth of his feelings for her.

He shivered as a cool breeze hit his wet skin, and he quickly finished washing and dried off. His mind cycled through the events of the day. He'd sent a telegram to the other sheriffs in the area to inform them of what had happened, including that he'd captured one of the outlaws. He wanted to notify everyone that the gang's activities were increasing in frequency and becoming more and more violent.

Allen had no doubt that they would have seriously harmed or killed anyone who tried to stop them. Luckily, everyone was either attempting to put out the fire or was terrified and ran instinctively.

He was exhausted by the time he climbed into bed.

Thank you, God, for protecting our people today. No one was seriously hurt. And please, let me get a good night's rest without any nightmares. In Jesus's name, I pray, Amen.

He closed his eyes, his mind on the beautiful redhead sleeping across the hall from him.

***

Allen gobbled his breakfast, kissed Virginia on the cheek, and flew out the door. He wanted to get to the sheriff's office as quickly as possible.

The outlaw was sitting on the cot, leaning against the wall, as though he didn't have a care in the world. He smirked at Allen as he walked in, hung his hat up, and sat down at his desk.

"Anything interesting happen?" he asked the two deputies.

"Nuttin'," George said. "Me 'n Seth sat here all night, playin' cards."

"Great. If you two wouldn't mind staying on for a while, we could use the help. Apparently, we need to clean out a nest of varmints."

"I'm willin'. Anna is gonna have another baby soon, and I could use the cash," Seth said.

"I'm up fer it. It's better than sittin' at home and listening to Becca's mom flap her gums all night," George said.

Allen chuckled. "Good. I'll see you boys tonight."

He sat down and went through a stack of handbills, searching for any of the wanted posters that matched the scoundrel sitting in his cell.

Aha, gotcha, he thought triumphantly as he pulled out a wanted poster for Fred Webbs. The bounty was two thousand dollars.

Allen leaned back in his chair and grinned at Webbs. "Well, look who we have here," he said, holding up the handbill. "We have a verified outlaw in our midst."

"You won't live long enough to collect the bounty," Webbs said, sounding amused.

"Oh, I think I will. The judge already has you on the docket tomorrow. You'll hang by the end of the week, and I'll have a pocket full of money." Allen shook his head. "What was the point of yesterday's mess?"

Webbs leaned forward and chuckled. "It was fun, hoss. I reckon we're keepin' folks on their toes. Life gets borin' after a while."

"Fun, huh? Is that what you're going to call it when you're dangling at the end of a rope?"

The outlaw laughed loudly, clutching his stomach as though that was the funniest joke he'd ever heard. "Is that 'sposed to scare me? I'll be outta here before you git the chance."

"I don't see anyone here to rescue you."

"They'll be here. The boys won't let me rot in jail or hang. They're a heck of a lot smarter than you think they are, and they'll have me out."

Allen shook his head and laughed. "So, who's the leader of this little gang you guys formed? You know, so I can be scared and all."

Webbs smiled widely. "You'll find out soon enough. Now, why don't you git to sheriffin' and let me sleep?"

Knowing he wouldn't get anything out of Webbs, he smiled at him pleasantly. Then, he brought out his paper, pen, and ink to write a letter to the territorial governor, Benjamin Franklin Potts, in Helena, letting him know that Frank Webbs had been captured and would face the judge tomorrow. He enclosed one of his copies of the handbill. Potts was known to champion law and order and would likely pay the bounty quickly.

Douglas stepped into the office and raised his eyebrows, nodding at Webbs questioningly. Allen just shook his head to let Douglas know that Webbs hadn't said anything. He handed Douglas the handbill.

"Nice one, Sheriff. Now you can buy a couple more registered Herefords."

"That's the plan. I'm going to take this to the post office and stop by to see Stephen."

"I'll hold down the fort," Douglas said. "I still have some reports to take care of."

He was glad Mary Ann was busy with her grandchildren, so she wasn't in the mood to chat. Everyone adored her, but she'd talk a person's ear off if she was able, and there was plenty to talk about.

Afterward, when he dropped by to check on his deputy, Stephen was fine and in good spirits. "Please let me come back to work. Abby is driving me crazy."

She crossed her arms over her chest and pretended to be angry with him, frowning and wrinkling her nose. "You're just mad because I won't let you walk anywhere except to go to the outhouse. Dr. Simmons said to stay off your feet for a week, and that's what you're going to do."

"I can see you're in good hands," Allen teased. "Good work, Abby."

"Traitor!" Stephen called out as Allen left.

He spent the rest of the morning writing reports and talking to the people who constantly trickled into the office. Some wanted to look at Webbs, and some wanted to know how he planned to handle it.

Allen always nodded to Webbs and said, "Can't talk about it now. Rest assured that all the sheriffs in the area are working hard to clean up the varmints."

His stomach rumbled loudly when lunchtime rolled around. He unwrapped the small bundle Virginia had carefully prepared for him this morning. She'd packed him a thick sandwich, an apple, and a small tin of cookies.

He thought about the kiss they'd shared last night. It had been completely unexpected, but as soon as she'd thrown her arms around him, something stirred inside of him. The feeling of her body pressed to his and the knowledge that she cared about him so much had made his heart thunder in his chest. Without thinking about it, he lowered his head to kiss her. She'd met him with a shy passion that made him ache with a need he never expected.

Allen ran his hand over his face and sighed.

He had come to care for Virginia. It started slowly when they spent a lot of time together poring over the books. Now, he realized she was a very important part of his life.

Sighing heavily, his mind traveled back in time when he'd loved another. Angelica had been the one he'd wanted to spend the rest of his life with, but fate had other plans.

I wonder if Angelica's mother still has Mother's ring. She's likely sold it by now, but if she still has it, I'd like to give it to Virginia, he thought, surprising himself with the observation.

He'd never thought he would want to lay eyes on that ring again, but now.... Virginia was changing everything.

At the end of his shift, George and Seth were settled in, and a strong warning was given to be on the lookout for anyone trying to rescue their guest.

"We'll blast 'em," George promised.

Allen smiled and nodded. Then, he saddled Blaze. "We're going to go see an old friend."

Blaze shook his head and whinnied as though he understood Allen's words.

The small cottage on the outskirts of town looked just as it always had. She had consistently maintained flower gardens around her porch, and a small vegetable and herb garden was flourishing in the back.

Allen hesitated for a moment before he knocked.

Suddenly, he was nervous about seeing Angelica's mom again at her home. Of course, he'd seen her in town when she came for supplies or to sell her sewing and other goods. But this was different. This was where he'd stood when his last dreams had shattered, along with his soul.

He knocked and waited patiently.

Mrs. Matthis opened the door and smiled. "Allen. It's so good to see you again."

Allen's palms were coated in sweat, but he managed to clear his throat and compose himself enough to answer. "You, as well. How are you?"

"I'm doing well," she said, her smile softening. "I'm still on this side of the daisies, and there's something to be said for that."

"Yes, ma'am." He hesitated for a second and asked, "I was wondering if you still had my mother's ring."

She nodded, and she didn't look all that surprised by the question. "I do. I've been waiting for you to come back for it. Give me a minute."

Mrs. Matthis closed the door and returned a minute later, holding a small box. She opened it to reveal a delicate gold ring adorned with three tiny diamonds embedded in it.

At the sight of it—once so familiar but now completely foreign—Allen's breath caught in his throat. Memories flashed through his head, images of Angelica wearing this very same ring, and he forced himself to swallow down the bile that rose in his throat.

"Thank you," he choked out, his eyes tearing up.

"You're welcome," she said, patting his hand. "Angelica would want you to have it, and she'd want you to be happy."

He couldn't help himself; he hugged her. She laughed and hugged him back, pulling him into her embrace. "Get on with you, now. You've got a woman at home waiting on you."

Allen rode back to the ranch with a smile, the ring in his pocket, now with a new purpose. Virginia had come to mean so much to him, and he wanted to make sure she knew just how much.

Chapter Nineteen

Virginia looked around the town as she drove Belle and Star down the main street, parking the wagon near Mick's general store. Her heart sank when she saw the remnants of the building. It resembled a sightless face, as the windows had been broken out and the interior walls were covered in blackened soot. The smell of burning fabric, leather, and other items hung heavily in the air. Her hand touched her throat as the acrid scent choked her.

She stepped out of the wagon and petted Belle and Star. "I'll be right back, ladies. I promise I won't keep you long."

As she turned around, she almost literally ran into Mick. "I'm so sorry. I need to watch where I'm going."

"No worries," he said, shaking his head. "How are you doing? I imagine you must have had quite a scare from yesterday's events."

Virginia nodded, raising her hand to rest over her chest. "It was pretty frightening. I've never experienced anything like it before. There was crime and fights in New York City, but nothing like what happened yesterday." She sighed. "I was just afraid that one of the kids would be hurt. Luckily, they all managed to get to the church before that happened."

"I hear you're to thank for that. Your quick thinking kept them safe."

Smiling, Virginia said, "It was a group effort." She pointed at the store ruins. "I'm so sorry about your store."

"Thank you. It'll be all right, though. I have insurance, so we're going to start rebuilding tomorrow. We have to tear down the rest of the walls because they were weakened by the heat." He gestured at the empty hull. "Luckily, there are enough supplies available here to get started, and the rest can come in on the train. It'll take about six to ten weeks to get the outer walls torn down, the debris picked up, the place rebuilt, and everything stocked again." Mick gazed at his ruined store and sighed. "I'm just glad that no one got seriously hurt."

"Me, too," Virginia said. "Let us know if we can do anything."

"I sure will. Take care of yourself."

She walked to the post office and the smaller general store in town. People greeted her warmly, smiling and waving, and sometimes even stopping to talk to her.

Virginia finished her shopping and made her way back to the wagon lightheartedly. She finally felt as though she belonged somewhere. The people in Butte were very friendly. Life at home with Allen was comfortable, and after the kiss they shared, she hoped it would get even better.

Aunt Fiona has no idea what she did for me, and probably would be upset that I'm so happy. I have so much more here than I did in New York City, and I'm not even talking about money.

The landscape seemed even more beautiful as she drove home, and peace settled in her heart and soul. A golden glow bathed the prairie, and the reds, whites, blues, purples, oranges, and yellows reminded her of some of the art she'd seen in the free galleries in New York City. At the time, she'd never imagined such real beauty existed since the city was so grey and drab, but the vibrant colors that made the world come alive actually existed here.

A warmth flowed through her as she thought of her handsome husband. His smile could make her knees weak, and Virginia admitted to herself that she loved him. That wasn't such a frightening thought now because she knew he cared about her, too. A part of her dared to hope that perhaps they would one day have a real marriage and maybe even a family.

Keith was at the barn when she arrived. "Hello, Virginia. I'll be happy to unhitch the wagon for you and take care of Belle and Star."

"Thank you. I appreciate it."

His smile was wide when he said, "If you go inside the stables and look at the second stall on the left, you'll see something incredible."

"Let me put away my groceries and such, first." She hurriedly took care of her chores and went to the stables.

Virginia gasped upon seeing a new foal, just two hours old, standing beside its mother. It was a chestnut with a dark brown mane and tail. "Oh, my goodness. You are so precious."

"He's beautiful, isn't he?" Ben said.

"I was thinking when I was coming home that being out here, I've seen so much beauty and amazing things that I would never have seen in New York City. Everything is so full of colors and life, and now there's this little fellow."

Ben grinned. "I'm glad you like it, and I'm glad you're here. Allen's relaxed a lot since you've come." He gently patted her back. "I need to get back to work."

Taking another long look at the foal, she smiled happily to herself and went inside to make fried chicken, mashed potatoes, gravy, green beans, and cornbread for dinner. She sang to herself while she worked. Never would she have guessed that her aunt's method of getting rid of her would have resulted in such happiness.

She giggled as she thought about what Aunt Fiona's reaction would be if she sent a letter to her, telling her about her life in Montana Territory and how happy she was.

When he came home, Allen was in a good mood. They enjoyed a great dinner together, and afterward, Allen sat with her as she read more complicated stories from the primer. She was very proud of herself, and Allen praised how quickly she learned.

"Maybe tomorrow we can work on writing if you've got time," Virginia said.

"We can do that. Writing is just as important a skill as reading. I'm sure you'll be writing novels before too long." Allen smiled at her with a warm look in his eyes that made her heart skip a beat.

All too soon, it was time for bed. She paused outside of her bedroom door, hoping that he might kiss her again, or at least hug her. Disappointment filled her as he said, "Good night" and went into his room.

Maybe the kiss was just an accident, she mused, now doubting what she'd thought to be so clear. *It had been a long, emotional day. He might just need more time.*

Virginia was more tired than she realized because she fell asleep almost as soon as she got into bed.

She was jolted awake in the middle of the night. A loud scream pierced the night air, making Virginia's heart stop. For a moment, she clutched her blanket tightly to her chest, her white-knuckled hands trembling.

"Allen," she whispered. "He's having another nightmare."

She'd heard stories about how horrific the War of the Southern Rebellion had been and the terrible scenes on the battlefields once the fighting was done. Some of the veterans who'd come home talked about the sounds and sights that still haunted them.

Virginia's heart hurt as she thought about Allen being forced back into one of the battles and living it all over again.

She bit her lip and slipped out of bed.

Taking a huge breath, she hesitated outside of his bedroom door, not sure whether she should risk going in. She remembered how angry he'd been last time. However, when he cried out again, her soul twisted into a knot, and she couldn't bear the thought of him in pain.

Virginia touched her lips and thought of the kiss they'd shared.

Maybe that changes things.

Quietly, Virginia slipped into Allen's room and moved the chair closer to his bed. Instead of shaking him awake, she gently took his hand.

"Allen, I'm here. You're in Montana Territory, and you're safe. The war is over. You have a new foal and a lot of new calves running around in the pastures. There is nothing to fear here. You're home." Her voice was very low and calm—the slightest whisper in the air. She hoped that it would reach the deepest part of his mind.

His screams subsided to soft cries, and he stopped thrashing around in bed. He squeezed her hand so tightly that she winced from the pain, but she didn't let go.

"You're safe, Allen. You're home in Montana Territory. There's no war here. Everyone here is safe and okay."

His eyes fluttered open, and he looked at her with blank eyes. For a moment, she was worried that he wouldn't recognize her and would be afraid. But, sure enough, recognition flitted through.

Virginia braced herself for another tongue-lashing like he gave the last time she'd woken him from a nightmare, trembling. She sucked in a huge breath and held it, cringing, waiting for him to snap. Instead, he gave her a loving look, his gaze so warm and so open, before he slowly closed his eyes again.

She exhaled slowly, relieved that he wasn't angry with her for coming into his room after he'd told her twice never to do that. He still held her hand tightly as he lay still in the bed, his nightmare vanquished.

His breathing evened out, and, positive that he was sleeping peacefully, she smiled and stood, ready to go back to her own room. She let go of his hand and tucked into bed.

"Stay here," he whispered.

Virginia could hardly believe she heard correctly and wondered if he was simply talking in his sleep.

A warmth filled her, and she looked at the man she'd grown to love.

He asked me to stay with him.

She wondered if he was merely talking in his sleep, but was afraid that if she left, he might have another nightmare. Her presence seemed to comfort him.

I guess he can be mad at me in the morning if he doesn't remember.

Crossing her fingers that he wouldn't be angry with her, she grabbed a blanket draped on the back of the chair and curled up on the foot of his bed, wrapping the blanket around her.

Maybe I can help him sleep the rest of the night. Heaven knows when the last time he had a good night's sleep was.

Smiling to herself when she heard Allen's soft snores, she closed her eyes, pleased that she could ease his pain a little.

Maybe this means that there's hope for more than just a marriage of convenience for us.

Visions of a yard full of laughing kids running around floated through her mind as she drifted off with a contented smile.

Chapter Twenty

Allen stiffened, and his heart pounded so hard that he thought it was going to explode out of his chest when he heard someone breathing softly in his room. Then, he felt something at the foot of his bed.

He slowly opened his eyes and was surprised to see fiery red hair poking out of a rolled-up blanket, sprawled across the bottom of his mattress. Gradually, the night's events crept back into his memory.

Another nightmare had taken him back to that day that he'd already relived a million times over. His brother's large eyes, full of agony, stared into his as Joseph struggled to breathe, each raspy breath sounding like a scream of pain. Blood trickled out of his mouth. Even in his last moments, though, Joseph focused on Allen. Joseph had always taken care of his little brother, and he wasn't about to let a little thing like a bullet in his chest stop him.

Allen watched as his brother told him to be brave and carry on, and held him close as he drew his last ragged breath.

This time was different, though. Out of nowhere, a gentle, soothing voice emerged, carried on the swirling wind around him. He felt himself being pulled away from the horrors and drawn back to the present.

Virginia was sitting next to him, talking to him softly and calmly while holding his hand. He wasn't enraged or humiliated to see her there. He could see the worry and concern in her face. There was no pity or a sign that she thought he was less than a man.

He was almost asleep when she pulled away from him, and he couldn't let her go. Allen remembered telling her not to leave.

Staring up at the rafters in the ceiling, he tried to process everything. Asking her to stay meant he trusted her, not with his physical assets, but with a part of himself that he'd tried to keep buried for ten years. It felt very comforting, awkward, and a little overwhelming, all at the same time.

Allen swallowed hard as he slowly sat up, trying not to disturb Virginia. He was very surprised and touched that she'd come to help him, especially after the way he'd snapped at her the last time. Yet, here she was, lying at the foot of the bed because he'd asked her to stay.

A lump formed in his throat.

He coughed quietly, never taking his eyes off of Virginia.

He wasn't sure he deserved her kindness, but appreciated it and recognized that was just who Virginia was—one of those gentle, good souls who would do anything, including risk her own life, to help someone.

Allen carefully slipped out from under the covers, trying not to disturb her. He opened his bedroom door and saw that hers was still open from the night before.

Slipping his arms under her, he lifted her, cradling her close to his chest. She was still asleep when he laid her on the bed, but her eyes opened when he pulled the blankets up to her shoulders.

She smiled at him. "Good morning."

"Good morning."

"Did your nightmare go away?" she asked, her voice dreamy.

"Yes, it did, thanks to you. I heard your voice, and it carried me away from the bad place."

"I'm so glad. I can't imagine how awful it must be for you." She pushed the covers down and started to swing her feet out of bed. "I need to make breakfast for everyone."

"No, I've got it covered today. Why don't you stay here and get a couple more hours of sleep?"

"Are you sure? I don't mind," she said, hesitating.

"I'm sure. I know you didn't get a lot of sleep last night, so get some rest. The men have been eating my cooking for the last ten years. I'm pretty sure they can suffer through another day of it."

Virginia giggled and nodded. She lay back down, and Allen tucked her in. He touched her cheek briefly with the back of his hand.

"Thank you for coming to me last night."

"You're welcome."

He smiled at her and left, closing the door behind him. He would never have imagined how much she would come to mean to him when he put the advertisement in the paper and began writing to Virginia's aunt.

Honestly, if he'd known, he wouldn't have agreed to have her come to the ranch. Allen knew that he'd been so terrified of forming any kind of relationship with anyone, except Ben, that he wouldn't have taken the chance.

Allen glanced at Ben's door and saw that he was still asleep. It was early. The sun was just now peeking over the ridgeline, starting to light up the valley below.

He dressed and headed downstairs to start breakfast. Normally, today would be his day at home to work on the ranch, but since Webbs was in jail, he wanted to be in the office, taking his turn to watch over the prisoner and making sure that none of his friends came to town, looking to cause trouble.

It was more likely that the gang members would try to break him out at night, but these men were very bold. There was no telling what they might do.

As he came to the kitchen, his heart nearly stopped when he saw that the front door was slightly ajar.

He clenched his jaw and walked slowly toward the door, grabbing the rifle from the corner of the kitchen. Neither Keith nor John would have come into the house before breakfast.

No one was in sight. However, someone had nailed a note to the front door.

He inhaled sharply when he read the words, "Return Webbs to us or we'll destroy the ranch and your pretty little wife."

Allen's heart nearly stopped, and a stone dropped into the pit of his stomach. His hands trembled, and he gripped the note tightly in his fist.

He ran back upstairs and pounded on Ben's door. It flew open as Ben wiped the sleep out of his eyes.

"What in the...?" Ben asked.

He handed the note to Ben. "The front door was open, and this was nailed to it."

Ben's jaw clenched, and all at once, any traces of sleep were wiped away. He growled, "They won't get away with this."

"I don't intend to let them," Allen said. "I need you to stay here and protect Virginia in case someone comes back. I'm going to send Keith to Coyote Creek and fetch Sheriff Hicks so we can make a plan."

"You've got it," Ben said.

"Virginia's still in bed. She had a bit of a long night, so I told her to get a couple more hours of sleep."

Ben nodded. "Be careful on your way to town. They might just be waiting to ambush you on the way."

"I've thought of that. I'll be careful."

Allen sped downstairs, taking two at a time. He grabbed a couple of biscuits and hastily washed them down with water before racing outside.

A sudden thought occurred to him.

Why didn't the dogs alert?

"Major! Thunder!" he called.

He whistled a couple of times, but they didn't answer.

A sinking feeling in his gut told him that something was very wrong. Not only would the dogs have torn apart anyone who came onto the property without permission, but they certainly would have come when called.

He walked around the side of the barn and found both dogs lying on their sides in the dirt with their tongues hanging out. Fearing the worst, he knelt beside Major and placed his hand on the dog's chest. He was still breathing, and Thunder was also breathing. They were both unconscious.

"What in the heck happened here?" Allen quickly checked the dogs but didn't see any obvious injuries. He rubbed his hands over his face and groaned. "I don't have time for this now. They seem to be okay."

He sped toward the bunkhouse and almost stepped on a couple of half-eaten steaks in the dirt. Allen picked up one of them and sniffed it.

"Ugh." The bitter smell of alcohol and opium wafted from the meat. It was also very dark—much darker than a steak should have been, even if it had been left out overnight. "Laudanum."

Allen shook his head and growled. "You'd think those darned dogs would know better than to eat laudanum-laced meat or to take food from a stranger."

He carefully carried the steak remains to the outhouse, tossed them into the pit, and rushed back toward the bunkhouse. He glanced toward the dogs and saw that both of them were trying to raise their heads.

They'll be fine once the drug wears off.

Keith and John were just waking up when he entered. Allen explained the situation and showed them the note.

"Keith, would you mind riding to Coyote Creek and asking Sheriff Hicks to meet me in Butte? Tell him that Webbs has refused to talk and tell him about the break-in at the house and the note."

"You got it, Boss," Keith said.

"There are some biscuits in the house, and I'm sure Ben's started some coffee by now. Virginia had a late night, so she's still resting."

Keith nodded. "No worries. I've lived weeks off of hardtack and jerky before."

Allen slapped him on the back and glanced at John. "I know you're only one man, but I'd like for you to check the pastures and make sure none of the horses or cattle have been messed with. Ben's going to hang around here in case they come back."

"Will do."

"Thanks, men. I appreciate it," Allen said.

Allen had Blaze saddled and was headed into town five minutes later. He absolutely hated leaving Virginia, but knew he could trust Ben to watch her.

Gritting his teeth, he gripped the reins tightly.

Webbs smirked when he walked into the office. "Got yerself a little visit, huh?"

"What makes you say that?" Allen asked.

"A little birdy told me." Webbs pointed to the window of his cell.

"Threatening notes are for school children," Allen said, doing his best to control his temper and not let Webbs see that he was agitated.

Webbs chuckled. "You're not going to think of school children when they visit your house and take care of your pretty little wife. I'm sure they'll be enjoying her company a bit before they kill her."

Rage exploded inside of Allen. His fists were so tight that his fingernails dug deep into the palm of his hand. He clenched his jaw together and narrowed his eyes, wanting nothing more than to open the cell and kill Webbs.

He worked hard to keep his voice very controlled and calm. "You're just lucky that the judge got sick, or you'd already be hanged. Don't worry, though, because I've heard that he's feeling a mite better now."

Webbs waved his hand dismissively. "I ain't afraid of that old man, and I can guarantee I ain't gonna hang. You can't keep your eyes on that little woman all the time." He laughed hysterically as though he'd just told the funniest joke in the world.

Allen sat down, ignoring Webbs. He wasn't going to give the man the satisfaction of knowing that he'd struck a nerve.

About an hour later, Sheriff Hicks strolled into the office. He glanced at the cell and said, "He doesn't look so tough to me."

Webbs just laughed. "Don't worry, Sheriff. When we're done tearing apart Butte, we'll make a special trip to Coyote Creek. We'll tear down every building in town and take what's owed to us."

"Nothing is owed to you," Sheriff Hicks said.

"Sure, it is. It's our tax for not killing everyone in the area." Webbs laughed evilly.

Allen shook his head. "The man thinks he's funny. He's been telling stories all morning, but he's the only one laughing."

"We'll make sure he's laughing when we're done with him and his gang." Sheriff Hicks nodded. "Should we talk outside?"

Webbs smirked and stretched out on the cot like he didn't have a care in the world. "Ain't it bad manners to talk about a fella when he ain't invited to the conversation?"

"Don't worry, Webbs. You'll hear all about it and get your turn to talk when you face the judge."

The two sheriffs walked outside. Allen felt a sense of urgency and dread. His gut told him that they needed to shut this gang down soon and for good, or their reign of terror would only get worse.

Chapter Twenty-One

Virginia woke with a start. Her room was lit up by the bright sun shining through her window. She jumped out of bed, her heart thundering in her chest. "Breakfast. I'm so late."

Then, she remembered that Allen said he'd make breakfast, and she needed to rest for a couple of hours. She inhaled deeply through her nose and wiped the remnants of sleep out of her eyes.

She smiled as she thought about how tender Allen had been with her. Virginia knew she was taking a risk when she went into his room last night, hoping to calm his nightmares. She'd never imagined he'd ask her to stay and that she'd fall asleep on his bed.

He carried me in here and put me to bed instead of waking me up and telling me it was morning. Allen wanted me to get more rest. He really does care about me.

Wrapping her arms around herself, she smiled as a warm wave washed over her. Her heart beat faster, and her stomach fluttered as she savored this new feeling of being cared about. No one had cared for her since her father died when she was ten. Now, this handsome man who stole her breath away every time she looked at him had proven that he did.

She stood up and quickly dressed, feeling lighthearted and happy. A smile curved her lips as she brushed out her long red hair and rebraided it, wrapping it around her head like a rosy coronet.

Virginia practically skipped downstairs, feeling a little giddy. She stopped short when she got to the kitchen. She'd expected Allen to be there, but the room was empty. There was no sign of the breakfast he'd promised to make.

Worry hummed in the back of her mind. That wasn't like Allen. If he said he was going to do something, then come hell or high water, he was going to get it done.

She checked his office, but he wasn't there either.

"He's not supposed to go into the sheriff's office today," she muttered. "I wonder if something happened?"

Drawing in a huge breath, she scolded herself. "There's no need to borrow trouble. He might have gotten busy. One of the horses might be foaling, or a bull might have busted through the fence again, and they're out rounding up the cows that got loose."

Noticing that most of the biscuits left over from the night before were gone, she figured that the men must have simply eaten those before they got to work. Her chest tightened, and she sighed heavily. A flash of guilt hit her in the stomach because she knew that the men needed a lot more than just biscuits to sustain them through the morning's work.

He told you to rest. You didn't do anything wrong, she reminded herself.

That didn't help too much. She picked up one of the biscuits left and put a dab of honey on it. There was a little bit of coffee left. Virginia nearly choked on it. It was more like tar than coffee.

She quickly swallowed her biscuit, chasing it down with a glass of water. After tying on her apron, she started to prepare for her morning chores, but the worrying buzz in the back of her mind hadn't eased. The uneasy feeling prickled the back of her neck, like an icy finger tickling her.

I'm being a ninny, but I know that I won't be able to get anything done until I know that everything is all right. He might be in the barn. A couple of his prized Herefords were getting ready to calf.

Virginia inhaled the scent of the wildflowers and sagebrush carried on the breeze. The trees and tall grasses gently swayed, and she could hear different birds carrying on.

Thunder and Major were lying near the barn. They lifted their heads, whined, and stood, walking toward her like newborn foals. If she didn't know better, she'd say the dogs were walking as though they were drunk.

The barn door was slightly open. She hesitated for just a moment as her gut clenched, telling her that something wasn't right. The cows mooed loudly, and a couple of them stomped their feet.

Fear clenched her heart.

Allen might've been hurt. I have to help him.

She rushed inside the dark, musty barn. "Allen? Are you in here?"

A faint scraping sound caught her attention. She stopped, listening intently, trying to figure out where it was coming from.

"Allen?" she called louder.

Her nerves were on edge, and she was breathing rapidly. Virginia had no idea why her anxiety was threatening to suffocate her.

Something's not right. Get out.

Footsteps, heavy against the hard-packed dirt floor, rushed behind her. She whirled around and screamed as a tall man stepped into a small stream of light. His hat was pulled low, hiding most of his features, but the evil grin on his face made Virginia's knees weak and her chest tighten with fear.

"Who—who are you?" she stammered. Her voice trembled in spite of her attempt to sound confident.

He took another step toward her. The menacing look on his face terrified her even more.

"My name is O'Toole," he said in a deep, foreboding voice that sent a shiver of fear coursing down her spine. "You tell your husband that he'd better return what belongs to us, or there will be consequences."

A tight knot formed in her stomach, and her heart threatened to rip itself out of her chest. Her throat tightened, and she struggled to breathe. She had no idea what Allen might have taken from this man.

"I don't know what you're talking about," she said, hating the quiver of fear in her voice.

O'Toole sneered. "He knows what he took from us."

Without warning, he lunged at her, wrapping his large hands around her throat and tightening like a vise. She gasped for air, panic exploding inside of her.

She tried to punch him and managed to scratch him in the face even as darkness encroached upon the edges of her vision. Her blood ran cold as she tried to fight back.

O'Toole laughed. "You're a little spitfire. I've heard that redheaded women have quite the temper."

Virginia's lungs screamed for air. She kicked out, connecting with O'Toole's leg.

"Don't make me repeat myself," O'Toole growled. "Tell your husband to return what's ours, or you'll pay the price."

Her heart hammered in her chest, and the world blurred around her.

He leaned in close. His hot breath brushed against her cheek, and the putrid smell of his breath made her stomach roll. "If he doesn't return it, we'll come for you instead."

She opened her mouth, but no sound came out. Then, just as suddenly as he'd attacked, O'Toole let her go, pushing her to the ground. Virginia landed in a heap, gasping for air.

"Next time, we won't be so gentle with you," O'Toole said. "Don't forget to tell your husband what I said."

His footsteps faded as he casually walked out of the barn as though he didn't have a care in the world.

Virginia lay against the cold, hard dirt for a few minutes, trying to breathe. Her throat screamed in agony, and a sharp pain pierced her lungs with each gulp of air she swallowed.

Finally, after several minutes, her vision cleared, and she was able to push herself back up with shaky, weak arms.

Allen. What have they done with Allen?

She put her hand to her temple. *If he were here, they would have attacked him instead of me.*

As she stood, a noise from the corner caught her attention. Ben was lying sprawled out against the hay bales. He was barely conscious, and a pool of blood encircled his head. A shovel lay near him.

"Ben," she croaked, kneeling down beside him. "Oh, heavens, Ben!"

His eyes fluttered open, and he tried to focus on her. He immediately reached for the back of his head, wincing with pain. Blood smeared his fingers.

"Virginia...did he hurt you?" he asked slowly as though he had to focus on every word.

"I'm fine." Her voice was shaky and raspy. "We need to find Allen. He said that if Allen didn't return something to him, then they were going to come for me."

Ben pushed himself upright and saw the shovel. "He hit me from behind. I didn't know he was in the barn. Allen went into town this morning. Whoever it was left a note nailed to the front door, warning Allen to return Webbs to them or they'd destroy the ranch and hurt you." Ben groaned as he stood up, his knees wobbly.

Virginia grabbed his arm to hold him steady, although she wasn't so stable herself. "He said his name was O'Toole."

"O'Toole?" Ben's face turned ashen grey. "We're lucky to be alive. He's one of the nastiest men alive."

They'd just started to walk out of the barn when John rode up. He jumped off his horse and rushed over to them.

"What in tarnation happened to you two?" he asked, panic in his voice.

In as few words as possible, Virginia explained about O'Toole's visit.

"Do you think you could hitch up the wagon? I'm fine to drive, but I don't know how to do that," Virginia said. "I suppose I should learn soon."

John peered at her closely, noting the bruises that had already formed around her neck. "Are you sure you can drive? Allen told me to watch over the ranch, but he'd have my hide if anything happened to you."

"I'm fine. I'll have a sore throat for a few days. It's nothing that a bit of honey and lemon won't cure." She hated that her voice was still hoarse, as John looked at her doubtfully.

Virginia put her hand on his arm. "Please. I promise that I'll be fine to drive. Besides, Belle and Star know the way to town. All I have to do is hold the reins. You have to make sure that O'Toole doesn't come back and destroy the ranch."

"Yeah, okay," John said, nodding, although Virginia could tell by his expression that he didn't like the situation.

John hitched up the wagon while Virginia and Ben went inside the house. She cleaned the wound with a cloth and cold water. Quickly making a poultice of yarrow and plantain to stop the bleeding and help prevent infections, she applied it to the large gash in Ben's head. Grabbing the linen bandages, she made a pad, pressed it against his wound, and then wrapped his head with a couple of strips of old shirts.

"I bet I look a sight," Ben said.

"Don't think that matters right now," Virginia said. "You can worry about what the ladies think later. Right now, we have to get to Allen. We have to warn him that it's O'Toole and that the man might not be patient enough for us to deliver the message."

"I can worry about Allen *and* the ladies," Ben said with his characteristic sense of humor.

"I'm glad to know that you're fine in spite of the fact that you're going to have a splitting headache for a few days."

"Literally," Ben said.

John had the wagon ready when they walked back out. He cast a doubtful eye at them. "I'm not sure about this."

"I feel a lot better," Virginia insisted. "I can breathe just fine, and I'm okay. O'Toole's not going to be waiting for us as we ride into town because he wants us to deliver the message."

Sighing heavily, John helped Ben and Virginia onto the buckboard, handed her the reins, and watched as they drove away.

Although she'd assured John that O'Toole was gone, both of them constantly scanned the landscape, looking for any sign that the outlaw might be lying in wait for them. Ben had the rifle on his knees, ready to shoot at any sign of trouble.

The trip took an eternity. Virginia forced herself to breathe normally and tried to still her thudding heart as they rode into Butte. Every noise made her jump. When the town finally came into sight, she was certain that she was about to jump out of her skin.

Belle and Star pulled up in front of the sheriff's office. Allen was standing outside with another sheriff. They looked up at Virginia and Ben.

She saw the fear written on Allen's face as the two men rushed over to the wagon. Then, his eyes dropped to her throat—to the marks she knew would be circling her neck.

Allen helped her down from the wagon and looked into her eyes, a mixture of fury and fear written all over his face. His brows were furrowed, and his lips were pursed. "Who did this to you?" he demanded.

"O'Toole," she said, her voice a bit raspy. "Ben's hurt a lot worse than me. He probably needs a doctor."

Ben, who'd been helped down by the other sheriff, said weakly, "I'm fine."

"I'll take him to Dr. Simmons," the sheriff offered.

"I'm good. He's just going to do the same thing that Virginia did. She washed it, put a poultice on it, and wrapped it."

"You're too stubborn for your own good," the visiting sheriff said.

Allen wrapped his arms around Virginia, holding her close to him. As his arms embraced her, she felt his muscles trembling, shaking with barely-concealed rage. "I'll kill O'Toole for this," he said fiercely.

And with the low tone of his voice and fire lighting his eyes, Virginia knew he was far from exaggerating.

Chapter Twenty-Two

Sheriff Hicks shook his head as they walked outside. "He's pretty confident that he won't face the gallows."

"I'm pretty confident that he will," Allen said. "It's too bad that the judge became ill, or Webbs would have already been sentenced. It's not him I'm worried about."

"It's the rest of the gang. You're already getting threatening letters, and Webbs hasn't even faced the judge yet. The outlaws will only become worse once he's sentenced. If he's actually hanged, you and your family won't be able to rest until they're all caught."

Allen nodded. "Normally, I wouldn't worry about the threat. I can hire enough men to watch my ranch and catch anyone up to no good. However, they're threatening Virginia, and that can't happen."

"I understand. We need to come up with a good plan on how to catch them," Sheriff Hicks said.

"Do you have something in mind?"

Sheriff Hicks hesitated and scratched his chin. "I just might."

Their conversation was interrupted when the wagon pulled up in front of them. Allen's eyes opened wide when he saw Virginia and Ben. A sinking feeling in his stomach told him something was wrong.

He rushed over to Virginia and helped her down. He immediately saw the bruises that encircled her neck. The blue and purple fingerprint impressions from large hands glowed against her pale skin. Her throat was swollen.

She looked at him with bloodshot, teary eyes. Her hair was disheveled, and a streak of dirt was smeared across her cheek.

Fury exploded inside of him. Blazing heat rushed into his face, and he gritted his teeth. Allen sucked in a huge breath, trying to control his rage and not scare Virginia. He wanted nothing more than to storm back inside the jail and rip Webbs from limb to limb.

"Who did this to you?" he demanded harshly.

"O'Toole," she said, her voice raspy. "Ben's hurt a lot worse than me. He probably needs a doctor."

Glancing over at Ben, he caught sight of the bandage wrapped around his head, soaked through slightly with blood. Ben looked terrible, and the image of his friend, his *brother*, being so injured just about pushed him over the edge.

His blood rushed in his ears, and his heart was pounding so loudly that he could scarcely make out the conversation as Ben and Sheriff Hicks debated taking Ben to the doctor's office.

When the discussion died down, Allen turned back to Virginia.

He pulled her close to him, angry with himself for not protecting her and furious with the man who dared to lay a hand on his wife *and* his friend. "I'll kill O'Toole for this," he growled.

Then, he looked over Virginia's head at Ben. "What happened?"

"I went into the barn to do the milking and check on the heifers. I had just stepped inside when he hit me with the shovel." Ben shook his head, and embarrassment and frustration shone in his eyes. He pressed his lips tightly together and groaned in the back of his throat. "I was knocked out cold and didn't come to until Virginia found me."

Ben rubbed his face. "I'm sorry. I should have been more careful. I didn't protect Virginia." His voice was hard and cold, his anger directed toward himself.

"This wasn't your fault," Virginia said. "You couldn't possibly know that he'd be hiding out in the barn. He'd left his note, and one would think that he'd have taken off, waiting to see if Allen would give O'Toole what he wanted."

"I didn't even think of checking the barn this morning. I just assumed that he'd have left after posting the note." Allen released Virginia, his stomach tightening with guilt. "Frank, will you escort them back to the ranch? I'm going to go find the blackguards who did this."

Sheriff Hicks shook his head. "That's not a good idea. There are several of them. The only thing that would happen is you'd get yourself killed, and then they'd still go after Virginia. Use your head."

Allen groaned, though he knew the older man was right. "What do you think we should do, then? I can't let them get away with harming my wife and Ben."

Virginia and Ben sat on the bench and glanced at the two sheriffs. Sheriff Hicks held out his hand to Virginia.

"I'm Frank Hicks, by the way. I'm the sheriff of Coyote Creek, about ten miles west of here."

Virginia shook his hand and smiled. "Virginia. It's a pleasure to meet you."

"You, as well, although I wish it were under better circumstances. Are you sure you don't need to see Dr. Simmons? Your throat is swollen and looks terrible." He paused. "And no offense, my dear, but your voice sounds awful."

Her smile widened. "I suspect that it will for a while. However, the doctor is going to tell me everything I already know and charge me a dollar for it." She held up one finger. "He's going to tell me to drink honey and lemon tea to soothe my throat, and drink willow bark tea for the pain." She held up a second finger. "He'll tell me not to talk and get plenty of rest." Virginia held up a third finger. "He might offer laudanum, but there's no way in the world that I'm getting near that stuff. I have no interest in getting hooked on it. I've seen what happens to people who do."

Sheriff Hicks and Allen glanced at each other.

"I guess she has a point," Allen said. "We need to get you back home so you can rest." He peered at Ben. "What about you? You took a shovel to the head."

Ben gritted his teeth. "I'm fine. The bleeding has stopped. The doctor can't do anything for me that I can't do myself, or that Virginia can't do."

Sheriff Hicks crossed his arms over his chest. "You don't know that. You could have a cracked skull."

Snorting, Ben shook his head slightly. "What's Dr. Simmons going to do? Crack it open the rest of the way? No, thanks."

Virginia giggled. "He was making jokes right after I bandaged his head. He was worried about what the ladies would think about him with the bandage wrapped around his head."

"I appreciate you being worried about me. But I'm not bleeding, and if it looks like I might need a stitch or two, well, I've heard that Virginia is a mighty fine seamstress."

She shook her head. "I know how to sew dresses and other clothes. I've never sewn a head together."

"It ain't much different. Instead of wool or silk, you're just sewing two pieces of leather together."

Virginia put her hand on her stomach. "Thank you ever so much for that image."

"You're quite welcome," Ben said. He looked at the two sheriffs. "What are we going to do about our outlaw problem? A man doesn't get to sneak-attack me and hurt my friend without me having something to say about it."

"*You* aren't going to do anything but rest," Allen said. "It wouldn't take much for your head to start bleeding all over the place again. Plus, you're going to have some major headaches, and you might even get dizzy or sick. If you go off half-cocked, you might end up with brain fever."

"I'm with Allen," Sheriff Hicks chimed in. "I can't make you go to the doctor, but I wouldn't have you riding with us. You'd be more of a worry and a distraction than you would a help. Besides, someone needs to take Virginia home and watch over her. You can still use your rifle, I assume."

"Yes," Ben said. "I won't miss, either."

Allen looked at Sheriff Hicks. "You said you had a plan before they arrived. What were you thinking?"

"I don't know how good it is, but my thought was that we could use Webbs as bait. You three can go inside the station and talk about the situation." Sheriff Hicks looked at Allen. "I know it'll be hard, but you can talk about how much you care about your wife and ranch and that no worthless scoundrel is worth losing them. You're going to let him go." He chuckled humorlessly. "Don't try to kill him when he starts taunting you, because he will."

Allen raised his eyebrows and stared at Sheriff Hicks disbelievingly. "You want me to let him go?"

"Yes. Only, I'll be a little ways off. I'll be close enough that I can keep an eye on him, but he won't be able to see me. I'll track him to the hideout." Sheriff Hicks saw that Allen was about to speak and held up his hand. "I'm not dumb enough to take them all on my own. I'll come back, we'll round up all of the men in town, and we'll take out the entire gang all at once. They can either surrender, and we'll collect the bounty for them and split it between us, or the outlaws will not survive the fight, and we'll still collect the bounty. It's a win-win situation."

Allen scratched his chin and thought about it. "I guess it's not the worst idea I've ever heard."

"Thank you. And trust me, I've had a lot worse."

"Do you want me to send Douglas and Stephen with you? Stephen's leg has healed, and the doctor has released him for duty."

Sheriff Hicks cocked his head to one side and thought about the offer for a moment. "If you want them to trail behind me, that'll be all right, I 'spose. We wouldn't want them to ride with me because that would be too much noise, and Webbs would know he was being tracked."

"All right. The three of us will go inside, and I'll tell Douglas to come out, and you can fill him in."

"Give us ten minutes before you release him."

Allen, Virginia, and Ben went inside the office.

"Douglas, can you step outside for a moment, please?" Allen asked.

The deputy nodded. Curiosity filled his eyes when he saw Virginia's bruises and Ben's bandage, but he didn't ask questions.

Webbs chuckled. "I like your neck decorations."

Virginia smiled sweetly at him. "I'm so glad that you like them. I'm sure you'll be getting some of your own soon. I hear that rope burns around the neck are all the rage in your line of work."

"Now, ma'am, don't get ahead of yourself. The only rope burns you'll be seeing is around Sheriff Strauss's neck when my friends come calling. I'm sure they'll have a tall tree and short rope waitin' fer him."

"Your friends? Well, bless your little heart. They're only brave enough to hit a man from behind with a shovel and attack a woman. Seems to me like they've got the courage of a week-old kitten."

Virginia turned her nose into the air and sauntered over to the chair in front of Allen's desk while Webbs sputtered profanities under his breath.

"Guess he's not as clever as he thought," Ben said. "Outwitted by a sweet woman from the city."

Even Allen chuckled. Getting Webbs riled up would make him more careless when he was getting back to the gang. He wouldn't be paying attention to Sheriff Hicks riding behind him.

After ten minutes had passed, Allen stood and stretched. "You know, Webbs, I'm feeling generous today. I've decided to let you go."

Webbs swung his feet off his cot and looked at the sheriff with wide, disbelieving eyes. "You're going to let me go, just like that?"

"Yep. I've had enough of your wretched breath stinking up my office." Allen walked over to the cell. "Come on, let's go. Put your hands through the bars."

Allen put cuffs on him so Webbs wouldn't try anything stupid in the office.

"I knew you'd see reason. I guess the little visit your foreman and wife got this morning made you see things our way." Webbs leered at Virginia. "Don't worry, sweetheart. We'll probably see you again."

Allen gritted his teeth, trying hard not to kill the man with his bare hands on the spot.

Remember, we've got a plan. We can destroy the entire nest of blood-sucking ticks at once.

He escorted Webbs to the front door, with Virginia and Ben trailing behind.

Webbs blinked rapidly when he stepped outside into the bright sunshine. He inhaled deeply and said, "I thank you, Sheriff. It's been a real treat spending time with you. I'm sure we'll see each other again really soon."

Allen was about to unlock the cuffs when Mayor Johnson and his wife hurried over.

"Sheriff Strauss, what in the world are you doing?" the mayor asked, glancing at Webbs and back at Allen. "You'd better not be thinking about releasing this criminal!"

Chapter Twenty-Three

Horses' hooves kick up the dust from the street behind them. The sun was bearing down on them, sending a tiny trickle of sweat running down Virginia's back. People were rushing around on the wooden sidewalks, talking and laughing. Sounds of metal on metal from the blacksmith shop filled the air, as did the neighing of horses.

A few people walked slowly by, gawking at the scene, casting nervous glances at them. Virginia and Ben stood to Allen's left. He was holding the shackled prisoner with his right hand.

Virginia's neck burned and throbbed. Her throat felt raw, and it was hard to swallow. She wanted nothing more than to get back home. She saw some comfrey and wanted to make a poultice to put around her swollen bruises. The plant, referred to as knitbone, helped bruises heal and reduce swelling.

She glanced over at Ben, whose pale face told her that he felt the same. She imagined he had an excruciating headache and needed to lie down, out of the intense heat. However, they were both compelled to stand by Allen.

Allen stiffened when he heard the mayor's words and saw Gloria looking down her nose at him. His jaw clenched, and the vein in his neck throbbed, letting Virginia know that he was frustrated and angry.

Gloria sniffed, and Virginia looked at her. The mayor's wife was dressed in a fine cotton print long-sleeved dress with tiny blue flowers all over it, decorated with lace trim around the neck and wrists. It had a tight bodice and a full skirt with a small bustle. Her bonnet was trimmed with feathers, and little curls framed her face. She looked more like a China doll than the wife of the mayor of a dusty mining town.

The mayor frowned at Allen, his arms crossed over his chest. He wore a charcoal cotton suit with a white shirt, a stiff collar, and a tie. Black polished boots and a bowler hat made him look like one of the dandies Virginia had seen walking downtown in New York City.

His voice was a low growl when he asked Allen, repeating his question, "What are you doing with this prisoner? You'd better not be thinking about letting him go."

"I think it's too risky for the town to hold him," Allen said. "The leader of his gang is a man named O'Toole, and he's known to be particularly vicious. He's made it clear that he'll hurt people until Webbs is released."

"You don't know what you're talking about," Mayor Johnson said. "Letting Webbs go isn't going to prevent O'Toole from hurting anyone. Besides, the best way to scare the outlaws is to hang this man and let his body be on display for everyone to see. That'll show them that we mean business, and we aren't going to tolerate their violence."

Virginia pointed to her neck. "He came to the ranch this morning and nearly strangled me to death." Her voice was hoarse and raspy, and a sympathetic look flashed across Gloria's face, but was gone in a second. "He said he'd come back and finish the job if Webbs wasn't released. O'Toole also hit Ben in the back of the head with a shovel, splitting his head open and nearly killing him."

The mayor and his wife looked at Ben and back at Virginia. Mayor Johnson sighed. "I'm sorry the two of you were hurt this morning, but that's the risk you take being a part of the sheriff's family. You both know that there are risks when the outlaws want to retaliate."

"He'll hurt other people in the community unless you do as they say," Virginia argued. Her voice trembled with frustration.

Her body was rigid, and she stared into the mayor's eyes, not bowing down to his condescending tone.

Mayor Johnson looked at her disdainfully, wrinkling his nose and pressing his lips together. "Mrs. Strauss, you're new around here. You come from the big city, where things are done differently. This is the Wild West, and we don't have the luxury of meting out justice the way you do in the city."

He looked at her as though she were a child, and his cutting tone infuriated Virginia. She bit her tongue, knowing she had to be polite for Allen's sake.

Gloria adjusted her bonnet and cleared her throat as though she was uncomfortable with the conversation.

What is wrong with this man? Doesn't he see there is something else going on here, or is he really that blind?

"Mayor, if you will..." Virginia started to say.

He raised his hand to cut off her words and stared at Allen. "We rely on you to keep this city safe. If you aren't able to do your job anymore, perhaps we should find someone new who can."

Webbs smirked. "Yeah, Sheriff Strauss. You can't even protect your wife and foreman. What makes you think you can protect this town? You're nothing."

Allen inhaled a long breath, trying to control his temper. He gritted his teeth and stared at the mayor.

"I can assure you, sir, that everything is under control. There is a method in my madness, if I might quote Shakespeare." He stood tall with his back straight and looked into the mayor's eyes as though trying to send him a message. "There is a plan to end this once and for all. Webbs is central to that."

"Your plan is to release me and try to save your pretty little wife," Webbs taunted. "It's a good one. O'Toole really put some fear into you, didn't he?" Webbs laughed loudly, catching the attention of everyone around them.

"I don't care about any plan you might have. Your job, as a sheriff, is to keep control of your prisoners, make sure they show up for court, and in his case, get him ready to hang." Mayor Johnson narrowed his eyes. "Remember that your salary is paid by the town, and it helps fund your ranch. I would hate to take that salary away from you and see your ranch fail."

Webbs stated, "Yeah. Everyone would know that you're a failure as a man, a sheriff, and a rancher."

Allen jerked the cuffs a bit, causing them to bite into Webbs's wrists. The outlaw simply laughed loudly again, like some kind of madman.

"Are you threatening me, Mayor?" Allen asked through gritted teeth.

Gloria picked an invisible particle off her dress and refused to look at Allen. Ben and Virginia stood tall, staring at the mayor as though daring him to admit that he was. The air around them stilled, and Virginia could hear her heartbeat in her ears.

Virginia knew that Allen was furious about being backed against the wall. With Webbs standing there and the plan already set up, he couldn't divulge anything to the mayor.

Webbs was shuffling his feet as though dancing and giggling like a schoolgirl. "Whatcha gonna do, *Sheriff?*" He emphasized the word as a taunt. "Are you gonna save yer job and put me back in the cell, or are you gonna save that perty little wife of yers and let me go?" He licked his lips. "Of course, now that O'Toole has seen her...."

Allen jerked the cuffs again, eliciting another bout of laughter from Webbs.

Mayor Johnson lowered his voice. "Look, I'm up for reelection and there are a lot of people wondering if I'm up for the job, especially after what happened at the festival. Every move I make is being watched carefully. Paul Wilson is telling everyone how weak I am and that he could do a much better job of protecting this city and bringing in new money, making it prosper." He paused and wiped his brow, wrinkling his forehead. "If you let this man go, it'll be seen as a weakness on my part. We're so afraid of the outlaws that we're going to give in to their demands."

He put his finger up and glared at Allen. "No. That's not going to happen. Put that man back in his cell, or turn in your badge."

The mayor turned, offered his arm to Gloria, and walked down the wooden sidewalk as though he didn't have a care in the world.

Webbs laughed. "I take it he won't be gettin' yer vote this election, will he?" His voice got low and serious. "So, whatcher gonna do?"

"I'm going to put you back in your cell, wait for the judge to get better, and watch you hang." Allen pushed him into the cell, shut the door, and unlocked his cuffs. "We'll figure out another way to get your leader and the rest of you devils, and we'll put you where you belong—in hell."

Sheriff Hicks, Stephen, and Douglas stormed into the office.

"What's going on?" the sheriff asked.

"The mayor shut down whatever game you fools had cooked up for me!" Webbs shouted with glee. "He told Sheriff Strauss here that if he let me go, he'd lose his badge."

Sheriff Hicks glared at Webbs. "Don't worry. This isn't over. There's more than one way to skin a cat."

Virginia was shocked at the phrase, but Ben whispered in her ear, "He means a catfish."

"Allen, I need to get back to Coyote Creek. Don't worry, we'll figure this out quickly." He glanced at Webbs. "I'll be back to watch you hang."

"You do that," Webbs taunted.

Sheriff Hicks shook Virginia's and Ben's hands and slapped Allen on the shoulders. "Keep me updated."

They watched him leave. Ben sat in one of the chairs and put his hand on his head, which seemed to amuse Webbs.

Virginia looked at Allen and shook her head. "He's constantly laughing and giggling like he's lost his mind. Has someone been sneaking in some booze, or has he gone completely mad?"

"No one has brought him anything but water," Allen said. "If he wasn't going to the gallows, he'd be a candidate for the asylum."

Stephen said, "We've got it from here. Why don't you take these two back to the ranch? Ben looks like he's about to pass out, and Mrs. Strauss doesn't look a whole lot better." He grinned ruefully at Virginia. "No offense, ma'am."

Virginia smiled. "None taken. It's been a rough day, and I'm sure I resemble someone who's been through a stampede, covered in dust and trampled along the way. Ben's not looking much better."

Douglas put his hand on Ben's shoulder. "Take them home, Sheriff, and keep them safe. We've got this taken care of right now. We'll send for you if there's any need."

Allen nodded. "Thanks."

Virginia thanked Douglas and Stephen and looked back at Webbs. He was smirking, and the glint in his eyes was enough to make her blood run cold.

Chapter Twenty-Four

Allen gritted his teeth as he, Ben, and Virginia stepped outside. He was furious with the mayor for interfering with their chance at possibly finding the entire gang and eliminating them once and for all.

Ben looked down the street to see the mayor and his wife talking to Mick. "The man is such a dandy. When the mayor was a kid, his father bought up a ton of land along the proposed railroad routes for next to nothing and then sold it at top dollar. The man was worth a million by the end of the war. He bought several mines out here and died, leaving our esteemed mayor with a lot of money and not enough work to keep him busy."

"Why does he want to be mayor so badly?" Virginia asked.

"Power and prestige," Allen said. "It makes him feel important. I'm surprised he hasn't tried to use his money and influence to get the president to name him governor."

"Right now, he's a big fish in a little pond," Ben said. "That does a lot for a man's ego."

"Yeah, I guess it does." Allen sighed. "Normally, he's not such a bad guy, but I guess he's worried that he'll lose his job. Then, what's he going to do?"

"Sit around the house and drive his wife crazy," Ben said.

Allen rubbed his temples. The stress from the day was starting to get to him. "Let me get Blaze. I'll drive the wagon home. He'll follow without me having to lead him."

"That horse thinks he's a puppy," Ben said. "You raised him since he was a foal and his dam died."

He quickly turned toward the corral where Blaze was munching on hay. Allen led the horse out of the stall, holding his halter. He put the saddle blanket and saddle in the back of the wagon and helped Virginia up.

Allen was going to help Ben up because his friend was still wobbly on his feet, but Ben beat him to it. "My head hurts, but there's nothing wrong with my legs."

"Did your hard head break my shovel?" Allen smirked. "Do I need to stop at the store and get another?"

"Seems someone's feeling clever, now," Ben said.

Allen grabbed the reins, and the horses headed back to the ranch with Blaze walking next to the wagon. He looked at Virginia, who hadn't said anything since they first left the sheriff's office. She was extremely pale, and the bruises had turned a deep purple. O'Toole's fingerprints were clearly pronounced against her ghostly-white skin. Her throat had swollen, and Allen worried whether she could breathe well.

"Can you breathe okay?" he asked.

She nodded. "It just hurts. I'll make some willow bark tea for Ben and me at home and make a comfrey poultice. I'll be fine." Her voice was hoarse.

That familiar fury exploded inside of him.

His heart raced and stomach clenched as he pictured O'Toole wrapping his hands around Virginia's neck and squeezing the life out of her. He couldn't imagine the fear she must have felt. Allen was very proud of her for fighting back. That took a lot of courage and control because most people instinctively put their hands on whatever was choking them to try to pull it away.

He glanced over at Ben, who was bent over. His elbows were on his knees, and his face was in his hands.

I'll kill O'Toole with my own hands.

Allen's hands tightened into white-knuckled fists as he replayed the scene of Ben's ambush and Virginia's attack in his mind over and over again. He clenched his jaw and every muscle in his body tightened.

Darn Mayor Johnson. We could have ended this today.

The horses plodded home while Allen continuously scanned the landscape for signs of the outlaws. Ben had the rifle, although Allen wasn't sure he'd be steady enough to shoot it. Allen had his pistols, but he knew that if the outlaws decided to attack, he and Ben would be greatly outnumbered.

He breathed a sigh of relief when the ranch came into view, but didn't feel completely safe until he pulled the wagon up in front of the barn. Keith and John rushed out.

"John told me what happened. Is everyone okay?

Ben almost fell out of the wagon, and John caught him.

"I'm fine. I just have a wee bit of a headache. Allen was worried about his shovel." Ben laughed weakly.

"The shovel is fine. I was using it to clean the barn," Keith said, grinning. "What can we do to help?"

Allen helped Virginia out of the wagon and wrapped his arm around her shoulders. "If you would take care of the wagon and horses for me, I'd appreciate it. Then, you two should keep watch, although I suspect the outlaws will strike at night if they intend to."

Keith nodded.

"How are the dogs?" Allen asked.

"They're fine. Hopefully, they won't take meat from strange people anymore," Keith said.

John laughed. "I doubt it. They're fed better than royalty, but they always want their treats."

Virginia smiled. "That's because they're hard-working animals and need bonus pay."

Keith and John looked horrified at the sound of her voice.

Virginia noticed.

"Don't worry. It sounds a lot worse than it really is. I'll be fine." She chuckled, although the sound was more of a gurgle. "I got in a few licks of my own. His face is scratched like he fought a mountain lion, and I got a good kick in a place where he's not likely to forget."

"I knew I liked you for some reason," Keith said. He looked at Allen. "Take them inside. We've got this taken care of."

"Thanks, men." Allen was glad to know that the ranch hands not only worked for him but were friends he could trust with his life.

Virginia opened up the cupboard and grabbed the herbs she needed for the tea and poultice, and the linens necessary to change Ben's bandage.

Allen shook his head. Virginia wasn't one to give up. She would keep going until she fell down.

A warmth spread through him as he looked at her determined face.

"Please sit down. I know how to do all of this, I promise." Allen led her over to a chair.

"But I—"

"But nothing. Sit there and relax."

He got the water boiling for the tea and then pulled out some dried comfrey leaves. Allen ground them, wet them with water until they were a thick paste, and spread them gently over Virginia's neck. He wrapped a clean linen bandage around it, making sure it wasn't too tight.

Allen checked Ben's bandage and groaned loudly when he saw the large gash on the back of his head. It had stopped bleeding, although Ben's hair was matted with the blood and poultice Virginia had applied, some having seeped through the bandage.

"You must have the constitution of an ox to take a blow like that and keep going."

"Takes more than a bump on the head to put me under. I guess they never got that message."

Virginia got up to pour the willow bark tea for herself and Ben while Allen reapplied the poultice and put a new bandage around his head. The entire time, he was seething inside, trying very hard not to show it.

That blackguard came to my ranch and attacked my family. I'll make sure he knows he made a grave mistake. At that point, I'm no longer the sheriff. I'm a husband and a brother.

Although Ben wasn't his blood brother, he loved the man as though he were. Ben had been there for him through the worst of times.

Ben finished his tea. "Thank you. I'm going upstairs to lie down." He held up his hand when Allen started to protest. "I've been up and moving around enough that I think I'm fine, except for the massive headache and hole in my brain."

"I don't think the hole quite reached your brain." Virginia grinned.

"Feels like it." Ben patted her hand. "You get some rest, too."

"I'm going that way," she replied.

Allen walked her to her room and hesitated by the door. She glanced at him, a new vulnerability suddenly settling in her eyes. "Please don't leave me. I can't fight back if I'm asleep."

He wanted to go back into town and talk to Stephen and Douglas to make a new plan, leaving Keith and John at the house to guard Ben and Virginia, but he could see that she needed him more.

His heart lurched and tightened like a fist, and a physical ache welled up inside him. Her words settled heavily on him. He looked at her trembling hands, holding her skirt in fists. The fear beneath her words wafted like an inferno from her.

Allen knew that he should get back to town and figure out how to stop these men from hurting anyone else. He knew that, but....

Drawing a slow breath, he bit his bottom lip. He nodded and walked into the room with her.

She climbed under the covers, dressed as she was, and he pulled the blankets up to her shoulders. Her hand snaked out, and he held it in both of his hands. It was so tiny compared to his.

He stared at her and noticed how frail and delicate she appeared. Allen knew that she was tougher than she looked, but the ordeal she'd gone through today would have terrified anyone.

Something stirred inside of him as he studied her. A deep, quiet ache consumed him. It wasn't pain, but a feeling he couldn't identify. He swallowed hard as he thought about how much he'd come to care for her. It was unexpected, as theirs was a marriage of convenience, and they had initially formed a simple friendship.

The warmth from her hand radiated inside of him. Her fingers had tightened around his, looking for comfort and safety. She trusted him and needed him. Considering her life in New York City, he was probably the first person she could trust in a long time.

The knowledge tugged at his heart, and he made a silent vow that he'd never let her down.

The house was eerily quiet, pressing down like a heavy wool blanket. He'd gotten used to the constant noise of Virginia cleaning, cooking, and moving around, singing to herself. Ben would often poke his head in for some of her tarts and to check on her.

Virginia's shoulders relaxed, and her eyes closed. Allen was glad to see that she was finally resting. It briefly occurred to him that he could go into town now, but he didn't want her to be frightened when she woke up.

***

Virginia sat upright and gasped loudly, her eyes wide with fear, when a loud pounding on the door echoed through the house. Allen was instantly alert, his heart thundering in his chest.

A knock like that could only mean bad news. Something's happened.

He leaped out of the chair and crossed the room with one stride.

"They're back," she whispered hoarsely.

"Stay here," he said.

"No, I'm coming with you." She kicked off the blankets and followed him downstairs.

Allen opened his mouth to argue, but decided that it would be useless. Virginia wouldn't listen, and they'd waste precious time.

"Stay behind me."

He grabbed his rifle off the wall mount and, with a practiced motion, pulled the lever, chambering a round. Allen tensed, ready to shoot, and opened the door.

A man whom Allen didn't recognize lingered on the porch. He wore buckskin pants and a buckskin jacket. His wide-brimmed hat was pulled low over his eyes. A pair of pistols hung in the holsters slung around his waist. He leaned against the door frame, one leg crossed over the other, arms folded over his chest, as though he didn't have a care in the world.

He didn't relax his grip on the rifle, not sure what to think about the person standing in his doorway.

"Who are—"

Behind him, Virginia gasped. "June?"

Chapter Twenty-Five

"You know this person?" Allen asked in disbelief.

Virginia nodded. "This is the person I met on the train. She sent me a letter. This is Shootin' June."

Allen lowered his rifle slowly, although still keeping a watchful eye on the newcomer.

Grabbing June's arm with shaking hands, Virginia pulled June inside the house. "You have to come inside. It's not safe out there."

Struggling to control her breathing, Virginia glanced around as though expecting to see a gang of evil outlaws spring out of thin air and attack them.

Allen shut the door behind June, his body tense and his eyes never leaving the other woman. Although he wasn't pointing the rifle at her, he hadn't released his grip on it either.

Virginia bit her bottom lip and looked at June. "I wasn't…we weren't expecting you."

"I know," June said. "I'm sorry to barge in on ya like this, but I needed to talk to ya."

Allen pointed to the sitting room. "Let's sit down in there."

Ben ambled downstairs, his bloodshot eyes squinting at June. "What's going on?"

"Ben, this is my friend Shootin' June. We met while I was on the train. She helped me out."

He held out his hand. "Virginia told us about you. It's a pleasure to meet you."

They walked into the sitting room. Allen and Virginia sat on the couch, and Ben took one of the chairs by the fireplace. June paced back and forth from the doorway to the fireplace and back again, in complete contrast to the calm demeanor when she arrived.

"Can I get you some coffee or tea?" Virginia asked.

"No, thank you." June stopped pacing and looked at Virginia and then at Ben. "What happened to you two?"

Virginia smiled to herself.

It's just like June to be blunt and jump straight to the point instead of beating around the bush.

"We were attacked by an outlaw this morning. Ben went into the barn to work, and a gang leader, named O'Toole, was hiding in the shadows and hit him in the back of the head with a shovel."

June glanced at Ben and raised her eyebrows. "Oh, no. Are you okay?"

"I'm still kicking and breathing, for now. It'll take more than a little bump on the noggin to take me out."

Nodding, June peered at Virginia. She shared her side of the story. "He strangled me, almost to the point where I was about to pass out. It was a warning because Allen put one of the gang members in jail, and O'Toole wanted him back."

"Oh, my goodness. Ya musta been terrified," June gasped, sitting next to Virginia and staring at the bandage around her neck.

"I still am." Virginia paused. "It doesn't hurt quite as bad because we treated it with comfrey, and I drank some willow bark tea. I reckon I won't be singing for a while, but I'll be all right."

June sighed heavily and rubbed the back of her neck. She took off her hat and set it on the table next to the couch. "By thunder, I was afraid of that."

Everyone's eyes bore down on June.

"You know, with my job, I sometimes run into some unsavory people. Well, I was in Silver Bow, doin' a shootin' demonstration, when I overheard a couple of men, askin' for people who could shoot ta join them." June inhaled sharply and rubbed her eye. "I heard them say that they were formin' a large army to attack a local town."

Virginia gasped and unconsciously touched her throat. Her heart raced, and she looked at Allen, who stared at June.

"What else did they have to say?" Ben asked.

"They said there was a sheriff their leader wanted ta get revenge on. One of the men said they were coming to Butte, and I remembered that's where ya said ya was livin', and ya said ya was gonna marry a sheriff."

June paused and turned her attention to Allen. "I asked them what the name of the sheriff was. They said it was Allen Strauss. They were mad because he'd arrested a member of their gang, and they wanted him back. They told the people they were talking to that they were gonna raid the jail, get their man back, and destroy the entire town in the process. They promised that anyone who joined them could keep whatever loot they got from the people and stores. They didn't say nothin' 'bout killin' or nothin', but to me, it sounded like they didn't care about the people in the town."

"How many men were there?" Allen asked.

"Three that I could tell. Not too many people were interested in joinin' them. Most folks just ignored them."

Virginia gasped in disbelief. "They wouldn't destroy the entire town just to get revenge and break their friend out of jail, would they?"

June fixed her with a serious look. "I wouldn't be here if I didn't believe them."

Ben groaned. "Look what they did during the festival. They burned down Mick's general store just to create a diversion so they could steal a few things from the booths in town." He rubbed his temple. "I don't think they would hesitate to destroy the town, not only for revenge but for a diversion. If they're riding through town, causing panic and chaos, looting the stores and people's houses, the sheriff and deputies aren't going to be at the jail guarding Webbs."

Virginia's heart sank. Ben made a great point. The outlaw gang had already proved that they wouldn't stop at anything to get what they wanted. If hurting and threatening Virginia and Ben wouldn't work, then destroying Butte would.

"Did you happen to hear who the leader of their gang was?" Allen asked.

June gestured toward Virginia. "They mentioned O'Toole, the same feller that did that to her. I heard someone in the crowd say that he was a ruthless, dangerous man." She pointed at Virginia's throat. "It seems they knew what they were talkin' 'bout."

"Did you hear anything about their plan, such as when they were going to attack and whether it was during the day or after dark?"

She shrugged. "I think they were plannin' on comin' today or tonight. I reckon' they'd talk 'bout that once they got everyone rallied up. My guess is that they'd do it at night when people are asleep."

Allen nodded. "That makes the most sense to me, too."

Virginia looked at Allen, tears prickling the back of her eyes and fear gripping her heart like an icy hand. Her breath caught in her throat, and she felt sick. She knew that he had to go into town to warn the mayor and the rest of the people, and she had to stay at the ranch. Otherwise, she'd just be in the way. She was scared that the outlaws would kill him and terrified that O'Toole would come back to the ranch to hurt her.

She wanted to cling to him and beg him to stay. The helplessness, fear, and pain she felt in the barn overwhelmed her, and she felt the pain in her lungs when she couldn't draw a breath.

I can't ask him to stay. He can't, and that would be selfish of me.

Allen stood. "I've got to go into town to warn the mayor and gather all the men to prepare. I'll send Keith to fetch Sheriff Hicks and get more backup. Those gang members will be walking into a death trap they can't escape."

"I'm coming with you." The hardness in Ben's voice told everyone that there wouldn't be an argument. "I've got a score to settle, and trust me, I'm well enough to hit what I'm aiming for, headache or no. I was hurt worse than this in the war and always managed to hit my target."

"I'll watch over Virginia. She's my friend, and I won't let nothin' or nobody hurt her." She narrowed her eyes and glanced at Allen. "I'm a better shot than most men. I don't miss when I aim my gun."

The tone of her voice and the fact that she earned a living with her shooting tricks convinced Allen. He nodded. "You take good care of her."

June returned the nod. "Ya know I will."

Virginia follows Allen to the door. She grabbed his shirt and looked into his eyes, trying to convey everything she couldn't say with that one stare. Then, fire exploded inside of her, spreading through her veins, when he lowered his head and possessed her lips, consuming them like a starving man devoured a steak.

Virginia felt the lightning strike as their hearts and souls met.

When Allen pulled away, he touched her face, gently, with the back of his hand. "When this is over, we'll talk, okay?"

She nodded slowly as she watched him walk away with Ben at his side. Then, she closed the door and locked it carefully.

June smiled. "Things seemed to have turned out good for the two of ya."

"Yes, I hope so," Virginia muttered. "I think so. I just wish this whole mess with these outlaws was over."

"It'll be over sooner than you think," June reassured her.

Virginia shuddered.

She was terrified to think that it might end with Allen getting hurt or—worse—killed.

Chapter Twenty-Six

Allen explained to Keith and John what June had reported. "I need one of you to alert Sheriff Hicks and the other to stay here and keep an eye on things."

"I'll ride to Coyote Creek. Keith went this morning," John said.

"You just want to have all the fun," Keith joked.

John snickered. "That's right. Maybe the girls will see me coming to the rescue, and they'll be all over me. Don't worry, I leave the ugly ones for you."

"Harass him later. Ride now," Allen ordered.

John quickly saddled his horse and headed off to Coyote Creek.

"Are you sure we can trust her?" Ben asked as they saddled their horses.

"Honestly, I don't know for sure, but we can't take the chance that she's lying about it. What would she have to gain? Plus, she did come out to the ranch to warn us." Allen sighed. "Virginia likes her."

Ben licked his lips and tilted his head to one side. "Virginia is a sweet woman and would like a rattlesnake until it bit her."

Annoyance flickered inside Allen, and he wanted to defend his wife, but he had to admit that Ben was right. However, he couldn't take the chance that June was telling the truth. If he dismissed it, and the town was destroyed, then he would have a lot of guilt on his hands.

Exhaustion and stress weighed heavily on his shoulders. His shoulders sagged. It seemed as though Blaze was moving through molasses, taking forever to cover the five miles to town. It even seemed too hard to breathe. The storm churning in his gut made him ill and reminded him that he hadn't eaten anything but a biscuit all day.

After an eternity, the town came into sight. They headed straight for the sheriff's office. As soon as they got into town and took care of the horses, Ben went in search of the mayor.

Allen went into the station. "Stephen and Douglas, please step outside with me."

Webbs walked up to the cell door and wrapped his hands around the bars. "Somethin' interestin' goin' on? The only time yer wanter talk outside is when it's about me."

"He's so full of himself that he thinks the world revolves around him," Stephen said.

"It ain't my fault that I'm the most interestin' thing this town's got," Webbs called out as the three men headed outside.

"What's up?" Stephen asked.

Allen repeated the story that June gave. "I don't know if I trust her a hundred percent, but something in my gut tells me that she's not lying."

Douglas sighed heavily and shuffled from one foot to the other. "We can't dismiss her offhand, anyway. It's better to be prepared for the fight and no one shows than to be caught flat-footed."

"Those are my thoughts. I need you to go rally up about twenty men. We'll need them to keep watch and be prepared in case something goes down," Allen said.

Stephen and Douglas quickly discussed whom they would each call upon and where they would station them, and then went their separate ways.

Just as they left, the mayor and his wife hurried up to him. "What's this all about?" the mayor demanded. "Ben said that some strange woman showed up at your house with a crazy story."

"Yes. A woman who performs at different shooting events visited us tonight. Virginia met her during her train ride here. She said she heard some men trying to recruit people to shoot up a town."

The mayor crossed his arms over his chest and stared at Allen through narrowed eyes. He pressed his lips together.

"You want to scare the entire town based on some woman's story?" Mayor Johnson asked.

"Well, would you rather ignore it and hope that nothing happens?" Allen asked. "If the gang does ride into town tonight, destroy the town, and hurt people, and everyone finds out you knew about it but chose not to act, I'm pretty sure you can kiss your reelection goodbye."

The mayor pointed his fat finger at Allen. "If we get people riled up and they don't come, then you can kiss your badge goodbye."

He and Gloria pushed past Allen and went into the sheriff's office.

"Who's that other man running for office?" Ben asked.

"Paul Wilson, I think."

Ben shook his head. "I think I'm going to vote for him for mayor. He doesn't even have to campaign."

Allen laughed. "Mayor Johnson isn't too bad most of the time. He's just stressed out with the gang raiding the town and the election. He'll calm down."

They went inside, and Allen rolled his eyes. Webbs was taunting the mayor and his wife.

"You two are a little old to be joining the gang, but I'm sure O'Toole would find a place for you. He'll be coming to town soon, and I'll be happy to put a good word in for you." Webbs looked at Gloria. "Those fancy clothes won't last you long out there, but I'm sure we could find you something suitable to wear. Can you shoot a gun?"

Gloria walked over to him, her heels clicking against the floor. She tilted her chin, and a slow smile spread over her face. "Webbs, I bet that I could outshoot you with these fancy clothes and high heels on and still have time to fix my hair afterward."

"Ooh, sassy. I like my women that way."

"You couldn't handle a sassy woman. She'd be more of a man than you ever could," Gloria shot back.

Webbs's face turned bright red, and he growled at her. "Let's see where that smart mouth of yours gets you when O'Toole comes to town."

She simply laughed, walked over to one of the chairs, and sat down, looking impressively bored.

Sheriff Hicks and several men arrived about an hour later.

Webbs practically ran to the cell door. "You're gathering the troops. Today's my lucky day. I'm getting out of here."

"Sit down, Webbs. The only place you're going is the gallows," Stephen said.

"You keep saying that. It sounds more like an empty threat than a promise," Webbs replied.

No one answered him.

They stepped outside, and Allen explained that they had several men around Butte, armed and waiting for trouble. Stephen and Douglas had alerted most of the town, and everyone promised to spread the word to their neighbors that everyone had to stay inside and lock their doors and windows.

"What do we do?" Sheriff Hicks asked.

"We wait," Allen said.

Sheriff Hicks told his men to spread out and keep watch. Then, he, Allen, Ben, the two deputies, the mayor, and the mayor's wife went back into the office.

Allen hated waiting more than anything else in the world. Anxiety crawled up his spine and squeezed his heart. On the one hand, he didn't want anyone to get hurt—and someone surely would if the gang showed up. On the other hand, he wanted them to show up not only because he didn't want to look foolish, but also to take care of this problem once and for all.

The mayor paced constantly, stopping only to check his pocket watch. Every few minutes, he looked at Allen, frowned, and muttered, "They'd better come," or "Something had better happen soon."

Every single time there was any kind of bump, a horse neighed, or something creaked, Gloria nearly jumped out of her skin. She sat in the chair, rigid, her eyes wide, holding the arms with a white-knuckled grip. Allen was worried that she'd have a fit of hysterics.

"Why don't you take Gloria home? She can lock the doors and would have the servants there to protect her," Allen suggested. "She's obviously frightened."

"Haha. She doesn't look so tough now, does she?" Webbs taunted.

Everyone in the room looked at him and said, "Shut up," at the same time.

That drew an amused chuckle from Webbs.

"No. I need her here with me," the mayor said.

Allen flexed his fingers. Every muscle in his body was as tight as a coiled spring and felt as though it were going to snap from the strain. The streets were deathly silent, and everyone was hiding in their homes, waiting for the imminent attack or lurking in the darkness, ready to protect their town. There was only the sound of the wind brushing against the building.

Everyone in the sheriff's office was silent, each person lost in their own thoughts, worried about whether the outlaw gang would come and what would happen if they did. Even Webbs had grown quiet, tired of harassing his captive audience.

The mayor's constant pacing and Gloria's gasping every few minutes if someone breathed wrong were about to drive Allen crazy.

Allen wondered if June had lied to him or if she had gotten the timing wrong. He stood and walked to the window, thinking he heard a shot ring out in the distance. Everyone stilled as the thundering of hooves was heard in the streets, and a couple of shots echoed in the night air.

Allen opened the door and saw a group of men charging toward the sheriff's office. "At least five of them are heading this way," he called.

His heart thundered in his chest when he saw a large group of men rushing to the bank while several others raced through town carrying torches. There were a lot more men than he could have predicted, and he wondered how they were going to fight them all.

"What's going on?" the mayor demanded.

"There are at least twenty or more men heading our way, and they're riding fast," Allen reported.

The shots were getting closer, and Allen wondered if they were shooting in the air or if the outlaws were fighting the townsmen.

One of the outlaws threw a torch at the millinery shop. Others threw torches in various businesses, and smoke wreathed out of the buildings.

The outlaws yelled and screamed taunts, such as "Yeehaw" and "Ya-hoo." "Let's clean this town out" and "Burn it down" echoed in the night air.

One of them yelled, "Come out, come out, wherever you are! We want to play."

More shots rang out as the men rushed out to defend their town. One of the outlaws screamed and fell to the ground. His horse reared in fright and bolted away.

Allen froze for a brief second. A sharp pain burned in his lungs as he struggled to breathe, and his stomach churned. He trembled, terrified that this would trigger a panic attack or a flashback. An image of Virginia's face formed in his mind, pushing the anxiety and memories of the war back inside him.

He grabbed his rifle and yelled, "Let's go, men! We're not going to let them win. This ends tonight."

Allen rushed out into the street and took aim at the man who was running toward the jail, shooting at Allen. He breathed in deeply and pulled the trigger.

The mayor and his wife went out the back door. They had pistols, but in spite of her bold words, Gloria wasn't up for a fight.

Sheriff Hicks, Ben, the deputies, and other men rushed outside and disappeared into the darkness to fight the gang members who were shooting up the town and trying to set the buildings on fire.

One of the men who'd come with Sheriff Hicks stood next to Allen, trying to defend the sheriff's office. An outlaw raced out of the shadows and took aim, shooting the man down beside him.

"It's just my arm. Don't worry about me," the man yelled, trying to scoot back against the building and into the shadows.

It seemed that June hadn't exaggerated when she said that O'Toole's men had recruited people to help them overrun the town. Outlaws came out of nowhere, swarming the streets like cockroaches.

The next few minutes went by as a blur of gunshots, screams, and shouts. Several men rushed Allen, and a couple stormed in from the back door. Allen took down two men, aiming for center mass.

Bullets were flying all around him, and the desk was splintering.

"Yeehaw. Get 'em, boys," Webbs shouted from his cell.

One of the men grabbed the keys off the wall and unlocked the cell. Fury burned inside of Allen as he saw Webbs being pulled out, and adrenaline pushed him forward. He shot at the man, but a bullet seared across his ribs. Allen grunted from the pain shooting through him. He gritted his teeth, steadied himself, and took aim.

Two of the outlaws took advantage of Allen's brief hesitation and slammed the butt of a gun into the back of his head. He spun around to confront his attacker, but another man kicked his legs out from under him. A loud *thud* echoed in the air when Allen hit the ground.

One of the men's boots slammed into Allen's gut, knocking the air from his lungs. Another boot connected solidly with his head.

Pain was all he knew, and then, the world went dark.

Chapter Twenty-Seven

The house was too quiet after Allen left. Every sound screamed in her ear—the tree branch hitting against the side of the house, one of the dogs barking, and the creaking of the floor.

Virginia made another cup of willow bark tea for herself and black tea for June, and then paced back and forth in the sitting room. She sat down for a few seconds and then stood back up to make a few more laps around the room, wringing her hands and picturing the worst in her mind.

She felt like she couldn't breathe, and it had nothing to do with her throat. Her heart thundered in her chest as she moved the curtain aside just enough to look outside.

Butte was too far away for her to hear or see anything, but her imagination showed her a shootout in town between the sheriff and his men and the gang of outlaws.

Virginia pressed her lips together and wrapped her arms around herself. Her stomach was knotted so tightly that she was growing nauseous.

"You're goin' to wear yourself out," June said, watching from the couch. "He'll be okay. He's got Ben and all of his other men."

"You can't know that. You said yourself that the gang members were recruiting people to go into town, loot it, and burn it down. By now, they could have an army." Virginia sighed and slumped down into the chair. "A lot of people are looking for a way to make a quick buck. That's why so many people got into the Gold Rush."

"I can't argue with that point, but I know men like Allen," June said reassuringly. "He's tough, and he cares about you. He'll do whatever he has to so he can come back to ya."

Virginia felt tears burning at the back of her eyes. "I fell in love with him. I can't imagine life without him."

June's eyes opened wide. "I didn't expect that. Ya were a mail-order bride because he needed someone to take care of the house for him. I figured you were just goin' to have a marriage of convenience."

Sighing heavily, Virginia ran her fingers through her hair. "Me, too. But he's been so nice to me. We started spending a lot of time together, and, well, it just happened. I didn't mean for it to. I didn't think he'd ever love me back." She bit her bottom lip. "I think he does care about me now."

Swallowing hard, she walked into the kitchen and pulled the linen bandage off her neck. She couldn't stand wearing it anymore—it felt as though it was suffocating her.

Her fear grew until she thought it was going to explode. "I can't lose him."

"Why don't we go to town to check on him?" June offered. "Ya can see that he's safe and sound. I'll protect ya if the outlaws have made it to town." She touched her pistols. "I've been itchin' for a fight, anyway."

Virginia looked at June for a minute. She wanted to make sure that Allen was fine, but she knew he'd be furious with her.

June raised her eyebrows at her. "Well, what ya wanna do? Are ya gonna sit around here all night, worryin', or are ya gonna go out there and check on yer man?"

"Let's go," she said at last, pushing all reservations aside.

Her desire to make sure Allen was okay overrode any concerns she had about her own safety.

They rushed outside, and June quickly saddled her horse, Remington. Virginia saddled Belle, grateful that Allen had taught her how to tighten the girth.

John came out of the barn. "Where are you going? Allen wanted you to stay here."

"I know, but I can't. I'm going out of my mind, worried about him. June will protect me. I promise that I'll tell Allen that you did everything in your power to stop me," Virginia said, mounting Belle.

"I can shoot ya in the leg if ya want," June offered with a grin.

John waved his hand at her. "That's a generous offer, but I'd rather keep both of my legs in good working order."

"Suit yerself."

"I should come with you to keep you safe," John said.

"Shootin' June is a great shot and can outshoot most men," Virginia said. "Please, stay here and keep the ranch safe for Allen."

John was clearly conflicted about what to do. He shook his head. "Allen's going to kill me for this, but all right, I'll stay. Be careful."

Neither woman spoke as they rode into town. A whirlwind of emotions exploded inside Virginia. Fear of losing Allen just when they'd started something beautiful together sat heavily on her chest, suffocating her, making her feel that she couldn't breathe in enough air, no matter how much she tried.

A sense of urgency made her want to push Belle faster. Only the knowledge that it wasn't safe to run in the dark kept her from kicking the horse into a full-on gallop.

Biting her lip against the sharp pain that coursed through her as images of Allen lying in the dirt street, injured or dying, she fought to keep from crying out.

I'm sure he's fine. You were terrified before when the outlaw gang came into the town during the festival and destroyed everything. He was safe, and he'd even captured one of the bad men.

Aunt Fiona always said she had an overactive imagination when Virginia would tell stories to her cousins at night to try to get them to sleep.

They could hear the gunfire before they reached town. Virginia gasped in shock as she saw the brief, bright muzzle flashes bursting from many different directions. Rings of smoke curled in the air, and brilliant orange, red, and blue flames licked the night sky.

"Allen," she whispered under her breath. "Please, Lord God in Heaven, please protect him. Keep him safe," Virginia prayed.

"It looks like they did it," June said, her voice loud, almost triumphant about being right. "I hope my warnin' came in time."

"I pray it did, too," Virginia said.

As they rode closer to town, the outlaws' taunts and jeers grew louder. Shots continuously rang out. Shrill screams from those hit and the terrified townspeople threatened to burst Virginia's ears.

Her heart nearly stopped as she saw two men jump off their horses and break down the front door of a house. A woman and two children ran out. The men followed soon after and threw a torch into the house.

Virginia wanted to help, but she had to find Allen first. When they got into the town, they put their horses into one of the corrals and crept through the shadows, hiding next to buildings, trying not to be seen by the outlaws.

"I haven't had this much fun in ages," June breathed excitedly.

"You think this is fun?" Virginia asked disbelievingly.

"Sure. It beats sittin' around, doin' nothing, and I'll get to practice my shootin'," June said. "I'll join the fight as soon as we find yer sheriff."

The sound of the hooves filled the air, as did the gunfire, screams, and shouts. Virginia barely heard any of it over the thunderous beating of her heart. Every muscle in her body was tight, and she held her skirt up with tightly clenched fists.

Another burst of light and the sharp report of a gun flashed right next to them. Her breath came in short, ragged spurts, and her mind screamed Allen's name.

They jumped back and pressed themselves against the blacksmith shop as two outlaws raced by. The two women ran along the wooden sidewalk until they were across the street from the sheriff's office.

Virginia and June waited for a couple more outlaws to ride past them before they darted across the street. The door to the sheriff's office was wide open. Webbs's cell was empty. Papers were scattered everywhere, and the splintered desks showed that a gunfight had clearly taken place here.

"Allen!" she cried.

She spotted his boots sticking out from behind one of the desks and ran over to him. He lay unconscious on the floor and was bleeding profusely from his head.

Virginia fell to her knees, grabbed his arm, and shook him. "Allen, wake up. Come on. *Wake up.*"

There was no answer.

Virginia put her ear to his chest, and her heart nearly stopped when she didn't hear anything.

June knelt beside him and pressed her fingers against his neck. "He's alive. He's just knocked out."

"Why can't I feel him breathing?" Virginia asked, her voice shrill with panic.

"Because he's breathing too shallowly. He's alive. I felt his pulse. That means his heart's beatin'."

"We have to get him to the doctor. Can you help me carry him out?"

"I sure can. Ya grab his arms, and I'll grab his legs. Do ya know where the doctor lives?"

"Yeah. He's down the street and to the left," Virginia said.

"Can ya carry him that far?" June asked.

"Yes."

They lifted Allen up and carried him to the door. June peeked out to make sure no one was coming, and they carried him out to the wooden sidewalk. They'd only gotten a few feet when a figure lunged out at them from the darkness.

June dropped Allen's feet and pulled out her pistols. Virginia stood, frozen in shock and fear, holding onto Allen's arms for dear life.

"Don't shoot. It's me, Ben."

"Show yerself," June demanded.

He stepped out onto the sidewalk. "What in blue blazes are you doing here? Allen told you to stay at the ranch where he knew you'd be safe."

"I had to come. I was so scared, and I was right. He's hurt," Virginia said in a pleading voice. "You have to help me get him to the doctor."

"We can't go there. The doctor's place was set on fire a few minutes ago. A couple of the men rushed in to get Dr. Simmons and his family out. The safest place might be in the sheriff's office, especially if they think they've killed him." Ben looked at Allen, half lying on the sidewalk and half held up by Virginia. "They already got what they came for."

Ben held out his rifle to Virginia. "Set him down gently and take this."

Virginia did as she was told. Ben bent down and picked Allen up as though he weighed no more than a child. June and Virginia followed him back into the sheriff's office.

"Drag that cot out of the cell," Ben ordered.

June hastily complied, and Ben laid Allen on it. He ran to the back room and returned with a small box.

"His side's bleeding," Virginia said, panting.

She couldn't seem to inhale enough air, and her chest felt as though it was going to explode.

"I need you to breathe," Ben said calmly. "You can't help me if you pass out."

She nodded, trying to control her breathing. Virginia held Allen's hand tightly. "Please, wake up. Please, I need you," she whispered to him.

Allen's shirt was stained with blood on his side. A black and blue bruise with a purple center had formed near his temple. His face was ghostly pale.

Ben unbuttoned Allen's shirt and pulled it aside. He pushed up his blood-soaked undershirt. Holding a half-empty whisky bottle he'd found in the back room, Ben poured the amber liquid over Allen's side. "Sorry, my friend."

Allen flinched and groaned but didn't wake up.

"It looks like the bullet just grazed him. Darn lucky that it didn't go deeper," Ben muttered.

He found an old shirt, ripped it into strips, and formed a pad. "Put this against his ribs here, gently," he ordered Virginia.

She obeyed, and Ben wrapped more strips around Allen's torso and pulled down his undershirt.

Virginia squealed as a shot shattered the window, sending glass flying everywhere. June crouched down, both of her pistols drawn, watching and waiting for someone to come through the door so she could shoot them.

She thinks this is some kind of game or show.

Shaking the thought from her mind, Virginia reminded herself that June had come to Butte to warn Allen that O'Toole's gang was coming for them, and she was here to protect her.

She drew a deep breath when she saw how much Allen's side had bled. "Is he...?"

Ben briefly touched her arm. "He'll be fine. It's just a graze. I cleaned it with the whiskey."

Virginia clung to Allen's hand and pressed her lips to it. "Please, wake up."

Picking up another strip from the shirt, Ben soaked it in the water from the basin and cleaned the blood from Allen's temple.

"There's just a gash in the skin. They didn't break his skull. He'll have a heck of a headache to match mine, but he'll be fine," Ben said. "That's a dangerous place to be hit, but it didn't kill him."

Virginia gasped, and a tear streaked down her cheek. She jumped when another bullet slammed into the building.

"We're sitting ducks here," June said. "I don't think they're ever going to stop."

Ben shrugged and looked at her. "There's nothing we can do until he wakes up."

Pressing her lips against his cheek, she whispered, "Come back to me. Please, wake up. Please. I can't lose you now." She hesitated for just a second and then whispered, "I love you."

Chapter Twenty-Eight

Allen paused while running through the field to catch his breath. The sky was bright blue, and white, wispy clouds floated above as if there weren't men on the ground and others trying to kill their own brothers.

It was in stark contrast to the thick smoke that threatened to choke him and the smell of blood that hung in the air. Allen was certain that he'd never be able to get the metallic taste out of his mouth, which coated his tongue just by breathing in the scent.

He caught a glimpse of himself in a mud puddle. "Joseph?" Allen looked at his hands and touched his face. "What in tarnation?"

"General Atwood has been shot. The enemy is advancing. We have to get to him!" the major screamed.

Forgetting about his confusion, Allen jumped on his horse, racing toward enemy lines.

"We can't let them get the general!" another man shouted.

Everyone held the general in very high regard, and they couldn't let the Confederates capture one of their men.

The cannons thundered from the ridge. Loud screams sounded as some of the cannonballs hit their mark.

A large crack ripped the air, and a searing heat burned through his chest. The round knocked him off the horse. He hit the ground hard, knocking the breath out of him. Allen tried to get up but couldn't. Through red-hazed eyes, he searched for his brother.

"Allen," he whispered as the ghost of himself knelt over him.

His voice rattled in his throat as he struggled to draw in a breath. He clutched his chest, fingers trembling as they emerged covered in blood. The red was slowly spreading over his blue coat.

Allen stared up at the image as he recalled the words Joseph spoke to him that day. He'd played them over thousands of times since he buried his brother. Only this time, it would be him who was buried.

He blinked his eyes, his gaze remaining fixed on the ghostly figure who stood over him as he tried to speak. "Allen...I...."

His body felt so far away. He couldn't move his legs, and he was cold—so very cold. The searing hot pain in his chest was more of a throbbing ache. He tried to suck in a breath, but couldn't.

The blood that filled his mouth was hot, sticky, and coppery. He could vaguely hear the apparition talking to him, but he couldn't make out the words.

Allen felt his heart slowing. He heard the cannons and rifles as they continued to explode, not caring that he was lying on the ground amid the boots and stomping horses. Men were screaming, and he couldn't help.

He was tired—so very tired.

The darkness started crowding in around the edges of his vision.

Allen heard someone calling out to him. It wasn't his brother, though. It was a woman's voice.

"Allen, I need you to come back to me. Please, I can't lose you now. I love you."

Virginia, he realized, like a light going off. *I'm married to Virginia.*

He turned toward her voice as the darkness receded from the edge of his vision.

She continued calling out to him, and he followed the voice. He was lying on his back, but not in the mud. Something wet dripped down his face.

He blinked, and the room came into view. Virginia's bright green, worried eyes stared into his. Her blurred face slowly came back into focus.

Virginia touched his cheek and smiled. "Thank God," she breathed. "I thought I'd lost you."

Fog still clouded his vision, and his head ached, but he couldn't help but mutter, "You're real."

"Yes."

"I dreamed..." he started, then stopped. "It doesn't matter."

She gently touched his face, and his breath caught in his throat. A rush of emotions coursed through him as his heart pounded a million miles an hour. A heat ignited in his gut as he looked into her face. Relief and a love so deep that it came from his soul washed over him.

He reached for her hand when another shot hit the side of the sheriff's office.

Ben came in from the back. "You're awake. Good. I was afraid we lost you. The gash on your head is pretty nasty. You were shot in the side, but it's basically a graze. It took a chunk of meat out, but nothing you can't live without."

June peeked out the window and then ducked when a bullet came flying through. "I'm really glad that yer awake, too, but we need ta get out of here. More of the gang is gathering out front, and they aren't gonna to be happy that Allen's alive." She looked at Allen doubtfully. "Do ya think you can walk?"

"I'll make it."

"It looks like the back alley is clear," Ben interjected. "We need to head that way. There's no way that, even with June's fantastic shooting, we'll live for more than half a second if we try going out the back."

Allen gritted his teeth. "Help me up. Where are we going?"

June rubbed her chin. "When I was riding in, I came in through the woods. There's a small cave back by the river that should be safe long enough to make a plan."

Ben nodded, and Allen said, "We know the place."

"We'll have to walk. It's too risky to try to get the horses."

Ben and Virginia helped Allen stand. He wobbled for a minute as dizziness made his head swim and nausea almost overwhelmed him. He inhaled three long breaths, trying not to be sick.

"You okay, man?" Ben asked.

"I'll live."

They slowly walked to the back room, and Allen heard June sigh with impatience.

I can't go any faster. You're lucky I'm not crawling.

The night air was cool, and Allen tried to steady his breathing, still faintly recalling the sensation of his lungs filled with blood from his dream.

Gunshots, screams, and yells were almost deafening. Flames licked the skies in several directions.

"What's happening?" Allen gasped.

"The gang members are burnin' down houses and businesses." June's voice was brisk and matter-of-fact. "We can't do anythin' to stop them. As Ben said, even with my expertise and his, there's no way we can fight them all, 'specially since yer so injured. We have ta get you to safety."

June led the way through the woods. Ben walked on one side of Allen, and Virginia was on the other, helping him navigate fallen branches, rocks, and holes.

His gut wrenched. He was running away when his neighbors' houses were burning. Those were the people he'd sworn to protect.

Maybe if I can sit down for a second and catch my breath, I can get back into it.

His head throbbed, and he was still seeing double, especially when he tried to look into the distance. His side burned, and a new pain tore through him every time he inhaled.

Allen began to feel uneasy as June led the way to the cave. She had mentioned seeing it when she rode through the woods on her way to Butte. He was fairly certain she had told him and Virginia that she'd been to Helena before. The cave wasn't on the way. Plus, the simplest route would have been to travel the same road that everyone else took. He hadn't been thinking clearly.

He was just about to say something to Ben when June turned around.

"Virginia, can ya come help me for a second?" June asked.

Virginia directed her question toward Ben. "Do you have him?"

"Yeah."

She touched Allen's cheek briefly and then caught up to June. Suddenly, June grabbed her wrist and started running with her in tow, dragging her along.

"June, what are you doing? Stop! Let me go!" Virginia yelled.

Despite her attempts to free herself, Virginia couldn't help but stumble along; June's grip was too strong, he assumed.

Allen tried to run after them, his heart thrumming and his blood rushing in his ears, but he tripped and nearly fell, only to be caught by Ben.

June pulled Virginia toward a group of men emerging from the darkness. A man, taller than the others, stepped in front of them. His hat was cocked back arrogantly, and he stood with his legs apart and arms crossed over his chest. The moon glowed ominously in the clearing.

Virginia yanked her arm from June's grip and landed a powerful right hook to June's jaw. She drove her elbow into June's stomach.

June grabbed Virginia's hair, her cheeks reddening as she spat, "You wench. You'd better be glad that O'Toole wants you alive."

"Let go of me!" Virginia screamed.

"O'Toole, I've got the woman," June called out. "I brought you the sheriff's wife, just like you asked."

A couple of gang members rushed toward Virginia and grabbed her. She kicked at them, and Allen thought she might have bitten one. Virginia kneed another one in the groin, and he punched her in the face.

Allen lunged, but Ben held him back. He tried to shake Ben off, but his friend wouldn't let go.

"They'll kill you, and you won't be able to help her," Ben hissed in his ear.

He watched in horror as they shook her, and one of them pulled a gun and pointed it at her head. "Be still, or I'll shoot you here and now."

"Put that away, Jamison. You can play with her after we're done," O'Toole said. "Unless, of course, the sheriff does exactly what he's told. Then, he gets his wife back."

He tried to run toward her, but Ben held him back. "We don't stand a chance. They want something," he whispered.

Allen barely heard Ben's words. His blood turned to ice, and his heart thundered in his ears. A red haze covered his eyes, and he shook with pure rage.

Something cracked inside of him.

He loved her, and he'd failed her.

June walked toward her horse tethered to a tree and mounted. She glanced at Allen and smirked as though daring him to say anything.

One of the gang members pulled Virginia onto his horse. She flung her head back and busted the man in the nose. Blood exploded everywhere, and the gang member spewed several curse words at her.

That's my girl. Fight back.

The man put his hand around her throat. "O'Toole wants you alive. Lucky for you, I'm really great at choking someone until they pass out, but not until they die. You'll be a lot easier to handle if you're unconscious."

She looked as though she was debating whether she could wrestle him off the horse, but must have decided that she was no match against the much larger man.

Allen's hands clenched into tight fists pressed against his sides. His eyes narrowed, and he snarled at the gang members.

"Leave Virginia out of this, and I'll do whatever you want," Allen called.

"You're going to do whatever we want now since we have your pretty wife as insurance," O'Toole responded. Then, he smirked at Allen. "If you ever want to see your wife again, meet us at the bank in an hour. Come alone, or I'll splatter her brains all over the place."

Chapter Twenty-Nine

Virginia growled low in her throat. She believed him and didn't want to be choked again. Her throat still hurt from O'Toole's visit. However, she couldn't just sit quietly and let him ride off with her.

She looked at Allen. His face was bright red, and he was shaking with anger. If there weren't ten men against one—and if he weren't injured—she knew that he would have attacked.

Allen didn't look good. His shirt was soaked through with blood from the gunshot wound in his side, and his head was still bleeding. Allen's face was ashen, and he appeared to be on the verge of passing out again.

Virginia shifted and tensed, getting ready to jump off the horse. The man behind her must have sensed her intentions because he wrapped his arm around her waist and pulled her tightly against him.

Gulping in a huge breath of air, she tried to steady her heart, which slammed against her ribcage.

O'Toole yelled out that if Allen wanted to see her alive again, he should come to the bank in an hour.

The group took off into the trees. Virginia strained to look at Allen, but it was hard to move. She could hear Allen calling out, but she couldn't understand what he was saying.

She wanted to scream, but bit her lip until the coppery taste of blood made her grimace. There was no way in the world that she would allow these people to see how terrified she was. Instead, she gritted her teeth and closed her eyes, reminding herself to breathe.

Allen will figure out a way to save me. I know he will. I just have to bide my time.

At the same time, she knew that there was no way she was going down without a fight. She might not win, but she wasn't going to just lie down and die.

The man behind her stank of body odor, tobacco, and something sharp, like kerosene, which made her want to gag.

Allen's face popped into her mind. Her heart lurched as she pictured the look of anguish on his face. His jaw had been clenched, and his hands were white-knuckled fists against his legs. Allen's chest had been heaving as though he couldn't catch his breath.

She remembered that Ben had told her that Allen didn't open up to others because he'd lost everyone he'd ever loved. His father and brother had been killed in the war, and his fiancée had died from the fever.

We're not going to add me to that list, she vowed. *We'll figure a way out of this, one way or the other.*

The moonlight filtered through the trees, and the fires from town lit up the sky. The gang didn't seem to be in a hurry to get to the bank.

I guess they figure they have time since they're on horseback and Allen and Ben are walking. Plus, Allen isn't in the best condition.

She pressed her lips together and closed her eyes.

My Lord God, please protect Allen and keep him safe. Please take care of the other people in this town and save us from these men. Show me what to do, and give me the strength to do it. In Jesus's name, I pray, Amen.

They rode up to the bank, and everyone dismounted except for the man behind her. Two men walked over to them, and Virginia was practically thrown off the horse. They caught her. Before she could fight, one of them squeezed the back of her neck so hard that she had to bite her bottom lip to keep from crying out. Another roughly grabbed her arms and tied them behind her.

The man holding her neck shoved her. "Walk."

It didn't take long for O'Toole to break into the bank, and she was pushed inside. The wooden floors creaked, and their boots made a loud thudding sound as the group tramped across the floor.

Virginia grunted as O'Toole flung her onto a hard wooden bench.

"Sit there, and don't move," O'Toole said. "I need you alive, for now, at least, but it doesn't really matter what condition you're in, does it?"

He laughed maniacally, and Virginia was certain that the man had gone completely insane.

"Why in high heavens are you doing this?"

"What? Robbing the bank? You really are slow on the uptake, aren't you? Banks have money. We like money." O'Toole said the words with exaggerated slowness.

"Really? I never would have guessed," Virginia said sarcastically. "I'm talking about all of this—terrorizing the town. Don't you think this is a little excessive just to rob a bank or to save one worthless man who doesn't seem to have the sense God gave a common goose?"

O'Toole snarled at her, showing his teeth, reminding her of a rabid wolf. "It's about much more than that, girlie."

"Then what?"

"Your husband, the great esteemed Sheriff Strauss, killed Sadie Carver."

Virginia shook her head and shrugged her shoulders. "Who is she, how did he kill her, and why?"

He got in her face, and Virginia tried not to gag from the putrid smell of his breath. "She was my girlfriend. We were going to get married."

O'Toole stood up and glared at her. Everyone in the room fell silent and stared at him. The fury in his voice was palpable, but there was also an undercurrent of hurt.

Virginia was surprised that a man like him had the capability to love anyone other than himself.

"Your husband killed her."

"There has to be more to the story than that. There's no way on God's green Earth that Allen would kill someone unprovoked."

"You think very highly of your man, but he's not as great as you think he is," O'Toole sneered.

"So, tell me."

"Strauss arrested Sadie after a bank robbery in Coyote Creek went wrong," he said through gritted teeth. "He turned her over to that cur Hicks."

Virginia wanted to say, "What do you expect? Robbing banks is illegal, and when you commit a crime, you run the risk of being arrested." However, she kept her mouth shut. She wanted to keep O'Toole talking.

O'Toole's face changed. For once, it wasn't the angry monster talking. Grief and regret clouded his eyes, and if Virginia wasn't sitting in a bank, tied up, with a throbbing eye and painful throat, she might have felt sorry for him.

"She was just a kid. We'd just celebrated her nineteenth birthday. Sadie was pretty, and she was wild. She had an independent streak, and boy, was she stubborn." He rubbed his forehead. "She wasn't made to be caged up and couldn't handle it like some people can."

"What happened?" Virginia asked softly, interested in his story in spite of her hatred for the man.

"That blackguard Hicks kept her locked up in jail for a few months until the judge got around to sentencing her for the bank robbery, and she spent another couple of years in prison."

She was a bank robber. What did she expect? A bouquet of flowers and an offer of marriage? Perhaps a hymn sung in her honor as she rode away with the county's savings? A woman who dances with the devil ought not to be surprised when her slippers catch fire.

As these thoughts rolled through her mind, she was careful to keep her face blank. Every second that O'Toole talked was a second that he was focused on her and not on what Allen might be doing.

"When she came out...." O'Toole shook his head and sighed. "She wasn't Sadie anymore. She couldn't stop shaking. Sadie never ate anymore and never slept for more than a couple of hours at a time. I would catch her pacing back and forth in the middle of the night."

"I'm sorry. That must have been hard."

"You're darn right it was," O'Toole spat out. "Whiskey was the only thing that seemed to quiet the demons she brought back with her that tormented her soul. Eventually, she drank herself to death."

Virginia bit her lip. Sympathy flickered inside of her, but she quickly shoved it aside. The ropes were biting into her wrists, and her arms and shoulders ached.

"I was with her when she died. She sat down next to me and told me she was sorry. Her breath was barely a whisper, and I knew that it wouldn't be long. Then, she laid her head on my shoulder, and she let out a long breath. She was gone."

O'Toole's eyes were shiny as though he was holding back unshed tears.

"I buried her that night, and I swore that I'd pay back Hicks and Strauss if it took my dying breath."

"It's very unfortunate that Sadie suffered like she did, and I'm sorry for it." Virginia paused and tried to move her shoulders to relieve some of the pressure in her arms. "This wasn't Hicks's and Allen's fault. Sadie chose to break the law, and the sheriffs were just doing their job."

O'Toole's face turned bright red, and Virginia saw the vein in his neck throb. "He was just doing his job?"

"That's what sheriffs do. They arrest people who break the law. That's their job. Sadie broke the law, knowing what would happen if she were caught. The judge sentenced her to prison. Neither Allen nor Hicks locked her away, and they didn't make her pick up the bottle after."

"You smug little wench." He backhanded her across the face so hard that it made her brain rattle.

White-hot pain erupted in her cheek, and she tasted blood. Instead of shrinking away from him as she did in the barn, she sat up straight, ignoring the painful pulling on her shoulders and arms.

She stared at O'Toole, her eyes blazing with anger. "You can hit me all day long if it makes you feel like more of a man. It won't bring back Sadie, and it doesn't change the truth that you refuse to see."

"I'm going to enjoy cutting your throat when this is all done," he spat at her.

"Allen will save me. I'm not worried," she said, trying to keep her voice as light as possible as though she really wasn't concerned. "I'd be worried if I were you, though."

He took a step toward her when June came inside. "Everyone's in their places. That way, if Strauss brought reinforcements, even though ya told him not to, they'll be ambushed."

Virginia's heart nearly stopped. She forced herself to appear calm, even though her insides felt like gelatin and she was certain they could hear her heart thundering in her chest.

She looked up at June, who wore a huge smile. "How could you betray me like this? We were friends, and Allen and I welcomed you into our home."

June shrugged. "Spending my life on the road means that I need money. I was doin' a show when I heard some men askin' for people to ride with them and clean out a town." She smiled at Virginia. "That part of the story was true."

Virginia glared at her.

"I met O'Toole. He said they were bound for Butte and plannin' on destroyin' the town. It would be a bonus if they could kill the sheriff. I told him I'd met ya on the train, and ya trusted me. We hatched a plan."

"I can't believe you."

June laughed. "You're so naïve. I knew there was a payday in my future as soon as I sat next to the bright-eyed, innocent city girl who didn't know anything about the West." She nodded toward the tall gang leader. "O'Toole made it easier than I thought."

Virginia licked her lips and tasted the blood that trickled from the side of her mouth. "You know, you reap what you sow. Eventually, all of this is going to come back around on you."

"I'm not worried 'bout that. Right now, I just want my cut from the bank robbery, and I'll be on my way."

"You're famous, remember? There will be a price on your head, and people will be looking for you no matter where you go."

"Are you tryin' to convince me to help you or somethin'? Forget it. As for me, I'll just change my name and my appearance. It won't be the first time." She glanced at O'Toole. "The hour's about up."

Right on cue, there was a commotion outside.

"O'Toole!" a voice shouted. "Come out here and face me like a man."

Allen, Virginia realized, her heart leaping. *I knew he'd come for me.*

Chapter Thirty

Allen gritted his teeth and pressed his hand hard against his side. It had started bleeding again when he'd tried to loosen Ben's grip.

"We have to go back and get her," Allen groaned.

Ben nodded. "That's what we're going to do. You can't just show up at the bank and think they're going to hand Virginia over to you. They'll kill you both. We have to come up with a plan."

They walked back through the woods as quickly as Allen could manage. The bullet may have only taken a small bite from his side, but it burned like fire, eating away at his skin.

Allen blinked a few times, trying to clear his double vision.

"They got you pretty good. Honestly, I'm surprised they didn't kill you. I told Virginia that we just had to wait for you to wake up, but honestly, I wasn't sure you would."

"It's going to take more than a couple kicks in the head to kill me," Allen said, suppressing the shudder that crawled down his spine.

The injury almost killed him, and he remembered the dream he had while he was unconscious. Virginia had saved his life.

He pictured her red hair and emerald-green eyes that constantly flashed her emotions. She wasn't good at hiding her feelings from anyone.

Allen bit his lip, and something tugged at his soul. He knew that she was the one for him. Virginia filled a hole inside his heart that he never knew could be repaired—not after his father, Joseph, and Angelica. He'd be cold in his grave before he let anyone hurt her or take her from him.

They walked in silence for a bit before Ben said, "This seems to be a strange way to carry out a bank robbery. Most of the robbers go into the bank while they're open, point the guns at the tellers, demand money, and high-tail it out of there."

"Yeah."

"O'Toole seems to have a particular grudge against you. The outlaws aren't necessarily known for completely burning down towns. Plus, he kidnapped your wife to lure you to the bank. Is there something you aren't telling me?"

Allen groaned and put his hand on a tree to keep from falling as he tripped over a stick. "About six years ago, he and his gang robbed a bank in Coyote Creek. I caught one of the robbers—Sadie Carver. She was O'Toole's girlfriend. I turned her over to Hicks since it was his territory."

"Oh..." Ben said, clearly not knowing what else to add.

"Yeah," Allen sighed. "She was sent to prison for a few years, and word has it that she didn't do well. After she got out, she drank herself to death."

"So, O'Toole blames you?" Ben filled in the gap.

"Me and Hicks. If O'Toole and his men get away from here, then my guess is that he'll do the same to Coyote Creek."

Ben was silent for a moment before concluding, "I guess we'd better not let them get away with it."

Allen shook his head and instantly regretted it, wincing at the spike of pain that shot through him. "Nope. I'm not planning on it."

Butte was eerily quiet when they got back into town. Allen and Ben went to the sheriff's station, which was covered in holes and half destroyed. Shattered glass littered the floor.

"Go get the mayor and have him meet us here—preferably without his wife. I'm going to see if I can round up some men," Allen started. "I have an idea, but we need to hurry. I don't think he'll kill her until I show up, since Virginia is his leverage, but I don't want to push it."

His heart lurched at the thought of the outlaws hurting Virginia, and that familiar rage started to boil in his veins, but he pushed it to the side for now. He couldn't afford to lose control. He needed to think clearly, which was hard enough to do with his headache.

Ben set off to find the mayor, while Allen went outside in search of the men. He encountered several, including Sheriff Hicks. They reconvened in the sheriff's office, where Allen outlined his plan. Exactly an hour after O'Toole gave the deadline, Allen walked up to the bank.

"O'Toole!" he bellowed. "Come out here and face me like a man."

He heard a commotion inside the bank, and then O'Toole appeared at the door with Virginia in front of him. He had one arm around her neck and a gun pressed against her temple. Two men stood behind them.

Allen took a deep breath to suppress the raging fire building inside him.

Stick to the plan.

"Walk really slowly to us. You're going to take us down to the vaults so we can collect what's inside," O'Toole ordered.

"Let Virginia go, and I'll do whatever you want me to." Allen was proud of himself for managing to keep his voice steady.

O'Toole laughed. "Not a chance. I don't trust you. You're just like every other snake in the grass. There's no way I'm going to take your word for it."

Allen worked hard to keep a straight face.

Just as I predicted.

"Come unarmed," O'Toole added.

He pulled his pistols out of their holsters and threw them on the ground. A couple of gang members grabbed them. Allen hoped that O'Toole wouldn't consider patting him down because he had two double-shot Derringer pistols hidden in his boots, as well as a Bowie knife.

"Let's get this wagon rollin'. Come on." O'Toole walked backward into the bank, pulling Virginia with him.

He walked slowly, pressing his hand to his side and exaggerating the pain and seriousness of the wound. Allen feigned wiping his forehead and rubbed his sleeve against the large cut near his temple, causing it to bleed again.

Ben's going to murder me for that. It took him forever to make it stop bleeding.

Allen glanced at Virginia as soon as he stepped into the bank and once again had to suppress his anger. Her hair was a tangled mess. Her hands were bound behind her back, and she had a black eye and a massive bruise across her right cheek. Dried blood from a large cut on the right side of her mouth made Allen want to kill O'Toole. His fingers itched to tear the man apart piece by piece right then.

He'll kill her first. Keep your cool. Breathe. We've got a plan.

"You don't like the way your woman looks?" O'Toole narrowed his eyes at Allen. "Sadie looked ten times worse than this, and it was your doing. At least your wife is alive—for now."

Don't say anything.

"We're going to the vault."

Allen crossed his arms over his chest. "No. Let Virginia go, and you and I will go down there together."

"Not a chance. You get the woman when I get the money inside the vault," O'Toole growled. "We'll walk downstairs together."

"Then only you, me, and Virginia go. Everyone else stays upstairs."

"O'Toole, I wouldn't..." June started to say.

"Shut up, June. You ain't in charge."

Allen looked at June. He'd never hit a woman before, even when arresting them, but he was certain that he could cheerfully strangle her for her betrayal of Virginia.

"All right," O'Toole conceded. "The three of us will go down. Claude, Seth, toss me those bags."

They looked as though they wanted to argue, too, but they did as they were told.

"Downstairs," O'Toole ordered, motioning to the steps that led to the vault.

Allen hated walking in front of him, but knew that O'Toole wouldn't shoot him in the back. He wanted Allen to open the vault, and he couldn't do that if he were dead.

He reached the bottom of the stairs and started to head toward the vault.

A loud thumping noise and a piercing scream filled the air. O'Toole had pushed Virginia down the stairs for seemingly no reason and was laughing like a crazed hyena, leaning over as he cackled.

Allen fought the red haze of pure fury that filled him as he ran over to Virginia's crumbled form. It took every ounce of his willpower not to pull his pistol out and shoot O'Toole. He had to get Virginia out of the bank first.

"Are you okay?" he asked.

Tears streamed down her pale face. Her lips trembled, and several scrapes appeared on her forehead and face. She panted as though she was trying to catch her breath.

"Keep steady. We're almost done. Trust me."

Allen was glad to see the resolve in her eyes. She pressed her lips together and gritted her teeth.

Nodding, she whispered, "I do."

"Aw, such a tender scene," O'Toole cooed. "The next one will be you picking up her dead body if you don't open that vault right now."

O'Toole swaggered over to Virginia, grabbed her arm, and yanked her toward the large metal box as if she were a rag doll. She winced but didn't cry out or say anything.

"As soon as I open this, you give me Virginia."

"That's what I said," O'Toole said, waving his gun at Allen.

Allen took a deep breath. He spun the large dial on the front of the vault, pausing at each number; the faint click of the tumblers was the only sound in the room.

With the final click, he threw open the vault door. O'Toole pushed Virginia to the ground and sped inside the vault, uncaring about his hostage at this point.

Allen hastily pulled Virginia to her feet, nudging her toward the stairs. "Run."

It was time to act.

Chapter Thirty-One

Virginia didn't think. The second that Allen pulled her to her feet and told her to run, instincts took over. She didn't stop to consider her next actions. She just moved.

She hit the first step hard. Virginia almost stumbled, her boot slipping, but Allen grabbed her arm and steadied her.

It was hard to run up the stairs with her arms tied behind her. She didn't feel any of the scrapes, cuts, or bruises. Her only thought was to get up and out of the bank.

She gasped when she tripped over her skirts, her knees hitting the hardwood.

Allen pulled her up, and she continued racing up the steps.

O'Toole's screams of rage echoed from the vault and into the room. "Get them!" he bellowed.

Fury vibrated in his voice, making Virginia's heart thunder in her chest. She gasped for air as she continued climbing for safety.

Loud, confused voices and what sounded like a stampede of a thousand cattle thundered on the main floor.

Virginia wondered how she and Allen were going to get out of the bank alive. There was no way they could fight all those people by themselves, especially since her hands were tied behind her back.

Allen stopped to pull something out of his boots. A shot rang out, buzzing by her ear. Allen turned around and fired a shot in return.

Virginia didn't look back. She didn't need to. The anger in O'Toole's voice was enough to send the fire of terror coursing through her veins. If he got hold of them, he'd murder them.

She could hear Allen breathing behind her. He was panting, as though he was struggling to catch his breath. Virginia had seen the fresh blood seeping out of his side and trickling down his forehead earlier.

"They're coming down. Don't stop for anything!" Allen yelled.

She charged into one of the gang members with her shoulder. He lost his balance and tumbled down the stairs, dragging another man down with him.

Allen struck the next man in the throat, grabbed his shirt, and threw him down the stairs. He kicked the third man in the knee. Virginia shuddered at the sound of cracking bones. The man screamed as he tumbled down the stairs.

"You pack of worthless idiots!" O'Toole screamed at the men lying on the basement floor. "You fools couldn't fight your way out of a barn."

As Virginia and Allen reached the top, more gang members rushed down the stairs.

"Keep moving. Plow through them," Allen growled.

Virginia didn't hesitate. She ran as hard and fast as she could, evading the grasping hands that tried to catch her.

A shot rang out, and Allen fired back.

"Go. Go. Go," he yelled.

Virginia's chest heaved. Her lungs burned, and her heart pounded in her ears.

The chaos seemed to work in their favor. Half of the men were scrambling downstairs while the other half stood by the front door, trying to block Virginia's and Allen's escape. They were stumbling over each other, seemingly unsure whether they should fight, chase after them, or run downstairs.

Someone fired a shot that flew over their heads.

He grabbed her arm. "This way!"

She tensed, anticipating the searing pain of a bullet tearing through her at any moment.

Allen half-pulled and half-dragged her to a narrow servant's entrance hidden next to a large shelf.

"Find them! Now! I want that wench in front of me!" O'Toole screamed furiously.

Allen pulled open the door and pushed her through. "Go. I'm right behind you."

She ran. Allen paused briefly to lock the door behind them. Several men and a few women stood in the alley, holding guns.

"You all right, Sheriff, Mrs. Strauss?" one of the men called out.

"We're fine. Don't let anyone out of here," Allen replied.

He pulled a knife out of his boot and hastily cut the rope. She nearly fainted from the pain as the blood rushed back into her hands.

Allen lifted her chin with two of his fingers. "I know it hurts, but just a few minutes more. Are you with me?"

Virginia nodded, her head heavy as she worked to stay awake.

He grabbed her hand and led her around to the front of the bank.

For a second, it seemed as if everything was frozen solid. She inhaled deeply and blinked several times. Absently rubbing her wrists, she stared at the people on the street. The entire town appeared to be standing outside the bank, most of them holding rifles, shotguns, or revolvers. Each of them wore an angry, determined expression.

Ben, Sheriff Hicks, and Mayor Johnson stood in front of the crowd.

"Are you okay?" Ben asked Virginia worriedly when he saw her.

"I'm peachy," she muttered. "Nothing perks a woman's complexion like being tossed around like a sack of flour," Virginia added, still rubbing her hands and wrists.

"At least you still have your sense of humor," Ben said. "I reckon the rest of you will heal. You're a tough cookie."

"Thank you."

Sheriff Hicks nodded to them. "As you saw, we have the entire place surrounded. Our men ambushed the gang members who didn't go into the bank. Your cells are crowded, and we have several of them tied up, gagged, and blindfolded with armed guards, tossed in the back of wagons, heading to my jail."

"We've sent word to sheriffs in Anaconda and Deer Lodge, as well as other nearby towns. We and Sheriff Hicks are keeping the gang members as well as June, while the ruffians they recruited are being farmed out," Mayor Johnson said. "I imagine they'll be dealt with harshly enough. I figured that the people around here would want to see O'Toole and his men swing for what they've done to our town."

"Excellent work," Allen said. He rubbed his hands together. "Everything has fallen into place, just as I intended."

Virginia listened to the men, but their voices seemed far away. Her head was spinning, and her vision was starting to blur. She put her hand up to her face and tried to breathe. Now that the danger was over, she felt every one of the bruises, cuts, and scrapes on her body. Her throat was killing her, and the scratches on her face throbbed. Her hands still felt as though she was being pricked with a thousand needles. She was sure that she was going to be sick soon.

Allen seemed to sense that she wasn't feeling well. He grabbed her hand and squeezed.

"Do you want Gloria to take you to our house to wait until Allen can take you home?" Mayor Johnson asked.

Virginia shook her head. "No. I want to see their faces when they're arrested, especially O'Toole's and June's."

"Is the money safe?" Allen asked.

Mayor Johnson nodded. "Even though I had my doubts when you first raised the alarm, I let Ben and a couple of other trusted men get the money out of the vault and take it to the church an hour ago, just like you suggested. Father Cahill and a couple of men have been sitting on it since."

Allen grinned and let out a laugh that was a mixture of relief and satisfaction. "O'Toole walked into an empty vault."

Their heads jerked toward the bank as the front door burst open and O'Toole, followed by June and the other gang members, exploded onto the wooden sidewalk. They stopped in shock at the wall of angry townspeople aiming their weapons at the gang members.

"Going somewhere, O'Toole?" Allen asked mockingly.

The man's face turned bright red, and Virginia thought he might explode from the anger. His entire body shook, and he pointed his finger at Allen.

"*You* did this. This is all on *you*. Tell everyone here how you murdered Sadie," he yelled, his finger trembling as he used it to emphasize his words.

"Everyone knows the story, O'Toole," Allen said as though he was already bored with the conversation. "The truth is, you aren't here because you're sad about your dead girlfriend. You're just a mean snake." Allen took a step closer to O'Toole. "And just like all mean snakes, eventually, they get their heads chopped off. Or, in your case, they swing from the gallows."

"This isn't the end!" O'Toole screamed as one of the men handcuffed him and led him to the jail.

Virginia glanced at June with a mixture of disgust and disappointment. "I thought you were a good person. I was pulling for you. You have the kind of grit and skill that most women get a chance to show. You could've gone so far and made a real name for yourself. Now, you're either going to spend a long time in prison or hang."

"I was yer friend. You can help me," June said pleadingly, her eyes now watering with tears.

Virginia shook her head. "No. I might be that naïve city girl that you thought I was, but that doesn't mean I'm an idiot. Fool me once, shame on you. Fool me twice, shame on me."

One of Sheriff Hick's deputies handcuffed her and put her in a wagon with a couple other men.

"Virginia, please!" she begged. "I had no choice. You know how ruthless O'Toole can be. He woulda killed me."

Her voice faded as the wagon rolled into the darkness.

"How many were there in all?" Allen asked.

"The best I can count was that O'Toole had thirty-three gang members who sometimes broke off into smaller groups, depending on the job. They'd recruited seventeen others to help destroy the town," Sheriff Hicks said.

Allen rubbed his forehead and sighed. "I hope we got them all. I want this done with."

"You and me both, brother. I'm heading back to Coyote Creek. You get your head and side taken care of."

Virginia glanced at Allen and gasped. Blood was still seeping out of his side, and his shirt was a bloody mess.

I almost lost him, twice. O'Toole came close to killing him and would have killed me.

Suddenly, she didn't feel so well. Her head was swimming, and her stomach rolled up in knots. Every inch of her body thrummed and throbbed with pain. A sharp pain squeezed her lungs, and her legs felt as though they couldn't hold her up any longer.

Her knees buckled, but Allen caught her before she could hit the ground.

"Virginia. Look at me," Allen said.

"I'm okay," she murmured, even as her eyes rolled back into her head and darkness enveloped her.

Chapter Thirty-Two

Two Weeks Later

"These people are very resilient," Allen said as he hammered the last nail into Widow Wilson's house.

Ben nodded. "Her house was burned to the ground, and she lost everything. She didn't give up; she got mad."

"If anything good came out of this, it's that we got to see what the people in Butte are made of. The community took care of those who lost their houses and belongings during the raid. Everyone stopped their everyday work and stepped up to the plate to rebuild."

"Keith and John wanted to do more, but someone had to take care of the animals and the ranch."

Allen put the hammer back into the toolbox and stretched. "O'Toole's trial starts tomorrow. Virginia has to be there. She said she'd rather scrub the pig pen with a toothbrush than go."

"Poor girl. She still looks like an angry cloud before a storm," Ben said.

"She's sore and walking slower, but you know nothing is going to stop her."

"Virginia is stubborn, just like her husband."

"What do you mean by that?" Allen said, pretending to be hurt by the comment.

"Who's been out here, wielding a hammer when the hole in your side still hasn't healed?"

"Things needed to be done, and I'm the sheriff."

Ben just chuckled, turning his attention back to their work. "I'm glad that all the houses have been rebuilt. Widow Wilson's was the last. Supplies were sent in from different cities and towns around the territory, and people even came to help. There are a lot of O'Tooles and Junes in this world, but there are a lot more good people than bad."

"Amen, brother," Ben cheered. "How about if I buy you a beer before we head home?"

Allen let his shoulders relax, and the look he shared with his brother was fond. "Sounds good."

***

O'Toole's trial was the first of all the gang members since he was the leader. Judge Joshua Parker had finally overcome his lung inflammation. It had been touch and go for a while, and Dr. Simmons wasn't sure he'd make it.

Judge Parker still had a slight cough, but he was doing well enough to preside over O'Toole's case. It would be his first since returning to the bench.

Mayor Johnson had offered to call Butte and ask for a traveling judge, but Judge Parker said, "Ah, heck, no. This one's mine."

Allen knew that every judge in Montana Territory would feel the same. O'Toole and his gang had been terrorizing the area for a very long time.

The small community building had been turned into a courthouse. The judge sat at a makeshift bench in front of the room. Tables were set up for the territorial prosecutor, Adam Jackson, and the defendants. Portable chairs were lined up in rows to accommodate as many of the townspeople as possible.

Allen whistled as he and Virginia walked past the line of people waiting to get into the building. The trial was set to start at eight, but it seemed like every single person in town was lined up by six.

Everyone greeted Allen and Virginia warmly. Everyone was eager to know how Virginia felt because she still looked like she'd gone three rounds in a boxing ring.

They took their seats in the front row, and Virginia grasped his hand tightly. "I don't want to be here."

"I know," he said, his stomach churning in sympathy. "You don't have to stay for the whole trial. You just have to tell the court what happened to you," Allen assured her.

O'Toole and his attorney decided to forgo a jury trial because every person in the entire Montana Territory would be biased. The territorial prosecutor explained the charges to the judge and the evidence he would present.

The judge glanced at O'Toole. "Where's your attorney?"

"I'll be representing myself. I don't trust anyone to do a good job, and I'm smarter than lawyers are anyway."

There was a smattering of giggles throughout the room. O'Toole turned around and glared at them. He was a lot less terrifying now, so no one was intimidated.

"I wasn't in my right mind when I did the acts I was accused of. I loved Sadie Carter. Sheriff Allen Strauss and Sheriff Frank Hicks murdered her. All I could think about was revenge. I don't deserve to hang or even do prison time because I was getting retribution for her murder." He paused and wiped his mouth with the back of his hand. Then, as if thinking of something else, he tacked on, "Also, June and my men put me up to robbing the bank."

Another round of giggles flooded the courtroom.

Virginia was the first witness for the prosecution. She explained how June tricked her and how she was treated by O'Toole. Of course, O'Toole accused her of exaggerating her bad treatment.

She narrowed her eyes and pressed her lips together. "Look at me."

Virginia rolled up her sleeves and held up her arms. The townspeople gasped when they saw the cuts, scrapes, and bruises that were beginning to heal. The rope burns around her wrists still glowed red.

"My legs look just as bad."

And with that, there wasn't much else she needed to say.

The trial only lasted two days.

By the end, Judge Parker glared at O'Toole through narrowed eyes. "Your crimes were heinous, not just the raid here, but throughout your career as an outlaw. During the raid, six people were killed, and dozens more were injured. You might not have pulled the trigger, but you gave the orders. I sentence you to hang by your neck until you are dead. The sentence will be carried out three days after all of the trials have ended. May God have mercy on your soul."

Everyone clapped when they heard the verdict.

Virginia shivered when O'Toole turned around and looked at her with a smirk on his face, and Allen wasted no time pulling her into his side.

"Are you going to come say goodbye, sweetheart?" O'Toole mocked.

She didn't get a chance to reply—not that Allen would've let her deal with him. The bailiff slapped cuffs on him and jerked him out of the courthouse.

Everyone nodded in satisfaction. That was the verdict everyone hoped for and wanted.

June's trial was next. She was very pale and appeared much smaller than usual. Her buckskin suit had been replaced with a calico dress, and her hair was pulled back into a tight braid. She raised her hand high, but Allen noticed she was trembling.

She had an attorney who tried to say that O'Toole forced her into helping him. However, Virginia repeated what June had said about knowing she could get a payday from the naïve city woman sitting next to her.

June took the stand on her own behalf.

"I didn't know anyone would be hurt or killed," June argued. "I thought we'd scare folks, take their money, and run. I knew O'Toole wanted to use Virginia as leverage to rob the bank, but I didn't think he'd hurt her."

"Why should we believe you?" her attorney asked.

"Because I told them everything I knew about O'Toole's hideouts and the names of all the gang members, includin' the ones who weren't in Butte at the time."

Although Allen didn't like it, he had to testify that she did provide valuable information that led to the recovery of a lot of money and the arrest of more gang members. He still wanted June to hang for her part in hurting Virginia.

Judge Parker sentenced her to fifteen years at the women's penitentiary in St. Louis.

The courtroom buzzed. Some people were relieved because they couldn't stomach the thought of a woman being hanged with the rest of the men. Others, especially those who'd lost a lot during the raid, didn't think justice would be served.

On the way home, Allen looked at Virginia. "What do you think about her sentence?"

Virginia paused. "I've been thinking about this for the last couple of weeks. I don't know that I believe her when she said she didn't know people would be hurt or killed. She's the kind of person who doesn't care who she hurts as long as she benefits. I'm pretty sure the only reason she sold out O'Toole was to help herself." Virginia sighed. "Still, though, I didn't really want to see her hanged."

Allen had to go to the rest of the trials. He was nervous about leaving Virginia home, although he knew that Ben, John, and Keith would die before letting anything happen to her, and someone would be close to the house at all times.

He'd almost lost her, and he knew that if she died, so would he. Maybe not physically, but everything inside him would.

Allen knew he loved her.

He just had to find the right time to talk to her about it.

I don't want to talk to her about us while the trials are still going on. I need all of this death and chaos done with before we discuss our future.

The trials continued for two weeks. Each of the gang members, including a not-so-smug Webbs, received the same penalty as O'Toole. Construction of the gallows started immediately. The men would be hanged five at a time, and their bodies dumped into a single mass grave.

Virginia refused to go. "It's enough to know that they'll be punished for their crimes and they can't hurt anyone else."

Allen didn't want to go either, but he was forced to because he was the sheriff. He didn't take any joy in seeing the men hanged. Most of the townspeople showed up to watch. However, unlike a lot of public hangings, there were no booths, food sold, or celebrations. It was simply a way for the people to claim their lives back so they could live without fear of O'Toole or his gang.

As they prepared to leave, the mayor clapped him on the shoulder. "Maybe life can get back to normal around here."

"I hope." He thought about Virginia, and the warmth pooling in his stomach pushed him to add, "Maybe it'll be even better."

Chapter Thirty-Three

A Month Later

Allen leaned against a fence post and sniffed the air, filled with the aromas of candied apples, pies, gingersnaps, roasted nuts, and meat. Everyone in Butte had turned out for the fall festival. People from Coyote Creek, Anaconda, and Deer Lodge visited Butte for the celebration.

It was the first time the town had gotten together after the raid. This morning, when they were setting up, everyone seemed a little tense, even though the gang members were gone. Gradually, though, everyone realized that they were safe. Laughter and conversation began to fill the air.

Mayor Johnson and his wife walked up to him, smiling. The mayor was way overdressed for the occasion, wearing a three-piece black suit with a red tie. His thumbs were hooked into his suspenders. Gloria was wearing a bright yellow dress with red roses on it.

You're definitely going to stand out with that dress, if that's your goal, Allen thought.

"Hello, Sheriff. I trust that everything is going well here."

"Everything is fine. It seems that everyone is having a great time," Allen said. "Congrats on winning the election, Mayor."

He didn't bother telling the mayor that he voted for the other man, Paul Wilson. Paul was a rancher and was a lot more down-to-earth than Jasper Johnson.

"Thank you. Your plan to bring down the O'Toole gang cinched it for me."

Allen nodded. "I was just doing my job. There was no way that I was going to let that man come into my town and hurt my people without doing everything I could to stop him."

"You stopped him dead in his tracks." The mayor gestured to the festival. "I know the town was doing fine after the attacks, but I hoped this would be a healing celebration. I wanted the people of Butte to know that they could gather and have fun without fear."

"Everyone seems to be having a good time," Allen said.

The mayor nodded. "Take care. The missus and I have to judge the pie contest. Lucky us."

Allen shook his head. He didn't dislike the mayor, but he still couldn't help thinking that the raid could have been prevented if the man hadn't stopped his and Sheriff Hicks's plan to let Webbs go and trail him. They could have arrested the snake in his den.

He grimaced as the twinge in his side reminded him that he was still tender. Doctor Simmons told him that the injury was one thing, but then Allen continued to run around "all over God's country," constantly tearing open the wound more and more.

Virginia diligently cleaned the wound, applied poultices of yarrow and comfrey, and ensured there were no signs of infection. He'd teased her about playing mother hen a couple of times. She'd just smiled and told him to quit squirming.

A group of children ran past him, laughing and chasing each other with wooden swords. They stopped in front of him for a small sword fight before running off again.

His heart beat a little faster as he caught sight of Virginia. She was giggling and kneeling on the ground next to a little girl with pigtails and a smudge of dirt on her nose.

She took his breath away. Her red hair trailed down her back in a long, thick braid. The green cotton dress with tiny pink roses that she'd finished yesterday made her emerald eyes even more vivid.

Virginia glanced at him and smiled. His heart skipped a beat, and warmth coursed through him.

Allen admired her so much. Her external injuries had healed, and she refused to let what happened to her get her down.

He'd asked her about it once.

She'd smiled at him and touched his cheek. "What happened, happened, and there's nothing that anyone could do to change it. I'm not going to let those bad people steal my happiness."

Allen hugged her, holding her close to him, letting her know she was the most cherished part of his life.

She pulled back and looked into his eyes. "Besides, you saved me, just like I knew you would."

Those words that conveyed her love and trust in him had nearly knocked him over.

Virginia was wonderful with children. At that moment, she was assisting the little girl in lining up her shot for the ring toss. They both laughed and clapped when the child got the ring over the neck of the milk bottle. Virginia handed her a small cloth doll. The little girl hugged her and skipped away.

Allen didn't realize he was staring at the scene and smiling until Ben poked him on his good side.

"You keep staring at her like that, and someone's going to think that you're sweet on her."

Chuckling, Allen said, "Maybe I am."

Ben snorted and grinned. "Well, it's about time. That woman's been in love with you for a long time. She even whispered it to you when you were unconscious the night of the raid, trying to bring you back."

"I heard her calling to me. That's what brought me back. She's my angel."

They watched her pick up a piece of chalk and walk over to the chalkboard that was set up at the children's games section. For a long moment, she stood there, frowning, her lips moving slightly. Then, she slowly and carefully wrote, "Gunny sack race."

She stood back and looked at her sign, smiling proudly. The letters were uneven, but they were clear.

Allen's heart welled up with pride. "She's been practicing writing every night, even when I'm not helping her. I could hear her sounding out the words under her breath in the kitchen as she wrote."

Ben nodded. "Two things about Virginia: She's very intelligent and can easily learn anything she needs to. She's also very determined. Once she sets her mind on a goal, she's going to achieve it, come hell or high water."

"She definitely wanted to learn." Allen ran his fingers through his hair. "I remember how embarrassed she was when she told me she never learned to read and write."

Ben patted him on the shoulder. "She also needed someone to believe in her and show her that she was worth the effort. You did that for her." He sniffed the air and rubbed his belly. "I'm heading over to Miss Brenda's turkey leg booth."

"Is it to get a turkey leg or to talk to Miss Brenda?"

Ben's eyes twinkled. "Maybe a little of both."

Allen made his rounds to make sure everyone was behaving, but still paid close attention to Virginia. He knew the threat was over, and he was being very protective, but now that he found the piece of himself that was missing, he couldn't bear to let anything happen to her.

After the gunny sack race, she changed the sign to "Gess the jellybeans." She misspelled "guess," but he was still very proud of her anyway. Someone quietly corrected the mistake for her.

Silent letters are confusing for everyone, he thought.

After she ran a couple more games, he approached Gloria. "Would you mind finding someone to take over the children's games for a while?"

She looked at him and smiled. "Of course not, Sheriff."

Madeline took over the games, and Allen held out his hand to Virginia. "Come with me. I want to show you something."

He led her to the wooded area behind the town. Instead of going toward the cave where June had betrayed them, he turned toward the river.

"Where are we going?" she asked after they'd walked for about half an hour.

Allen gently squeezed her hand. "You'll see. We're almost there."

They passed by an ancient, fallen tree and a herd of deer munching contentedly on the undergrowth.

Eventually, they arrived at an overlook atop a ridge. The scent of pine trees filled the air, accompanied by wild thistle blooming everywhere with its bright purple flowers.

She gasped as she took in the sight below. The prairie was painted gold with tall native grasses growing everywhere. Bright green fields sprawled with crops that would be harvested soon, and the silvery ribbon of the creek meandered across the land.

"Look over there," he said.

The church practically glowed in the afternoon sun, and tiny dots of people swarming around at the festival looked like a bunch of busy ants getting ready for the harsh Montana Territory winter.

"It's absolutely beautiful," she said, her eyes shining as she observed her surroundings.

"I come here when I need to think. It gives me a sense of peace."

She reached for his hand without speaking. Virginia didn't have to ask what he was searching for peace from. She'd seen him when he had his nightmares.

He turned toward her and looked into her bright green eyes. His heart filled with love for the woman who'd turned his life upside down in just a short amount of time.

"I brought you up here because there's something I wanted to talk to you about."

His heart raced, and he was surprised at how nervous he was.

She tilted her head and looked at him.

"When I put that ad in the paper, looking for a mail-order bride, I wasn't looking for a wife or a companion. I needed someone who could cook and clean the house. I even told Ben that I didn't care what you looked like or if you were a shrew because I didn't intend to have any kind of relationship with you."

Virginia smiled and dipped her head. "I kind of got that idea when I arrived."

"When I discovered what your life had been like in New York, I figured I was helping you. At least here, you had food, your own room, and you were safe." His voice was low and rough. "It turns out that you helped me. You helped me learn to be patient and to look at the world again without bitterness. You turned me back into a human being instead of a shadow of myself."

Her beautiful emerald eyes widened, and she licked her bottom lip as she listened.

Allen reached into his pocket and pulled out a small box. He slowly got down on one knee and opened the box.

Virginia gasped and put her hand to her mouth.

"I should have done this from the start and asked you properly. At the time, I didn't want anything more than just a quiet life without any hassle of caring about someone."

Virginia looked at him, speechless.

"I want you to be a part of my life, more than just a housemaid. I want you to be my wife and partner in all things. I want to stand up in front of God and promise that I'll love and protect you, build something lasting with you, and mean it. I love you. Will you be my wife in the true sense of the word?"

She dropped to her knees in front of him. "Yes," she whispered. "I want that more than anything. I love you, too."

He slipped the ring on her finger, and it fit perfectly. Then, he pulled her close to him, lowered his head, and pressed his lips against hers.

The world around them disappeared as he gently touched her face. She tasted faintly of peppermint. The kiss deepened and became more passionate, sending a flash of lightning coursing through his body.

She wrapped her arms around his neck, opening her mouth to his gentle push. Allen was lost in the scent of vanilla and lavender and her warmth.

When the kiss finally ended, he rested his forehead against hers.

"I never thought I'd be so happy," she said. "I never imagined I'd find love."

"Me, either," he murmured, his eyes stinging with tears. "Thank you for teaching me how to love again."

They stood, and he wrapped her up in his arms again, holding her close to him. Together, they lingered there in silence, looking over the town below.

Allen knew he'd finally found the peace he'd been looking for.

Epilogue

Four Years Later

Virginia rubbed her eyes as the sunlight streaming through the window gently woke her. She lay still for a minute, enjoying the early morning quiet. The air was cool, and she snuggled under the familiar weight of the blankets. She inhaled deeply, loving the scent of the sheets, which smelled faintly of the special lavender soap she made to wash them in.

The birds were chirping, and the house creaked. Sounds from their ranch filled the morning air. They knew breakfast would be coming soon if Keith and John weren't already at it.

She turned her head slightly to look at her handsome husband sleeping peacefully next to her. One arm was bent beneath his pillow. His curly brown hair was tousled like a little boy's after playing all day. Allen's chest rose and fell in a smooth, even rhythm.

Virginia smiled. It had been more than a year since he woke up in the middle of the night, screaming, his body covered in sweat, with wild, unfocused eyes. There were a few times that he thrashed around so much she was afraid he'd accidentally hurt her.

She'd always reach for him, whisper his name, and caress his face until he realized that he wasn't in the war anymore. Sometimes, he was able to snap out of the nightmare quickly, but other times, she had to be patient with him.

The last one had been so hard. He'd called out Joseph's name over and over again, and she could hear the anguish in his voice. When he woke up, he held her tightly, and his body shook as though he was sobbing.

Maybe he'd finally given himself a chance to grieve because he'd slept peacefully every night since then. Perhaps he finally realized that he was loved and he was safe.

She smiled as she thought about how his hand always reached across the bed for her and pulled her close to him in the middle of the night. The love inside of her burned hot, and she knew that a lifetime with Allen wouldn't be enough.

Virginia studied his face, her eyes tracing the faint scar on his temple. Her fingers itched to touch it, but she didn't want to wake him up.

"You're staring at me again," Allen murmured, his voice gravelly and deep from sleep. He cracked one of his eyes open and grinned at her.

Virginia laughed. "Maybe I am. I love looking at you."

Allen rolled over on his back, groaned, and stretched. He glanced at her, touched her face gently, and asked, "Why?"

"Well, for one, I can. You're mine, so I've got the right to admire the handsome man lying next to me."

"Mmm-hmm," he said.

"I love how you look so happy and peaceful. You smile in your sleep."

He looked at the ceiling for a minute, blinking the sleep out of his eyes. Then, he turned on his side and grinned at her.

"You make it easy to be happy and peaceful."

She swallowed hard. Butterflies erupted in her stomach. A now-familiar warmth began in her belly and flowed through her.

"Thank you. It makes me feel like I'm doing something right."

He brushed a kiss across her forehead. "If there's anything right in my life, Virginia, it's you. Don't you ever doubt that. I can't imagine life without you."

Her throat tightened, and tears pricked behind her eyes. Even though he had told her the same several times, his words never failed to make her heart beat faster. She was amazed that sometimes his love for her could catch her off guard and remind her just how deeply she loved him all over again.

Allen pulled her close to him, wrapping his arms around her. Her head rested on his chest. He smelled faintly of the pine she infused his soap with. The warmth from his body enveloped them.

They lay in the quiet morning for a while, neither of them in a hurry to get up.

"What's the plan for today?" Allen asked.

"We're meeting Ben, Brenda, and their kids for a picnic, remember? They're hosting it at their ranch to celebrate Caleb's birthday."

"That's right. I knew it was coming up, but the day slipped my mind."

"Are you going to be able to come with us, or are you Sheriff Strauss today?"

"Of course, I'm taking the day off. I've recently learned that spending time with my family is more important than anything else in the world." He rubbed his hand up and down her back. "Stephen and Douglas can handle any trouble that comes in."

She shifted onto her elbow and smiled at him, tracing his face with her fingertips.

"I love you so much," she said. "I never would have guessed that this type of love was even possible."

"It wasn't until you met me." He smirked.

Virginia lowered her head and pressed her lips against his. His smirk softened into a grin against her lips as he pulled her tightly against him. The smoldering ember inside of her burst into a flame of aching want and need.

"Mama!" a little boy's voice cried. "Mama."

She fell back onto the bed and groaned. "No. It's too early."

"Daddy!" a tiny voice called out.

Allen laughed. "I believe our children are summoning us. The last one downstairs cooks breakfast."

He jumped out of bed and hastily pulled on his clothes before rushing out the door to Hannah's room.

Virginia popped out a few minutes later. "Not fair. I have a few more things I have to put on than you do."

Allen laughed as he carried Hannah downstairs. "All's fair in love and war, sweetheart. Cooking breakfast is all about war."

Shaking her head, Virginia went into Joseph's room. "How are you, Baby Boy?"

"Hunnry," he said, rubbing his tummy.

"I guess we'll have to see what we can do about that."

She lifted him out of his crib, even though he could easily escape from it whenever he wanted, and cradled him close to her.

At two, Joseph was every bit the active boy that his uncle and father were. She had to keep a close eye on him because he was into everything. He was extremely curious, and his three favorite words were "What this?" and "Why?"

Virginia loved it. She hoped it would continue as he grew up so he would learn about the world.

Hannah was happily sipping milk from the white glazed ceramic vessel with blue flowers painted on it while sitting on Allen's lap. The narrow spout let Hannah drink her milk without getting it all over herself.

She set Joseph in his chair and kissed Hannah. "What would you like for breakfast this morning?"

"Bubewwy pancakes," Joseph said, clapping his hands.

Allen grinned. "What he said."

He placed Hannah in her high chair. Then, he kissed Virginia on the cheek. "I'll cook the bacon if you make the pancakes and eggs."

"That sounds fair." She smiled at him.

Virginia continued to grin as she cooked. She could still remember the horror and terror she felt when her aunt told her that she had to come to Montana Territory to marry a man she'd never met. Now, she had a life she would have never dared to dream of.

She smiled as she thought of the letter she'd mailed to her aunt, thanking her. Virginia had told her about the ranch and what a kind, loving husband Allen was. She'd described Hannah and Joseph and told her aunt that she loved her life.

Allen and Virginia had gotten a good laugh over Aunt Fiona's reply:

Virginia,

I received your letter and noted your gratitude, though it surprises me to hear such praise for a match you initially fought so vehemently. It seems time has softened you, or perhaps Allen has proven better than I expected.

You speak of happiness and fulfillment—how fortunate for you. Life does not often reward the ungrateful, yet it appears to have done so for you, in spite of your youth and defiance. I trust you will not forget who ensured your position, even if you prefer to cloak your thanks in sentiment rather than recognition of necessity.

Still, if your life is as splendid as you say, then I suppose you owe me even more than you imagined.

Fiona.

"She's such a delight, isn't she?" Allen said.

"I guess that's one way to put it. I have to say that I might have been flaunting my good life when I wrote the letter, and to find peace. I closed that part of my life forever."

They'd burned Fiona's letter.

It's only been four years, but it seems so long ago. Thank God that, in His wisdom, He brought me here.

"Hunnry!" Joseph yelled, snapping Virginia out of her memory.

Allen tore up small pieces of bacon for the kids, while Virginia broke up pieces of pancakes and scrambled eggs for the kids.

Breakfast was always a mess, but a lot of fun. Something was always dropped or spilled, and of course, the kids wore as much as they ate.

"I have to say that at least it's not boring," Allen said.

"Are you having fun?" Virginia asked.

He nodded. "I never would have guessed that I could have this much fun."

"Good, because that fun is about to increase by one."

Allen stared at her with a blank expression before he grasped what she was trying to convey.

"You're...? We're gonna have...?"

She grinned. "In about six months, we'll have a new addition to our family."

Allen jumped up, grabbed her, and twirled her around in a circle. "I love you," he gasped, his cheeks red from the force of his smile.

"And I love you," Virginia returned, meaning it with her whole heart.

THE END

Also by Nora J. Callaway

Thank you for reading "**The Sheriff's Unexpected Wife**"!

I hope you enjoyed it! If you did, here are some of my other books!

My latest Best-Selling Books

#1 An Unexpected Family in Montana

#2 A Governess at His Door

#3 Sheltered by the Mountain Man's Love

#4 The Rancher's Bride

#5 Faking Their Hearts on the Trail

You can also check out **my full Amazon Book Catalogue at:**

https://go.norajcallaway.com/bc-authorpage

Thank you for allowing me to keep doing what I love! ♥

Printed in Dunstable, United Kingdom